WHEN YOU KISS ME

~ Maine Sullivans ~

Lola & Duncan

Bella Andre

WHEN YOU KISS ME

~ Maine Sullivans ~

Lola & Duncan

© 2020 Bella Andre

Sign up for the New Release Newsletter
http://bellaandre.com/newsletter
www.BellaAndre.com
Facebook ~ Instagram ~ Twitter
facebook.com/bellaandrefans
instagram.com/bellaandrebooks
twitter.com/bellaandre

Lola Sullivan has been stared at by men since she was thirteen years old, but no one has ever seen the *real* her. Not until venture capitalist Duncan Lyman walks into her textile design studio, and they're drawn to each other on every level. When deep passion sparks between them, along with a powerful emotional connection, they stay up all night together. By the time the sun rises, she's sure she's found The One.

Duncan never imagined a woman like Lola existed—she is just as beautiful on the inside as she is on the outside. He trusts her in a way he's never trusted anyone else, and he tells her everything. Everything but the dark secret from his past that could destroy their budding love. It took thirty years for Lola and Duncan to find perfect love…but will it take only thirty seconds to destroy it?

A note from Bella

Books have always been the one thing I can count on to brighten my day and give me solace during difficult times. All my life, I've taken a book with me wherever I go in case I can squeeze in another few minutes of reading. When I began writing about the Sullivan family in *The Look of Love*, I discovered that I loved writing just as much as reading.

Getting to spend time every day with the Sullivans has brought me so much joy, and I can't tell you how happy it makes me to receive your emails and messages on social media letting me know that you feel exactly the same way!

Women like Lola Sullivan—strong and feisty, yet more vulnerable than they want to admit—are some of my favorite heroines to write about. Especially when they can't help but fall head over heels for an incredibly romantic man like Duncan Lyman.

I hope you absolutely love their emotional and sexy story.

If this is your first time reading about the Sullivans, you can easily read each book as a stand-alone—and there is a Sullivan family tree available on my website (https://www.bellaandre.com/sullivan-family-tree) so you can see how the books are connected!

Happy reading,
Bella

P.S. More stories about the Maine Sullivans are coming soon! Please be sure to sign up for my newsletter (http://bellaandre.com/newsletter) so that you don't miss out on any new book announcements.

CHAPTER ONE

In all the years that Lola Sullivan had been teaching classes in her textile design studio, she'd never had a student like *him*. Several inches taller than six feet, Duncan Lyman had broad shoulders, a square jaw, and piercing blue eyes.

As she went to greet her new student, she had to resist the urge to check her hair and smooth her dress. She would never hit on a student. Besides, she was firmly in a there-was-no-point-in-dating stage in her life, as every date she'd had in the past year had been a *massive* disappointment. Without fail, no matter how promising a man seemed at first, he inevitably assumed she couldn't possibly have such bountiful curves and also have the brains to add two plus two.

She approached him with a smile. "Hello, I'm Lola Sullivan. You must be Duncan?"

His handshake somehow managed to be warm, firm, *and* innately sensual at the same time. "It's nice to meet you, Lola." He held on to her hand for just long enough that her heartbeat started racing. "I've been looking forward to your class." His voice matched his looks, all low and rumbly and gorgeous. Just the way he said her name made her stomach flutter. She'd never realized before how sensual *Lola* could sound.

At a surprising loss for words—she wasn't known as the quiet one in her family, that was for sure!—she gestured for him to take a seat at the large worktable. Turning to speak to her ten students, nine of whom were women between the ages of forty-five and sixty, she said, "I'm so pleased you're all here today. Before we begin, I'd love to know what each of you hope to get out of the class."

All nine women were working toward second careers in textile and pattern design. Only Duncan had a different goal. "I'm interested in cartography. Hand-drawn maps, specifically. The reviews I read of your classes say you're a gifted teacher."

Lola felt like she was glowing from his compliment as she said, "I have an antique hand-drawn map hanging on my living-room wall, so I'm definitely a fan of cartography. I just hope I can help you with the skills you're looking for."

He gave her a smile that made her heartbeat pick up again. "I'm sure you will."

It wasn't until one of the other students cleared her throat that Lola realized she was still staring at him. More than a little alarmed by how quickly a handsome face and deliciously sexy voice had turned her head, she adopted a brisk tone. "If all of you would please turn to the printed materials, I'll go over today's class plan."

Thirty minutes later, her students were working on the first assignment of the day. Though she enjoyed teaching beginners, she was pleased to see that they were an advanced group. And head and shoulders above everyone else was Duncan.

For the next several hours, she gave each student as much individual attention as she could. Unfortunately, as soon as she began working one-on-one with Duncan, her heart began to race again. It didn't help that he smelled so good, like a refreshing breath of the sea, or that he was even more attractive close up. Sitting beside him now, she noticed not only the flecks of gold in his blue eyes, but also that he already had a hint of a five o'clock shadow on his jaw, though it was barely noon. He was wearing a beautifully tailored button-down shirt and had on a watch from an exclusive brand, but he still looked so rugged. Duncan looked like a man who'd been born to climb mountains and cut down trees. Or, given his appreciation for hand-drawn maps, to build and sail ships around the world.

Duncan was likely wondering why she continued to stare at him instead of teaching the new drawing skills he'd signed up to learn. She silently berated herself for acting like a schoolgirl with her first big crush. Working to clear her expression of any possible hints of attraction, she said, "Not many of my students have used dip pens and calligraphic nibs before. Watching you work with them this morning, I'm thinking you could teach me a thing or two."

It wasn't until the words were out of her mouth that she realized how they sounded. First, that she'd been *watching* him all morning. And second, that she was fantasizing about all the things he could *teach* her...

Her face flaming, she intended to move away, desperate now to put some space between them so that she could beat her unruly hormones back into submission. But his intense gaze held her captive. Spellbound in a way that no other man ever had before, without so much as a touch, or a kiss.

"I've been watching you too," he said, his deep voice resonating through every cell in her body. "Your talent is astonishing. Even your quick sketches when you're illustrating a point are more polished than I could ever hope for my work to be." His gaze moved to her hands, then back up to her face, making her skin tingle as though he had actually touched her. "Show me, Lola. Tell me your secrets."

Lola knew he was simply asking her for drawing pointers. And yet, somehow it felt like he was asking her for more. For something she hadn't given a man since college. Not only for her deeply held secrets, but also for a piece of the heart she had learned to keep carefully protected.

The sound of laughter from two students at the other end of the worktable brought her back to reality. She forced a smile, the kind she would give to a friend, rather than someone whose sheer presence made her breathless. "Have you ever tried the Number Five Superior School Pen by Tachikawa?"

When he shook his head, she pulled one out of her tool drawer for him. "It holds ink well and is stiff enough to help you maintain thin lines, but has enough flexibility so that you can vary the thickness when needed."

He drew several lines from .2 mm to .4 mm wide. "You're right, this is an excellent pen." The smile he gave her warmed her all over, in places that had been cold for a long time.

Jumping up from the seat she'd taken next to him, she said, "Who's hungry?" When everyone agreed that they were ready to break for lunch she suggested, "Let's go down the street to my mom's café. She makes the most delicious home-cooked Irish food you will ever eat."

When they got to the restaurant, Lola planned to make sure she sat at the very opposite end of the table from Duncan. Otherwise, she risked making a fool of herself...again. And yet, once all of her students were seated, Lola realized she had lost the game of musical chairs. Because the only seat available was the one beside Duncan.

A few of her students gave her surreptitious smiles. Lola barely held back a sigh. Clearly, some of the women had noticed her reaction to him and had visions of pairing them up.

Normally, Lola would be happy to play along and harmlessly flirt with him. But nothing felt normal today.

Still, once everyone had ordered and started to chat with one another, she couldn't sit there and ignore him, could she? "You're very talented. How long have you been working as a cartographer?"

"That compliment means a lot coming from you," he said with a smile that made her heart skip around inside her chest some more. "Especially since I'm just a hobbyist. I have a long way to go if I ever want to call myself a cartographer."

"Hand-drawn maps are a dying art, aren't they?" Thankfully, talking about art helped her relax around him.

He nodded, then gave the waitress a smile as she brought over his coffee. Aileen's face went bright red at his attention before she ran off to giggle with the other waitress. Clearly, both women found him extremely attractive.

"I admire modern-day mapmakers," he said, "but a part of me feels like you lose a bit of heart and soul with a digital map. Whereas, all the imperfections on hand-drawn maps are what give them such character." His grin was ridiculously sexy as he added, "At least, that's what I tell myself about my mistakes—that it gives my maps character."

It was extremely rare for Lola to meet a man who was both humble and good-looking. Most handsome men, in her experience, loved to expound on their seemingly endless virtues. What's more, Duncan had been a perfect gentleman in class, both with her and with the other students. And she couldn't agree more about imperfections being a crucial part of any piece of art. Some of her best designs had come from mistakes.

She was just thinking how much her mother would like him when Beth Sullivan pushed through the kitchen doors to come say hello to the group.

Lola got up to loop her arm through her mother's. "This is my mom, Beth. She's responsible for this amazing food."

"And an amazing daughter too," a student named Janice said.

Lola's mom grinned. "The most amazing daughter in the world."

"Just wait until I tell Cassie and Ashley you said that," Lola teased. "I always knew I was your favorite."

Beth laughed. "Sometimes it's a minefield having seven children," she joked to the group. "Now, I'd love to hear more about all of you, if you have a few minutes to chat with me before you head back to class."

Everyone was delighted to share the details and pictures of their projects. Lola's mom had a way of bringing out the best in everyone. All the while, however, Lola knew her mother was taking special note of Duncan.

Beth Sullivan badly wanted each of her children to find their one true love. The same powerful love that Beth shared with Lola's father, Ethan. Though her mother's matchmaking had yet to work, she hadn't given up. Clearly, from the gleam in her eyes as she looked between Lola and Duncan, she was dreaming of wedding bells.

"Now, Duncan," Lola's mom said in her gentle Irish accent, "tell me why you're here today."

The smile he gave her mother only made him more handsome, which undoubtedly filled Beth with *far* more matchmaking encouragement than she needed.

"Lola has a reputation as a brilliant teacher," he told her mother, "and after one morning in her class, I can confirm that she is indeed brilliant, on all fronts. Although I'm sure you don't need me to tell you that."

Beth beamed at him. "I'm very glad to hear you think so too. I'm sure it couldn't have been easy to carve out time away from your wife and children on a Sunday."

Lola almost groaned out loud, and it was only by great strength of will that she didn't drop her head into her hands. She was a full-grown woman. If she wanted to hook up with Duncan, she could manage it on her own without her mother's help, thank you very much.

But she had no intention of hooking up with him, because she was *done* with men. Lola had run out of fingers to count the lies she'd been told over the years by men she'd dated.

That they were single.

That they were solvent.

That they weren't controlling.

And that they respected her brain and talent as much as they lusted after her body. That was the biggest lie of all—and the one that cut the deepest.

Lola didn't have it in her to be disappointed again. Besides, she was perfectly fine staying single. She loved being a doting aunt to Kevin and Ruby and any other nieces and nephews who were sure to come along in the future. Frankly, getting a half-dozen cats and being a happily eccentric spinster whom no one lied to sounded nice.

Fortunately, Duncan didn't seem bothered by her mother's less-than-subtle information-fishing expedition. "It's just me in Boston, so I haven't left anyone behind."

"Mom," Lola interjected before Beth could say anything else, "I think Annie needs you back in the kitchen." Lola took her mother's hand and pulled her to her feet. "I'll be back in just a minute so that we can get back to work in the studio," she told the group, keeping her smile in place until the kitchen door swung closed behind them.

"Seriously, Mom," Lola said when they were out of earshot, "that was *mortifying*."

Beth didn't look the least bit sorry. "Duncan is gorgeous, clearly intelligent—and he couldn't take his eyes off of you."

Working to cover up any outward sign of her own interest in him, Lola replied, "You have no way of knowing if he's actually interested in me. And besides, even if you're right and he is, *I'm* the one who isn't interested in dating anyone right now."

"I know dating hasn't always been easy for you, honey. You are such a wonderful woman, with so much love inside of you." Beth pulled Lola into a hug. "I just want you to be happy."

Lola instantly forgave her mom for asking Duncan

such an embarrassing question about whether he had a wife and kids waiting for him at home. After all, Beth had only her best interests at heart. "I am happy, Mom. And if one day I magically fall head over heels in love like you and Dad did, I promise I won't fight it. But for now, you're going to have to accept that I'm unlikely to have a whirlwind love affair with a man who signed up for one of my classes."

Her mother finally looked contrite. "You've always been special, Lola. Right from the moment you were born, your father and I knew that you had broken the mold. You're right to hold out for someone who appreciates every part of you. I'm sorry I meddled. Could we blame it on the fact that Duncan reminds me a little of your father from way back when, so I couldn't help myself?"

"You're right that Duncan is easy on the eyes," Lola agreed. "He's incredibly talented, and modest too."

When Beth's eyes started doing that twinkling thing again, Lola knew she had better make her escape before the matchmaking devil inside of her mother rose back to the surface.

"Thanks for feeding my students so well for lunch. I'll see you at dinner on Friday."

She gave her mother a kiss on the cheek and was about to head back into the restaurant when she decided to make a quick pit stop in the bathroom. She wasn't tidying her makeup and hair for Duncan. But if people wanted pictures with her at the end of class and they posted them on their social media feeds, she wanted to look her best.

She meant what she'd said to her mother. Nothing could be more unlikely than falling head over heels for one of her students and ending up madly in love with him.

No question about it, Lola's heart was safe from a fairytale, whirlwind romance.

CHAPTER TWO

Duncan Lyman was a man who lived by a fierce code of ethics. He didn't lie. He didn't cheat.

And he sure as hell couldn't seduce his drawing instructor…even if she was the most extraordinary, and beautiful, woman he'd ever met.

Everything about Lola Sullivan drew him closer. Her sparkling eyes, full of such intelligence and interest in everyone and everything around her. Her talent, the scope of which he knew he had only barely glimpsed today. Her laughter, which seemed to come so easily and so freely, and which had managed to light up the dark places inside of him in a way few things had in a very long time. And on top of everything else, the attraction that he had felt sparking between them throughout the day. An attraction so heated and potent that at times he had felt as though they were touching even when they were across the room from one another.

Despite their undeniable connection, however, given Lola's reaction to her mother's obvious attempt at matchmaking, she was practically wearing a *Keep Away* sign on her back. He'd been shocked to realize Lola was single, when guys must surely be begging her to be with them every second of every day.

Then again, what man could possibly be good enough for Lola Sullivan?

Duncan knew he wasn't.

Every day since he'd walked away from his family's venture capital firm and started his own, Duncan had worked to make amends to the people who had been hurt by his brother Alastair's crimes. Lola's class was the first weekend he'd carved out for his own pursuits in five years. And even then, the only reason he was in Bar Harbor was because Gail, his office manager, had given Lola's class to him as a birthday present. Gail had made it clear that she would be insulted if he didn't use her gift. She'd made more than one concerned comment over the years about the long and punishing hours he spent in the office, and she clearly wanted him to take some time off for himself.

Duncan had been charmed by Bar Harbor immediately upon arriving in town earlier that morning. He'd always loved being by the sea. It was different here than Boston, though. The big-city smells and sounds had been replaced by a laid-back, small-town feel. When he'd driven in from the airport, he'd been pleasantly surprised to realize that only a mere handful of blocks from downtown Bar Harbor was nature at its finest. With rocky, windy shores, the Maine ocean was both stunningly beautiful and a serious force to be reckoned with. Lush green trees and forests covered nearly every bit of land that hadn't been domesticated, and when Duncan rolled down the window of his rental car, he'd breathed in pure, unpolluted oxygen.

Now, Duncan breathed in Lola's intoxicating scent as she leaned over his shoulder to show him a more effective way to use the new nib she'd lent him. He was not only learning a great deal from her, he was also encouraged by the positive remarks she made about his work, especially given that she seemed to know quite a bit about the specialized world of hand-drawn cartography.

Her office phone rang and when she saw the number, she made her apologies to the group. "I don't normally take calls during classes, but this is a distributor I've been hoping to work with."

After everyone said it was no problem, she picked up the phone. Though she pitched her voice as low as possible to keep from distracting her students, Duncan was sitting close enough not only to overhear, but also to see her face in profile.

Unfortunately, both her tone and expression soon changed from pleased to disappointed.

"Surely," he heard her say, "you can decide whether you want to distribute my textiles without meeting for dinner again? I've already given you my sales figures and new designs." Her frown deepened at the person's response. "Whether I'm single or not has nothing to do with a potential business partnership." She pressed her lips together hard at the reply, her skin flushing with what looked to Duncan like a mix of frustration and anger. "I'm in the middle of teaching a class, so I can't discuss this any further. But based on today's conversation, I don't think my company is a good fit with yours. Good-bye."

She looked a little shaken as she hung up the phone, and Duncan realized his fingers had clenched around his pen.

Lola took a moment to compose herself before turning back to her students with a smile. "Sorry about that. Now, who needs help with something?"

He wanted to ask her if she was all right. He also wanted to know how many times she'd had to deal with such blatant sexism. But she obviously wanted to move on as if it hadn't happened.

Too soon, the workshop came to an end. Lola showered everyone with compliments on their work, drawing them even more under her spell. Her mother, Beth, was best described as warm and adorable. But while Lola was warm, she was also *dazzling*. On every level—personal and professional.

As Duncan and his fellow students had worked on their drawing projects throughout the day, she had done several great freehand drawings to show them the techniques she wanted them to master. What's more, the textiles pinned around her studio looked extremely marketable. While she seemed happy in her small, sunlit studio in Bar Harbor, and she'd mentioned working with retail stores throughout Maine, she could easily go global. All it would take was the right investor behind her. And, of course, not having to deal with sexist jerks like the man she'd spoken with on the phone.

Duncan quickly justified the need to stay behind after class by telling himself that since she had helped him with his drawing skills, now he could return the favor by offering suggestions about potential avenues to grow her business. LS Textiles could become an international powerhouse, and he'd love to help her get there. Plus, he couldn't stand the thought of not seeing her again. The sooner he could see her smile and hear her laugh, the better.

Though the students hadn't known one another to begin with, they included him in their warm embraces at the end of class. A tall, muscular man, he always went out of his way to make sure people didn't feel threatened by his presence, and he was glad that everyone had been comfortable with him in class. He also appreciated the way the women insisted he stay in touch as part of their newly formed drawing group.

After the other students had left, he said to Lola, "I know you've already given up your day to the class, but I'd like to speak with you about something. Could I convince you to have a quick cup of coffee with me?"

When she paused before replying, he was surprised to realize that she was going to turn him down. Duncan couldn't remember the last time a woman had said no to one of his invitations. But Lola wasn't like any other woman he'd known.

But instead of saying no, she asked, "What do you want to talk with me about?"

His invitation had clearly made her wary. But was it him specifically who made her wary? Or was it men in general? He knew enough beautiful women—although none as stunning as Lola—to understand that beauty wasn't always a bonus. On the contrary, it could be a huge burden when a woman wanted to be taken seriously. Her phone call that afternoon with the distributor proved that in spades.

"I'd like to speak with you about your business," he clarified, to make sure she knew he wasn't planning to hit on her, even though eight hours with her in a group class wasn't nearly enough.

She frowned. "Were you unhappy with the class?"

"It was great. You're a fantastic teacher. But it's

your textile designs I'd like to discuss. As I said earlier, cartography is just a hobby. I work in venture capital."

A faint expression of disappointment moved across her face, though her tone was more teasing than condemning as she said, "And here I thought you were one of the good guys."

"Every day, I do whatever I can to be a good guy." Though he wasn't sure he'd ever be able to wipe his slate completely clean, he'd go to his grave trying. "I'd be happy to walk you through my portfolio of companies so that you can see that the people I work with are honest, hardworking, and talented. Whatever time you can spare to talk with me about your company, I'd appreciate."

Again, she made him sweat as he waited for her reply. Men, he figured, sweated in Lola Sullivan's presence a great deal.

Just then, her stomach let out a loud grumble. She laughed as she told him, "I need at least five meals a day to keep chugging along, and I'm afraid I was talking so much that I skipped most of lunch. I've actually been hankering for Irish steak with potato scones. If you've got thirty minutes or so, I can make enough for both of us in the café's kitchen."

Duncan was more than happy to stay for as long as she wanted him around, even if he had only her hunger pangs to thank for it. As they headed down the block to the café, he tried not to ogle her spectacular figure, but it wasn't easy when every inch of her was perfect, from her glossy dark hair, to her luscious curves, all the way down her long legs to her stiletto heels. Compared to Lola, the size-zero blondes with Botoxed faces from his Boston hometown looked pale and insignificant.

The guy who convinced Lola to give him a chance would be very lucky indeed. And even though he knew she deserved to be with a far better man, one without dark skeletons in his past, Duncan still couldn't help but wish *he* could be that guy.

Other men on the street didn't bother trying to disguise their interest in her. Duncan had noticed the same thing when they'd gone to the café for lunch—people's eyes constantly followed Lola. Without exception, men drooled. And the women with those men frequently shot Lola jealous glares. Lola didn't seem to take any notice, but Duncan knew she must be aware of the way people reacted to her. Yet again, it struck him that being gawked at everywhere she went had to be disconcerting. Hugely so.

In the café's kitchen, she introduced him to the staff, then set them up in a corner by an unoccupied stovetop. She gestured for him to sit on a nearby stool while she took out a frying pan and myriad ingredients from the industrial fridge, then began to chop potatoes deftly after turning down his offer to help, saying she was happy to cook.

Noting how comfortable she was in the commercial kitchen, he asked, "Did you ever think of being a chef like your mother?"

"No, although I have spent a lot of time in this kitchen. All seven of us have worked here at one time or another when our parents needed us to help out."

He thought back to the lovely woman he'd met at lunch. "Your mother looks so calm, and so youthful, I can barely wrap my head around her having raised seven kids."

"She's actually quite the firecracker," Lola informed him with a smile. "It's the lilting Irish accent that fools everyone."

Her smile was so stunning, he forgot what they were talking about for a moment. All he could do was stare at her, drinking in her incredible beauty. Until her quizzical glance, and then her slight frown as she realized he was staring at her, snapped him out of it. Still, while he had invited Lola for coffee to talk business, now that he had a chance, he couldn't resist finding out more about her. "What was it like to grow up as one of seven?"

"Honestly," she said as she finished peeling and chopping, then steamed the potatoes, "there have been times when I've wished I was an only child. Usually when one of my brothers or sisters is hitting me over the head with something. But the rest of the time, I'm really glad to be a part of such a big family."

"Where are you in the lineup?" She didn't seem like either the oldest or youngest. On the contrary, she seemed more like a middle child who refused to be forgotten.

"Are you sure you want the full rundown of my family members? There are so many of us that it could take all night. And you're here to talk about my business, not to draw the Maine branch of the Sullivan family tree."

Duncan couldn't think of anything better than sitting in this warm and cozy café kitchen listening to Lola tell him about herself. And if it took all night…well, he'd be more than willing to stay up until sunrise with her. "After meeting you and your mother, I'm curious about the rest of your family." Lola and Beth were obviously close. It was the kind of tight-knit relationship he'd only ever had with his brother.

Until he'd learned the truth about Alastair's crimes.

Lola's voice broke Duncan out of his dark thoughts. "Okay, but when you start to lose track of names, don't say I didn't warn you. As you've probably already guessed, Mom grew up in Ireland. She came to America after she met my dad, Ethan, in County Cork. Dad is one of four brothers, although my Uncle Jack passed away quite a while ago. And we have Sullivan relatives all over the world. My brother Hudson is the firstborn. He's married to Larissa, and they live in Boston."

"Do you get to Boston often to see them?" Duncan shouldn't be hoping Lola was a regular visitor to his hometown, when he had no business setting his sights on her. But he couldn't help wanting to see more of her anyway.

She looked a little sad as she shook her head. "When Hudson and Larissa were first married, we used to spend a lot of time together. But these past few years, I don't see nearly as much of them as I'd like to. Lately, he's been coming up here without her for family events, which is a bummer." She frowned as she stirred onions in the pan. "My brother Brandon is next in the lineup. He opens hotels all over the world. We don't see enough of him either, although he can be a little bit of a you-know-what, so that's not all bad."

But Duncan could tell she didn't mean it. She would have loved to see Brandon more often. That's when it hit him. "Is your brother the founder of the SLVN hotel brand?"

Lola's pride in her brother's achievements was evident as she grinned. "That's him. He works too hard, though," she added, the grin fading. "Then there's my brother Rory, who lives nearby and is a furniture maker. Although saying he makes furniture is like saying Louis Armstrong simply played in a band. Rory is also madly in love with Zara, who makes fantastic glasses frames."

"It sounds like there are a lot of makers and entrepreneurs in your family."

"Our parents always encouraged us to follow our hearts and to trust that money would follow passion."

"That's pretty rare." Duncan hadn't known his father well enough by the time he died to know what he would have encouraged Duncan to do, but his brother, who'd raised him from the age of six, had ended up being more concerned with money and power than anything else.

"My dad had a whole other life before he met my mom," Lola told him. "To hear him tell it, he made all the wrong choices, for all the wrong reasons, for a really long time. I'm sure it was more nuanced than that, but he ended up completely changing his life after going to Ireland and meeting my mom. Which is probably why he always says the only thing he truly wants is to know that we're happy."

"Are you? Happy, I mean." Duncan knew he shouldn't ask Lola such an intimate question. Just because she was making him something to eat and telling him about her siblings didn't mean she was inviting him into the inner recesses of her heart.

But he needed to know the answer. Though he had

known her for only a handful of hours, Duncan was surprised to realize that Lola's happiness already meant a great deal to him. He'd hated seeing her frown so deeply during her business call today—a call that hadn't actually been about business at all.

Her hand stilled over the pan, the spatula hanging in midair, as though she was thinking about whether to let him in deep enough to give him an honest answer.

At last, she raised her eyes to his. "Most of the time, I am happy." It was the first time she'd let her defenses down around him, and her honesty stole his breath away. "And those times when I'm not...well, I just try to remind myself that I have so much to be grateful for and so many people who love me that I love back just as much."

There.

Then.

It was the moment Duncan fell. Not just for Lola's beautiful face and stunning smile. Not just for her immense talent.

But for her heart.

Duncan couldn't think of anyone he knew who loved with their whole heart. Truly loved with everything they were.

Not until now.

Until Lola.

CHAPTER THREE

Lola's gaze held his, and for a moment, he thought he might not be the only one falling. But then she broke the intense connection and said, in a purely conversational tone, "Anyway, back to my family. My sister Cassie is a wizard with candy. You wouldn't believe the things she can make with sugar. Honestly, I'm not the one you should be talking to about investors. Cassie and Rory are far better candidates."

Before he could reply, she looked down at the stovetop as if she'd only just remembered that she was cooking. "I've been waxing on so much about my family that I almost burned our meal." She took the pan off the heat. "Although I still need to tell you about Cassie's fiancé, Flynn, and his little girl, Ruby. Flynn is a brilliant screenwriter, but what's more important is that he's an amazing dad. Ruby is the cutest kid in the entire world, apart from my sister Ashley's son, Kevin. And even though I know no one wants to see pictures of other people's nieces and nephews, I'm still going to show you some while we eat."

Lola plated their food, which they took to a small yellow table with matching yellow chairs under the shade of a leafy tree behind the café. Though they couldn't see the harbor from their seats, the sounds and smells of the waterfront wafted through the air.

They dove into their meals, and as the flavors hit his tongue, he was blown away all over again. "I had no idea steak and potatoes could taste this good. You're a wizard at everything you touch, aren't you?"

Most women would eat up his compliments. But Lola gave him a small, slightly wary smile. Almost as though she thought he was simply telling her what he thought she wanted to hear. He had to wonder how many men over the years *had* told her whatever they thought would get her to fall for them, even if it was a lie.

Duncan sensed it wouldn't be easy to earn her trust. At the same time, he could imagine just how good it would feel to know that Lola trusted him.

And to be able to trust her with everything he'd kept inside for so long, all his dark secrets...

"Irish steak with potato scones is my one and only specialty," she told him. "My mom makes everything else better. But I'm glad you like it." She took another bite and made her own sound of satisfaction. "I love teaching, but at the same time it's pretty exhausting. This was exactly what I needed to get my energy back."

They ate in greedy silence for a few minutes. Finally, he was replete enough to say, "You've told me about four older siblings so far. Are you the fifth?"

"Nope. My brother Turner is eighteen months older than me. He's an animator who's worked on a ton of movies. I'm sure you've seen at least one of them, but suffice it to say he's really good at what he does. He's also the mellowest of all seven of us. Although," she added with a sparkle to her eyes, "there's a part of me that wouldn't be surprised to find out he has a secret life none of us knows anything about." He was glad to see that talking about her family had made her relax again. "I was born next. And then last, but not at all least, is Ashley. We're a little more than a year apart, so we're super close. Her son, Kevin, is eleven, and I adore him to bits. His father, however, who was barely more than a sperm donor, is a total waste of space." She whipped out her phone to show Duncan the promised pictures of Ruby and Kevin, who were both cute kids. "And that," she said with a flourish as she put away her phone, "is the long and winding list of my immediate family." She pointed her fork at him. "Your turn. Do you have any siblings?"

"One brother who's ten years older." He worked to keep his expression and tone even. "His name is Alastair. He also lives in Boston."

Duncan had never told anyone about how everything he'd once believed to be true about his brother had turned out to be a lie. No one except the lawyers, who had ended up being as dirty as his brother. But Duncan was surprised to find he wanted to talk to Lola about it.

He'd met her only this morning. And yet, he felt such a strong connection with her. Of course he was attracted to her. What red-blooded man wouldn't be? But what she made him feel went so much further than just desire.

"What about your parents?" she asked, probably wondering why he wasn't already offering up the information. "Cousins? Aunts and uncles?"

He shook his head. "My parents died in a small plane crash when I was six. I have no other living family on either side. It's just me and my brother."

"Oh, Duncan." Her face was wreathed in sympathy. "I'm so sorry."

"I don't really remember my mother and father." His father had been too busy with his illustrious career to pay much attention to his second son, and according to his brother, their mother had been little more than a trophy wife. All Duncan remembered about her was that she hadn't been warm and sunny like Beth Sullivan. "My brother raised me. He also brought me into the family business after I graduated from college."

"Wow, he sounds amazing."

Duncan tensed in his seat despite trying to stay at ease. "He did a lot for me." That much was indisputable, given that Alastair had made sure neither of them ended up in foster care. He'd also taught Duncan how to ride a bike, and swim, and sail a boat. But after his brother had twisted up everything with his crimes, Duncan hadn't been certain if his good memories were actually even true. "We don't work together anymore. I left his company five years ago to start my own." But Duncan wasn't here to moan and groan about his life. And no matter how much he wished otherwise, this meal they were having together wasn't a date. He took the opportunity to say, "I'd love to hear more about your business. When did you first become interested in textile design?"

Though her eyebrows rose at his abrupt change of subject, she didn't push him for more information about his brother. "I majored in art and design in college. There wasn't a specific major for textile design, but my professors were happy to help me craft one. I created my first fabric line as part of my senior thesis project. Fortunately, I had also taken a few classes at the business school on marketing and sales, so by the time I graduated, I was ready to roll with my own company. I've dabbled a little bit in fashion design, but textiles are where my true passion lies, so that's where

I've decided to keep my focus from now on. My sales and retail contracts have grown in a slow and steady way, and though I don't have anyone on payroll, I work with a handful of freelance contractors."

"I'm extremely impressed with what you've built," he said, "and I'm positive that with the right investor behind you, your business could grow very quickly."

She shook her head. "I'm not interested in working with any investors."

He'd rarely met anyone who wasn't interested in selling more and making more money. "Why not?"

Her expression clouded over. "It's a long story, but suffice it to say that my mother's best friend from when they were growing up in Ireland—a woman I think of as my second mom—had a terrible experience with investors. They promised her the world, then turned around and dropped her cold, but only after convincing her to part with her savings first. Mom and I are sure the stress from it all was instrumental in her breast cancer diagnosis."

His heart was in his throat. Everything Lola was saying hit so close to home. Too close. He hated knowing how many entrepreneurs signed bad deals and ended up losing everything they'd worked so hard to create. "Is she all right?"

Thankfully, Lola nodded. "It was a long road of surgery, chemo, and radiation, and we all pitched in to help, but it was another huge setback on top of her business faltering. The most amazing part of the story, though, is how she's always insisted that it's a waste of time to wish she could go back into the past and change things, and that it's far better to accept things as they are and move forward from where she is now."

It was a concept that Duncan had spent five years trying to wrap his head around, with limited success. He would give anything to go back in time and change things. To clearly see everything he hadn't wanted to believe could be true. Simply trying to make good decisions from here on out didn't seem like enough.

"I'm sorry to hear about everything your friend went through. That's exactly the kind of business practice I most abhor."

She smiled. "Well, I'm glad to hear that there are some good venture capitalists out there. Speaking of which, what exactly is it that you invest in?"

"Anyone whose ideas have promise, ranging from pioneering work with renewable resources in fashion, to environmentally friendly farming and food production techniques, to building new and better prosthetics for children."

"You must sleep really well at night."

He wished he did. "I like the people I work with." He had completely changed his focus after starting his own fund. While profits mattered, helping good people mattered more. "And I like knowing I'm supporting businesses that will in turn support others."

"Plus, you have cartography." Before he could remind her that it was just a hobby, she asked, "Do you have any photos of maps you've drawn? I'd love to see them if you do."

He pulled out his phone and showed her a picture. "A friend of mine from college was born and raised in Paris. I knew how much she missed it, so I made this map for her."

"Duncan…" Lola looked up from his phone. "This is *so* much more than just a map." She studied it, using her fingers on the screen to enlarge the sections she wanted to see more clearly. "You've not only drawn the Eiffel Tower, the Arc de Triomphe, Notre Dame, the Bois de Boulogne—but this border decoration is also incredible."

No one's praise had ever felt so good, or meant so much to him. "I took inspiration for the border from eighteenth-century French maps."

Her eyes suddenly went wide. "I assumed you'd drawn this map on paper. But is it actually on vellum?"

He nodded. "It wasn't easy to get the inks to stick."

"I've never been patient enough to work with vellum," she told him. And then, "Just as I thought during class, you don't need me to teach you anything. This map is a work of art. I recently read an article about how the market for old maps is booming. You could make a living doing this."

Though he wanted to bask in the glow of her confidence in his artistic abilities, he simply smiled and reminded her, "It's just a hobby. I'm not an artist."

"You are," she insisted, her eyes lit with passion. Passion he had already become addicted to, though they hadn't so much as touched. "In addition to selling originals at galleries and taking commissions from individual buyers, you could draw maps of your favorite places and sell signed prints from your website."

He held up his hands. "Whoa...still just a venture capitalist here."

"No," she said with a firm shake of her head, "you're so much more than that. While I think you are doing amazing things for the companies you're supporting with your investment firm, you have real talent. Talent I would hate to see wasted." She leaned forward over the table, so close that he could see a flush of excitement on her cheekbones. "You can't honestly tell me you haven't thought about trying to squeeze in more time for your art, can you?"

He surprised himself by saying, "Secretly, I have." There was no one else he would admit this to. But Lola made him want to open up in a way he hadn't opened up to anyone in years. Certainly not since his trust had been betrayed by the one person he'd trusted above all others. "That's why I'm glad I had the opportunity to learn from you today. And I have recently hired someone at a high level to help me run the company, although her role is to work alongside me, rather than replace me."

"But if she ended up doing a really great job with your clients," Lola said, "wouldn't that mean you could give your other dreams some room to breathe?"

Yearning filled him. Yearning that he'd squashed down and done his level best to ignore for decades. Because while spending time drawing maps was something he had longed for since he was a child, for the first thirty years of his life, he'd done whatever he could to make his family proud. And then for the last five years, he'd been hell-bent on trying to right his family's wrongs. It wasn't until today, when Gail had sent him to Bar Harbor to learn drawing skills from a brilliant and beautiful woman, that he'd been able to give in to his own dreams for a short while.

He was on the verge of rejecting Lola's suggestion when it hit him. Maybe they could make a trade? "How about I agree to mull over your suggestion…if you agree to mull over mine about opening yourself to the potential upsides of working with an investor? An honest one, rather than a crook, whom I would personally vet for you."

She huffed out a laugh. "I should have seen that coming." She thought about it before replying. "Normally, I would never agree to think about taking on an investor, but since I really do think you should be spending more time on cartography, I'll make an exception. Let's shake on it."

She held out her hand. And when he clasped it in his, there was no other way to describe the sensation than as *pure electricity*.

Both of them stopped. Held on.

It could have been awkward, or maybe even funny.

Instead, it felt like *everything*.

For a few moments, they simply kept holding on, staring into each other's eyes. Moments that meant so damned much, more than anything in Duncan's life ever had before.

"Do you—"

"What if we—"

They both spoke at once. Laughing, Lola said, "Do you need to get back to Boston right away? Or is there any way you might—"

"I can stay."

She gave him a look of unfettered joy—exactly what he was feeling himself. Had anyone in his life ever looked at him like that? If so, he couldn't remember it.

Because all he could see, all he could feel, all he wanted was Lola.

CHAPTER FOUR

Lola had never been so impulsive before.

All her life, she'd been running from men who were trying to catch her. Until today, when she'd finally met the one she wanted to run *toward*.

When Duncan looked at her, he seemed to actually *see* her. He asked her questions he seemed to want to know the answers to, when every other guy only pretended to listen to get her into bed. She also loved how ethical Duncan was in his work and how he didn't brag about his success or wealth.

She should have been scared about throwing caution to the wind and risking her heart on a man she'd met only that morning. But with Duncan, even her wildest dreams suddenly seemed possible.

And she'd never know for sure if he could be *The One* unless she risked everything tonight on her heart—and his too.

She waited for the little voice in her head to pop up with a warning. *He's too good to be true. You should be careful.*

But that voice didn't come.

Amazingly, when she was with Duncan, her fears, her worries, her beliefs that she was never going to find the person she was destined to be with disappeared.

"Tell me everything," she said. "And don't leave anything out."

"Right now," he replied in his deep, sexy voice, "*everything* can be summed up by telling you that I've never felt this happy in my whole life."

There was nothing better, nothing nicer he could have said. "I feel the same way."

Unfortunately, the chiming of the clock at City Hall reminded her that they were counting down to his return to Boston. "When is your flight?"

"Eight o'clock tonight." He looked at his watch. "But even if I left now, I wouldn't make it in time." His gaze was intense as he looked back up at her. "I believe there's another flight out at seven in the morning, though, so I wouldn't need to leave for the airport until four a.m. That is, if you want me to stay?"

She sucked in a breath. The idea of Duncan staying all night was wonderful.

It was also terrifying.

As if he could read her mind, he said, "I would never pressure you to do anything you aren't comfortable with. I can find a hotel room in town for the rest of the night."

But she didn't want that. She wanted him in her home. Her *bed*. As soon as possible.

"I don't want you to stay in a hotel." Her heart was pounding wildly, as though she'd just asked him to marry her instead of simply inviting him back to her cottage for the night. "I meant it when I said I want to get to know you better. And..." She took a breath. "I know we've only just met, but I can't help wanting *you* to get to know *me* better too." Right from that moment in class when he'd asked her to tell him her secrets, it had felt like he'd been asking about more than just calligraphy pens. It had felt like he'd been looking all the way down into her soul—just the way he was now.

His answering smile only made her heart beat faster. She'd never known a smile could be so sensual. And when he stroked his thumb across the sensitive skin of her palm, it sent shivers—of heat, not cold—through her. "Anything you want to tell me about yourself, Lola, I want to hear."

She should have been second-guessing her impulse to share her secrets with him. But she felt calm, steady, and surprisingly sure that she should tell him something she'd held inside for years. "When I was a freshman in college, I dated a guy who was the same age as my parents. He was a businessman in New York, but he was often in Bar Harbor seeing clients. I knew my dad would totally freak if he found out, so I refused to let anyone take pictures of us in case they ended up online. I didn't even tell my sisters, so they wouldn't accidentally let it slip."

Duncan didn't seem taken aback by the age difference, although he did ask, "Was he good to you?"

She'd never told anyone the truth about her relationship with Frank before. How could she when she hadn't been able to confess to even having the relationship, let alone talk with anyone about how bad it was?

"Not really." Her next words came out in a rush, as though they'd been waiting all these years for the chance to be spoken. "Frank said all the right things and made me think he actually cared about me, when the truth was that he just wanted what every other guy wants…" She let her words fall away, but Duncan's expression had already darkened.

"Did he hurt you?" Duncan's question vibrated with barely quenched fury at this man he'd never met, and likely never would.

She swallowed hard. "Frank wasn't physically abusive, but…" He'd gotten inside her head with his constant comments about how sexy she was when she dressed in the extremely revealing clothes he bought her—and how nothing she'd ever achieve in life could possibly triumph over the face and body she'd been given. He'd made her feel like she was nothing more than a sex toy. An object to be bent and shaped to his needs, her own needs be damned. "I was still so young." Young enough not to realize that his "compliments" were actually meant to demean her so that she'd cling to him and look to him for guidance on how to live her life. "I didn't know how to stand up for myself. All I knew was that he seemed smart and powerful, and I couldn't believe he actually wanted to be with me."

"Lola." Duncan hadn't let go of her hand and now he squeezed it tightly. "You can't blame yourself for dating him. *He's* the one to blame for not treating you right. Hell, you were only eighteen years old. He should have stayed away from you."

"You're right," she agreed. "He should have. And once I finally figured that out, after he told me I should drop out of school to live with him in New York and be a sexy trophy on his arm, I broke up with him." The relationship had only lasted a few months, but the emotional scars of wondering if she really *was* only a pretty face had remained for a long time afterward. "It took realizing he didn't actually care about me or my future to finally knock sense into me. And," she added, "when he didn't seem to want to let me go, I started taking Krav Maga classes, just in case he, or some other guy in the future, didn't want to take no for an answer."

Duncan's jaw tensed even further. "You said he

didn't hurt you."

"He didn't. But by that point, I realized I needed to be prepared for the worst." She exhaled a long breath. "You know what? It feels good to have gotten that secret off my chest after all these years." She hadn't realized what a huge burden it had been keeping it in for so long. She smiled at Duncan, the weight she'd been carrying around for so long finally gone. "Okay, now it's your turn to confess one of your secrets."

He was silent for a long moment, as though he was warring within himself over what to tell her. Finally, he spoke. "I told you I stopped working with my brother. But I didn't tell you why." The light in his eyes dimmed even more as he told her, "I found out five years ago that Alastair isn't the person I thought he was. I didn't want to believe the things I discovered about him were true. Especially after the way he stepped up to raise me after our parents died."

Just as she had never told anyone her secret, she had a feeling Duncan had never told anyone this either. And though he wasn't yet giving her any specifics, whatever his brother had kept from him had clearly shaken him to his very core.

He looked pained as he continued, "I'll never stop regretting that I was blind to his faults for so long. For far too long."

Her heart broke for him. "I'm so sorry that you lost

your parents and then were so badly disappointed by your brother. But look at how well you turned out. You're a good man, Duncan." It had taken only a handful of hours for Lola see it. Her mother had seen it over lunch, as well, when she'd said that something about Duncan reminded Beth or the man she loved. "I could tell that from the start." She was the one tightly holding his hand now. "The more time we spend together, the more certain I am about you." She paused a beat before asking, "Are you still in contact with your brother?"

He shook his head, a sharp turn of his head from left to right. "I haven't seen or spoken to Alastair in five years." Duncan blew out a breath. "I didn't mean to darken the mood. Let's talk about something else." He tried to smile as he suggested, "Why don't you tell me your happiest memory?"

In the same way that Duncan had hated to hear about Frank's treatment of Lola, she hated to know that Alastair had been so awful. She wanted to ask more questions, wanted to know if there was anything she could do to help him heal. But she could also see how much Duncan wanted to move on from the painful memories. So she would share a happy one with him, rather than pushing for more information just yet.

"I have so many happy memories." She had been

blessed with a great family, with a life she loved. Of course she'd had her fair share of struggles, but she couldn't deny how lucky she'd been. "When I was eight years old, we were at the park celebrating Hudson's birthday. It was such a pretty day. I can still remember how blue the sky was, how the air smelled like flowers, and how everybody I loved was there." She was glad to see Duncan's smile grow as he pictured the scene. "I was wearing my favorite dress. It was bright yellow with beautiful watercolor flowers. Brandon teased me, saying he needed to put on sunglasses because it was so bright, but I didn't care what he thought. I loved that dress and wore it until the fabric eventually began to shred. Mom ended up incorporating a piece of it into a quilt I took to college. I still have it draped over an armchair in the corner of my bedroom."

Heat flooded her face simply from the mention of her bedroom. She'd never been a woman who flushed at the thought of going to bed with a man, but everything felt different with Duncan. Far more special. Even simply holding hands and talking about their lives.

"Everyone else wanted to play badminton," she went on, "but Mom must have known that I would rather draw, because she had a pad of drawing paper and pencils for me in her bag. They weren't just any pencils—they were watercolor pencils, which I had seen in an art store and coveted ever since. When she showed me how to use the pencils and then a wet brush to get the watercolor effect, it suddenly felt like anything was possible."

"You have a really great mom."

"I know." Even if Beth Sullivan was an indefatigable matchmaker. Although, maybe that wasn't such a bad thing, considering her mother had been completely right about Duncan. "Anyway, I used those watercolor pencils to draw absolutely everything. My family, our dog, strangers in the park, the trees, the birds, the flowers, the buildings around the square. I'd never realized just how colorful life was until that day. From that point forward, I've always brought a notebook and pen or pencil in my bag. And if my creative well ever feels like it's running a little dry, all I have to do is think back to that magical day in the park and I'm ready and raring to create again."

"What a beautiful memory." He looked as happy for her as he would have had the memory been his own.

"Now it's your turn," she said. "Tell me one of your happy memories."

"When I was a kid, my brother and I—" His expression darkened before he regrouped. "We sometimes went to the park near the Harborwalk in

Boston to kick a ball around. One afternoon, a storm blew in, and we took cover from the rain in the Boston Tea Party Ships and Museum. They were hosting an exhibit of hand-drawn maps, and even though I was only six years old, I was floored. I had always liked drawing, but there was something about the beauty and the precision of that specific kind of drawing that called to me. Granted, I was a boy obsessed with the adventure stories Alastair read to me, especially the ones that came with hand drawn maps of islands in the front, so that probably played into my interest in traditional cartography."

"I love hearing about where your inspiration came from." And now, more than ever, Lola wanted to know how things could have gone so wrong between Duncan and his brother. What had his brother done? But since she didn't want to risk making him sad again, she said instead, "You must also have a lot of happy memories about the businesses you've funded and the people you've helped turn dreams into reality."

Duncan's expression shuttered despite what she'd thought would be an innocuous question. "It's been a huge privilege to work with so many people who are making a difference in the world." With that, he picked up their plates and stood. "I'll take these into the kitchen and put them through the dishwasher."

She'd never met a man less inclined to talk about

himself. At the same time, given that he'd opened up a little bit about his fraught relationship with his brother, he didn't seem to be trying deliberately to keep secrets from her. It was more that he found the subject too painful to focus on for too long. Given that she never liked to dwell on her own painful experiences, even with her family, whom she trusted completely, she understood Duncan's reticence. Soon enough, she was confident they would let all of their walls down with each other.

It was yet another thought that should have surprised her, but with Duncan, everything she'd once believed to be true about relationships felt like it had been turned on its head.

Instead of going slow, she wanted to move fast.

Instead of holding things in, she wanted to share.

Instead of keeping her walls up, she wanted to let them all fall.

Instead of being afraid to open up, she wanted to trust him with everything.

And how sweet was he to offer to take care of the dishes? It was both considerate and sexy. Most guys were so focused on being macho and taking whatever they thought they could get, that it never occurred to them that giving, helping, and being kind were the ultimate in *sexy*. Of course, Duncan's broad shoulders, square jaw, and piercing blue eyes didn't hurt. "There's something I'd really like to show you in town before you head back to Boston," she said before he walked away with the dishes, "but I need to make a quick call to confirm that we can get in after hours. Once I've done that, I'll come help you clean up."

Duncan headed into the kitchen while she dialed Turner's cell phone.

Her brother picked up on the third ring. "Hey, Lola. What's up?"

"I was hoping you could let me and a new friend into the Maritime Museum tonight." The building was closed for the night, but as her brother volunteered there once a week, she thought he might be able to make an exception.

"Sure, I can let you in for a bit," Turner said. "Who's the new friend?"

"His name is Duncan." Though Turner was the mellowest of her brothers, even he had his Neanderthal moments. Which was why she added, "I like him. So be nice."

"I'm always nice."

While that was true, she couldn't help but think that Turner, as she'd said to Duncan, was keeping a lot more beneath the surface than any of them could guess. She suspected it would bubble up one day when the right woman came along, and nothing her brother did to shove it back down was going to do a lick of good. "See you in fifteen."

By the time she walked into the kitchen, Duncan was done cleaning up. "Why don't we take my van, since I'm the tour guide tonight?"

The café had closed while they were eating, so she locked up before they headed out. The Sullivan Café was open from seven in the morning until four in the afternoon. Her mother had set those hours so that she could always be home to make her children dinner, play games before bath time, and then tuck them in. Even after they'd all left home, her parents had kept the same hours for the café, apart from a special event pop-up dinner here and there.

Wishing Duncan had the support of a family like hers rather than a brother who had disappointed him so deeply, she consoled herself with the thought that when they were officially dating, the Sullivans would all support him too.

She barely caught her thought. *When* they were dating. Not *if*.

But amazingly, instead of being afraid of how quickly she was falling for Duncan, she was simply happy.

Happier than she had ever been before.

CHAPTER FIVE

Lola's van was big and blue, with her logo painted on the side. The brightly colored illustrated flower on a white background evoked both style and emotion. It was the perfect brand ambassador for both Lola and her business—everything about her was bold and colorful, yet warm and accessible at the same time.

"My van is always a little messy," she warned him. "I just need to move a few rolls of fabric off the passenger seat, and then there will be room for you."

"Let me help you with those. They must be heavy."

She shot him an amused look. "I have strong arms." She proved it by easily hefting the large stack of fabric bolts and moving them to the back of the van.

No question about it, Lola was a strong woman on all fronts. "As impressive as your upper-body strength is," Duncan said, "it's more impressive that you can do so much in such high heels."

"I own flats and tennis shoes, but I don't wear them unless I absolutely have to." She looked down at her feet. "These heels are some of my favorites." Her shoes had a bright floral print and sashes that tied around her ankles. "They make me smile every time I look down and see them."

He hadn't realized shoes had the power to make people happy, but now he got it. "They're making me smile too." Her smile was so bright he nearly gave in to the instinctive need to pull her into his arms and kiss her. Before he could, he remembered about the man she'd had to deal with on the phone that afternoon and her story about her ex. Both men only wanted to use her to sate their own selfish needs and desires.

Duncan would never do that to Lola, no matter how much he wanted her.

They got into the van, and she started the engine, then pulled into traffic. "I think you're really going to like where I'm taking you," she told him.

"Wherever we go, whatever we do, I already know I'm going to like it, because I'm with you." He winced at the way the words came out. "I know that sounds like a sappy line, but I swear it's not."

"It *does* sound sappy, but that's okay, because I'm thinking exactly the same thing." She reached for his hand over the gearshift. "We can be sappy together," she said with a grin.

Again, he wanted to kiss her until they were both breathless. Instead, he lightly stroked his fingertips over the back of her hand. The little shiver that ran through her gave him a good indication of how deeply she was responding to his touch, even the barest one.

She shifted her attention away from the road long enough to meet his gaze. "It's crazy, isn't it? This. *Us.*"

"It is crazy," he agreed. "I didn't see this coming. Didn't see *you* coming into my life like this."

Lola Sullivan wasn't just a wonderful daughter, sister, aunt, and businesswoman—she would also be an amazing wife and mother. It was a startling train of thought for him, given that he'd never before thought seriously about marriage or children. But after little more than eight hours with her, he could already see their future together with perfect clarity.

"I didn't see you coming either," she told him. "How could I when I had decided to completely shut myself off to the idea of being with anyone?"

Though he was glad she wasn't seeing another man, his gut clenched. "Because of what happened with Frank and trouble from men like that distributor on the phone today?"

She shot him a look. "You heard that?"

"I didn't mean to listen in. But what I caught wind of didn't sound good."

"It wasn't. But I'm used to it and he's dealt with now." She seemed a little wary again as she added, "Even before I met Frank, dealing with men was always kind of difficult for me. It's hard to explain..."

But he understood why. "People probably think you get handed everything on a silver platter and that everything is easier for you." He didn't need to say the words *because of your looks* for them both to understand that was the reason. "But that isn't true, is it? Instead, you end up having to fight to be taken seriously, don't you?"

He could tell she was uncomfortable with their conversation by the way she shifted in her seat and frowned, deeply enough to create tiny grooves on her forehead. "Let's just say that I've learned to stand up for myself in the business world. And when it comes to my personal life...well, the truth is that I haven't found many good, kind, confident-but-not-egotistical men coming into my world. Especially ones that cause my heart to race like crazy and make me want to spill all my secrets to them." Thankfully, a beat later she was smiling again. A smile that transformed her expression into pure joy as she said, "Not until you, Duncan."

Even as he drank in her beautiful smile, guilt moved through him at her unabashedly positive view of him. Yet again, he wanted to tell Lola the truth of everything that had happened when he'd worked with his brother. But though the words were on the tip of his tongue, he couldn't get them out. Not when he knew his admission would cause everything that was beginning between the two of them to abruptly end.

One day soon, he would tell her. He wouldn't be able to live with himself if he didn't. But right this second, when they were only just beginning to admit their feelings to each other, he couldn't risk losing Lola.

Not when he'd only just found her.

At the very least, though, he had to say, "You shouldn't give me too much credit."

"See?" she exclaimed. "That's exactly what I'm talking about. I don't know a single other man who would have told me to think less of him instead of more. None of the guys I've dated had an ounce of modesty. And none of them truly wanted to be with *me*."

"You're one of the most intelligent, determined, talented people I've ever known, Lola. I want to kiss you breathless," he said, intent on being as honest as he possibly could with her. "But I also want to know your hopes, your dreams, your past, and your plans for the future."

"I want all the same things from you." She paused a beat before adding, "Even though everything is moving so fast."

"I won't hurt you, Lola. And I'll never underestimate you, not in any way. I promise."

She pulled into the parking lot of a building on the oceanfront, then turned off the ignition and unbuckled her seat belt, shifting to face him. "I know you won't.

I've felt it all day. Practically from the first moment we met." She lifted his hand and laid it over her chest, where he could feel her heart beating strong and steady beneath his palm. "I feel it here. It's the same thing I feel when I look into your eyes. I know I can trust you. And you can trust me too. Because I'm not going to hurt you either."

They were leaning in toward each other, and he could almost taste her lips, almost feel her beautiful curves pressed against him when, suddenly, there was a loud bang on the window.

They jumped apart like two teenagers caught making out. But it wasn't a disapproving parent outside the van. It was a man in his thirties who shared a distinct resemblance to Lola.

She rolled her eyes, huffed out a breath. "I'm going to kill him," she muttered. "That's my brother Turner. He has the code to the building, so he's letting us in. Although I'm afraid I'm going to have to tear off at least one of his limbs first."

Even as she grumbled about their first kiss being thwarted by her brother, Duncan could hear the love and affection in her voice. Because her family clearly meant everything to her.

Once you were in Lola's heart, you were there permanently. She would do absolutely anything for the people she loved. To protect them. To care for them.

To make sure they were happy.

Duncan had never wanted anything more than he wanted to be one of those fortunate people. He would give and do anything, change any part of himself and his life for her.

When they got out of the van, her brother smiled at Lola but merely bared his teeth at Duncan.

"Turner," she said, "this is my friend Duncan. Duncan, this is my totally overbearing brother." She scowled at Turner, her voice slightly grudging as she added, "Thanks for coming to let us into the museum. If you'll give me the code to open and lock up, you won't need to stay."

Turner shook his head. "I've got no problem staying until you two leave."

"You're acting like we're going to have sex all over the building." Her eyes suddenly lit with mischief. "On second thought, maybe that isn't such a bad idea."

While it was clear to Duncan that she was only trying to wind her brother up in retaliation for his overprotectiveness, Turner looked ready for a fight. "You'd better not do anything in there with my sister," he growled at Duncan.

Lola whacked Turner on the shoulder. "*Stop it!* I was kidding. And if you so much as set one foot inside the museum before we're done, I won't be responsible for my actions." She took Duncan's hand and led him away.

Though Turner didn't look at all happy about it, he stayed where he was. Duncan tried not to laugh or even smile. He got the sense neither sibling would appreciate it. At the same time, it was heartening to see how natural their dynamic was. Even when one person was irritated and the other was concerned, no one said anything hurtful or wounding.

The same had not been true of Duncan and his brother. On the contrary, Alastair was a master at ramming a knife into your back when you were least expecting it. It didn't matter whether it was family or business—winning was all that mattered. Along with never being made to look like a fool.

And still, Duncan hadn't been able to see through his brother's lies. Hadn't been able to separate family loyalty from the crimes taking place right under his nose.

"Sorry about Turner," Lola said.

Her voice brought Duncan back to the present, away from his own family and the dark past that never seemed far behind, no matter how long and hard he tried to outrun it.

"Don't apologize for anything," he said. "Your brother is just looking out for you."

"Despite his behavior tonight, he really is a nice guy," she agreed. "Like I said before, he's the most easygoing of all my brothers."

Duncan's eyebrows went up. "Note to self—wear armor when meeting your other brothers."

She laughed, the sound incredibly sweet. "I can't wait for you to meet them all. Soon, hopefully."

Had Turner not still been watching them with laser vision from the parking lot, observing their every movement, every point of contact, Duncan would have kissed her, now that he was confident that it was also what she wanted. Instead, he said, "I'd like to meet them all soon, too. I have several business matters I need to deal with urgently in Boston this week." Namely, discussing the possibility of having his new hire, Anita, take over some of his day-to-day duties so that he could spend more time in Bar Harbor. "But after that, I'm suddenly finding myself inspired to clear my schedule."

She looked like he'd just given her the greatest possible gift. "Is there any chance you could come back by Friday? That's when we have our weekly family dinner at my parents' house, and then everyone can meet you."

"Friday will work." He'd make sure of it.

She beamed at him, her smile the brightest ray of sunshine he'd ever seen. One that staggered him with its beauty.

"Knowing you'll be back soon will help me be a

little less sad about you leaving in the morning." She looked a little startled by what she'd just said. "I meant it when I said I'm not normally so impulsive. Normally, I would never blurt out any of these things to you, but I can't help myself. Not when this, you, us—it all seems so right." She moved deeper into his arms, curving hers up around his neck. "It might sound crazy, but I can already see you sitting beside me at my parents' dining table laughing with everyone." She took his breath away all over again as she stared up into his eyes. "And you know the craziest thing of all? I'm not even the tiniest bit scared about giving my heart to you."

It didn't matter anymore that her brother was still watching them. Hell, it wouldn't have mattered if a tornado was thundering toward them.

He had to kiss her.

Duncan put his hands on either side of Lola's face, drinking her in for a moment before finally covering her mouth with his.

She tasted like lemons, and sunshine, and heat, and passion.

She made every nerve, every cell, every fiber in his body come to life.

She made him want, and need, and desire.

And she made him *believe*. Believe in the possibility of a beautiful future. Believe in love after he'd lost all faith in it.

Her kiss infused him with such joy. Joy he never wanted to end. Joy he never wanted to lose.

Joy that he silently vowed he would never, ever betray. No matter what.

"*Wow,*" she breathed as they both finally came up for air.

Their foreheads still touching, he smiled into her eyes and echoed, "Wow." And then he had to say, "I can't believe your brother hasn't come over here to slug me yet."

Still looking a little dazed from his kiss, she nodded. "We should probably go inside before he changes his mind." She drew his arm even tighter around her waist. "I'm never wobbly on my heels, but I think I'd better hold on extra tight to you right now to make sure I stay steady."

He liked that he made her legs a little shaky. She made his shaky too.

The building she took him into was old, and he could see and smell the years, the history, the past in every wood plank on the floor, in the walls, in the timbers of the roof. The windows were old, wavy glass, and there was a chimney in one corner.

"This maritime museum was once a fisherman's house. And when he was old enough to retire, he started drawing nautical maps."

Duncan had temporarily forgotten that he had come to Bar Harbor for any other reason than to be with Lola. His passion for her had taken over everything else. But as she led him toward a glass case and he looked at the antique map, he was infused with a deep appreciation for the art made by the fisherman who had once lived here.

"Amazing." The lines on the map weren't perfect. The fisherman hadn't been a trained artist, by any means. But a deep and abiding love for the sea was in every stroke of his pen. It was clear that the fisherman understood the heart of a nautical map in a way a non-sailor would never be able to. "I could study this map for hours."

Lola was equally rapt. "Just looking at it makes me feel like I know the man who lived here."

He turned to her. "I was struck the same way by you and your fabric designs. Who you are, what you believe, what matters to you, how you look at life—all of those things are in what you've created."

Lola's lips were on his before he could take his next breath, tasting him, teasing him, driving him absolutely wild. "I don't want to stop," she said in a husky voice several minutes later. "I just want to keep kissing you and kissing you and kissing you. But if I do that, I'm pretty sure we won't stop at just kissing...and then my brother really *will* kill you. So I'm going to force myself to put a moratorium on it until we're out of sight of his beady little eyes." She let go of Duncan's hand and pointed toward a glass case on the far left wall. "You go look at that map." She nodded toward a display case on the right wall. "I'll go look at the one on the other side of the room." Her eyes lit with renewed fire. "Later, we'll compare notes." She made certain to infuse the words *compare notes* with so much heat he couldn't possibly misunderstand her intent.

They laughed as they moved apart. Duncan liked everything about Lola. Not only that her kisses burned through every inch of him, and that she was a vision of beauty, but that she made him laugh.

He had never hoped to have a relationship like this, had never really seen a truly great couple in action before, certainly not with his parents or any of the couples in his Boston circle.

Who would have thought that coming to Bar Harbor for a one-day drawing class would mean having all of his dreams come true?

Even the ones he hadn't known to dream.

CHAPTER SIX

Lola felt like she was living in a dream. One she never wanted to wake from.

They didn't speak as they left the museum and drove back toward town, her hand held tightly in his. She loved sitting beside Duncan, holding his hand, knowing the breathtaking kisses they'd shared in the museum were about to turn into so much more.

Lola never slept with a guy on the first date. Truth was, she hadn't slept with many men at all. The problem was that guys looked at her and expected every inch of her to be perfect, without a lump or a bump in sight. Even worse, they expected her to live up to their ultimate fantasy.

But she was only human. A normal, flesh-and-blood woman. She wasn't perfect. Anything but. Plus, none of the men she'd been with had measured up to *her* fantasies.

Lola knew without a doubt, though, that Duncan would be different.

She pulled up beside his car where he'd parked it

outside her studio, but before he got out of her van to follow her back to her house, he kissed her again, another slow, sensuous kiss that promised all her sizzling-hot fantasies would soon become reality.

After he got out of her vehicle and into his, she worked to catch her breath as she led the way toward her cottage, only two blocks away. She couldn't remember ever feeling so full of anticipation.

Lola had walked, biked, and driven these tree-lined streets her entire life. She'd been happy before. She'd felt excited. But she'd never felt like *this*, like every inch of her skin was buzzing, like she could barely keep her heart from beating its way out of her chest.

Even better, she didn't have to wonder if Duncan felt the same way. Not when every sign pointed to their being of one mind. One heart. And soon to be *one* in the sexiest way possible…

Lola parked outside her cottage, with Duncan taking the space behind her. "Even if you hadn't told me which home was yours," he said as he got out of his rental car, "I could have picked it out. Your spirit is in every inch of it."

"I bought it three years ago, once I felt confident enough with my business to take on a mortgage. My family helped me paint it, although they joked that I unearthed colors never before seen by the naked eye."

"It's bright, and fun, and perfect for you, Lola."

She agreed. She loved her cottage, loved her garden, and got along great with her neighbors. Everything about her life in Bar Harbor suited her perfectly, and she had never wanted to live anywhere else. Along with the colorful wooden façade painted in a riot of magentas and sea blues and yellows, the garden was ripe and luscious with flowers and fruit trees. In the setting sun, it looked more beautiful than ever.

Lola wasn't a natural gardener, not like her brother Hudson, a landscape architect. But she loved flowers, loved trees, loved growing fruits and vegetables. She loved to go into the garden on a quiet morning or evening to sip a cup of tea and watch the birds and the butterflies and the ladybugs, and breathe in the sea air.

She couldn't wait to share those moments—*all* her moments—with Duncan.

"Come inside." She tugged him up the brick pathway, which Turner had helped her lay, then up the stairs of her painted porch and into the house, which, like most locals, she rarely locked.

"Your door is unlocked." He frowned. "Is someone already here?"

"It's very safe in Bar Harbor. And whenever I do decide to lock the door, I always manage to lose my key, so I end up having to bust in through a window anyway." She gestured to the formfitting pencil skirt of her dress. "Shimmying through a window wearing this isn't easy." She dropped her bag onto the entryway table, then said, "Why don't I open a bottle of wine? We can take it into the living room. And then we can finally *compare notes*." She'd never felt quite as sexy as she did walking into the kitchen, knowing his eyes were drinking her in with every step she took. "Merlot okay?"

But instead of answering from the entryway, his voice came from just beside her ear. "It's perfect."

As he wrapped his arms around her, it was wonderful to relax into his chest, closing her eyes, breathing him in. It took her far longer than usual to get the cork out of the bottle and pour the wine.

Turning slowly in his arms, she handed him a glass. "To tonight and all the wonders yet to be discovered."

"To you, Lola Sullivan, the most incredible woman I've ever met."

They clinked, sipped...and then wine was forgotten, their glasses left on the kitchen counter as they couldn't wait another second to unleash their passion.

Passion that had been building from the first moment they had set eyes on each other.

Passion that couldn't be denied.

Passion that Lola knew was going to fulfill every sexy fantasy she'd ever had, while also filling her heart.

Duncan's mouth found hers again, tasting, taking,

giving. His kiss was everything she wanted, somehow both gentle and rough at the same time. Raw and desperate and breathless.

And so, so, so *good*.

And then he was raining kisses over her cheekbones, claiming her mouth again before moving south over her chin and then her neck. She arched against him as his mouth and hands sent unparalleled pleasure through her.

He ran his hands down the length of her body—from curve to hollow and back again—as he kissed her. His touch brought every inch of her to sensual life. She felt teased, tempted, as he deliberately moved so slowly that she was constantly on the verge of crying out for him to rip off her clothes and take her right then and there against the kitchen cabinets.

At last, he approached her breasts—moving even slower now, so slowly that she thought he might never get there. Her heart was beating halfway out of her chest, pounding against his hands, and she couldn't breathe. Couldn't manage to inhale any oxygen at all. Not until he...

She gasped as he finally curved his large hands over her breasts. *"Duncan."* She'd never felt like this before, never been so incredibly glad for her abundant curves. Not until this very moment when he touched her this way.

He captured her lips again, their kiss even more desperate now. His eyes were burning with such heat his gaze nearly seared her as he said, "I need to feel you, Lola. I need to see you. *All* of you."

"Yes." She had never begged a man for anything before. Even when she was eighteen and still hadn't come fully into her own, she'd understood that it would be akin to giving up her power. But she knew instinctively that she didn't need to hold the word back with Duncan. Not when he would never, ever use her need for him against her. *"Please."*

He carried her over to the couch, but instead of laying her down on it, he put her on her feet, letting her curves slide against his hard heat until she was standing again.

Her heels had barely made contact with the floor when, without saying a word, he put his hands on her hips and turned her so that she was facing away from him.

His silent command of her body rode the edge of dominant. It was so damned sexy that her knees nearly went out beneath her.

She knew he'd never do anything to hurt her, but that didn't mean she wanted him to treat her like porcelain either. She'd never been able to find that perfect middle ground where she could give in to her innate sensuality without being reduced to a sex object.

But with Duncan, she could finally be sexy without worrying about how he'd see her afterward.

With Duncan, she could finally be herself and open her heart all the way.

And if she hadn't been one hundred percent open with him earlier when they were talking about their pasts? If she hadn't yet confessed her most secret fears? Well, she told herself, there would be plenty of time to get to all of that. Soon.

But not tonight. Not when she didn't want to focus on anything except Duncan's kisses and caresses and the growly sound he made deep in his throat as his lips skittered over the bared skin between her neck and shoulder.

Her dress was perfectly fitted to her figure, and she'd felt comfortable in it all day. But now the fabric felt as though it was scratching her overly sensitive skin, and with her breasts on the verge of overflowing the bodice, she was desperate for Duncan to take it off.

And as he ran his hands up from her waist to the top of the zipper, she felt as though he was marking every inch of her as his.

Oh yes, she was all his.

Lola held her breath as she waited for him to drag the zipper down. Instead, he continued to tease her with his left hand, sliding it around to her front so that he could pull her against him.

As her hips nestled against his erection, her breath came out in little pants. *"Please,"* she begged again.

"Tell me what you want." His words were hot against her skin, his touch even hotter as he finally drew the zipper down. "Tell me what you need."

"You."

Duncan turned her to face him again and captured her mouth with his. She melted even more into him, so lost in his kiss that she didn't realize he'd started to slide her bodice from her shoulders until he broke away from her mouth so that he could strip it away completely.

Before he could tease her any more than he already had, she reached for the clasp at the front of her bra and undid it, shrugging it off a second later. Taking his hands in hers, she drew them over her bare breasts.

Oh God. It felt so good. He felt so good. The heat of his hands, the slightly callused skin cupping and stroking her flesh, the ragged sound of his breath as he took everything she wanted so badly to give him.

She was *this close* to tipping over the edge when he stopped and said, "I don't deserve you."

She didn't know why he was saying that. All she knew was that he was wrong. "You do. And I deserve you too."

And then she was threading her hands into his hair and kissing him. He tasted so damned good, his skin faintly salty as she ran her mouth over his five o'clock shadow.

Lola wanted to memorize every moment in his arms so that she could mark this in her mind as the moment her life changed forever.

At last, she'd found the happiness she'd secretly been searching for.

CHAPTER SEVEN

Duncan had never felt so lucky.

No man could ever be worthy of Lola Sullivan. No mortal could possibly deserve the crazy pleasure of having her luscious curves pressed against him while she rained kisses over his face and lips.

And yet, somehow, some way, Duncan had found his way to Lola.

To her smile.

To her laughter.

To her open arms.

To the sinfully sexy sounds she made when she was desperate for his touch.

But even though Duncan knew he didn't deserve her, how the hell could he walk away from her when she was offering him the most precious gift in the world? Not just her body, but her heart.

He'd never wanted anything so badly as he wanted to be in her heart. Because for all that his body was crying out for hers, the warmth and honest emotion in her eyes were what made him catch his breath.

Lola was, hands down, the most stunning woman he'd ever seen, but her beauty was so much more than physical. Her beauty came from the inside, from a totally pure heart. More pure than he'd known a heart could be.

A million times more pure than his...

He drew back to look into her eyes, and what he saw in them floored him. No one had ever looked at him this way, as though she needed him more than she needed anything else, even her next breath.

I think I'm falling in love with you. The words hovered on the tip of his tongue. Only the worry that she might freak out if he said them so soon held them back. He couldn't bear the thought of scaring her off with the three little words he'd never said to anyone. Words he'd never so much as *thought* about another woman.

"Do you have any idea how much I want you?" His voice vibrated with desire. "Do you have any idea how desperate I am to hear you cry out with pleasure when I put my hands, my mouth on you?" He brushed the pad of his thumb over her full lower lip, and he nearly groaned as her tongue flicked out to taste him. "Do you have any idea how much I love hearing you gasp when I touch you?"

"Touch me again, Duncan." She pulled him down to the couch with her. *"Love me."*

Her words, and her obvious joy at being with him,

flipped a switch inside of him. She wrapped her legs around his hips as he levered up with one arm so he could watch her reaction as he used his free hand to cup, stroke, tease her breasts. Her eyes fell closed as she writhed beneath his touch, so damned responsive that it wasn't enough just to touch her, he had to taste her too.

Sweet Lord, the taste of her against his tongue nearly undid him…

Even if he never experienced anything more with Lola, this would be far more than Duncan had ever dreamed of.

Wanting to give her pleasure beyond her wildest imaginings, he laved her breasts with his tongue as he ran his hand over her stomach, loving the way her body tensed in anticipation as he slid his thumbs into the sides of her panties and drew the sheer fabric down her gorgeous legs.

For a long moment, he simply let himself drink her in. Her smooth skin. The faded scars on her knees where he guessed she must have fallen as a child playing with her siblings. The little freckles beneath the curves of her breasts. Every inch of her took his breath away. Until looking wasn't nearly enough, and he had to taste her again, had to touch her again.

He greedily took her mouth as he cupped her sex. She was so wet, so hot, as desperate for his touch as he was desperate to touch her. She arched against him, her hips instinctively moving so that his fingers slipped over, then inside her slick flesh.

He'd never come closer to the edge of control as he did at the feel of Lola's curves, her sweet scent, the taste of her lips against his, the bucking of her hips as she tried to take him deeper.

As he slid his thumb over the center of her arousal, all it took was one long moan from her throat to snap his remaining control. Moving like a man possessed, he drove her crazy with his hand against her sex while running kisses over her breasts, then down her abdomen.

In the exact moment he tasted her on his tongue, she cried out his name. Nothing had ever sounded better. He could spend his whole life making her come over and over again and never get enough of it. Never get enough of *her*.

Her inner muscles clenched against his fingers as he continued to pleasure her with his tongue. And as she gasped and writhed beneath him, everything in Duncan's world came down to giving Lola as much ecstasy as he possibly could.

Duncan's past and the future seemed to disappear completely, leaving only this perfect moment with Lola.

"That was *beyond* amazing," she said once he had

moved back up to hold her in his arms. Her skin was rosy and flushed from her climax, her lips full from their kisses, her eyes shining with what looked like anticipation. "I can't wait for what comes next."

She started to unbutton his shirt, and the pleasures awaiting him threatened to overwhelm what was left of his sense. His conscience.

It was impossible to think straight when they were this close, her skin flushed a beautiful rose, her chest still rapidly rising and falling in the aftermath of her release. He'd never wanted anything so much in his life as he wanted to make love to her. And he knew she wanted that just as much by the way she wrapped her arms around his neck and looked into his eyes.

Only, even now, he couldn't completely forget his past—or hers. Not only that he was nowhere close to being a saint, but that she deserved a man who would do whatever it took to prove to her that she was far more than just a beautiful face and a hot body.

Drawing from his deep well of control, he lifted his mouth from hers.

"Duncan?" She blinked at him, her gaze slowly refocusing. "What's wrong?"

"I don't deserve you."

"You're the only one who does."

She reached for his chest again, but he caught her hands in his. One more touch, and he'd be lost, forgetting what he needed to do.

"I'm not good enough for you," he insisted. "But when I look in your eyes, I desperately want to be worthy of you." It nearly killed him to say the rest. "Which is why I can't make love to you tonight."

"What?" She looked stunned. And, worse, hurt. "Why can't you?"

"That came out all wrong." Damn it, he hadn't meant to hurt her. Hurting Lola was the very last thing he ever wanted to do. "Of course I want to make love with you. More than I've ever wanted anything in my whole life." He tried to corral his thoughts into some semblance of order. "But I don't want you to think I came to Bar Harbor because I was angling for a one-night stand. I swear to you that it's the very last thing I want. I want us to have more than just one night together. So much more."

"I want that too," she said. "And you don't have to worry. I know this isn't a one-night stand. Our connection…" She stared into his eyes, her heart in hers. "I've never felt anything like this before, Duncan. Not with anyone else."

Her clear confirmation that she felt exactly the way he did nearly shook his resolve. "I haven't either," he said softly. But he still needed to ask, "How many men have treated you the way you deserve to be treated?"

She shook her head, his question seeming to hit her

hard. "Apart from my family—" She dropped her gaze. "None."

"Let me woo you." The intensity in his voice made her gaze connect with his again. "Let me romance you. Let me adore you the way you deserve to be adored."

CHAPTER EIGHT

Lola's body was still humming from the incredible orgasm Duncan had given her. She felt sated, deliciously so, and yet…

She wanted *all* of Duncan. Wanted to feel his body wrapped around her. Wanted to feel his strong muscles pressing her into her bed. Wanted to twist up her sheets together as they made wild, passionate love.

She'd been stunned when he'd held himself back, and then when he'd told her he couldn't make love to her tonight. It had been the very last thing she'd expected him to say. The very last thing any other man she'd been with would have said.

And it would be so easy to seduce him into changing his mind. Truthfully, she was so darned tempted to do just that.

But at the same time, he was right that no other man had ever put her first. Men had lavished her looks with praise, they'd practically written sonnets about how sexy she was…but no one had ever truly adored her or romanced her. All they'd ever wanted was physical pleasure for themselves.

So if Duncan wanted to prove his devotion to her, she would let him.

And she would adore *him* even more for it.

"Okay. I can do it. I can wait. At least I can try," she said as she licked her lips, wanting him more and more every second. "I have to be honest, though. I'm not sure I'll be able to withstand wanting you this much for too long."

His gaze was intense, full of heat *and* emotion. "I'll never forgive myself if I screw up things with you. I've never felt like this about anyone else. Never thought I could. Not until you smiled at me, and held my hand, and made me feel like dreams *can* come true." He stroked her cheek. "I want to savor you. Everything about you. Inside and out. I want to hear about your childhood, and your experiences in high school and college, and then everything that happened after that. I want to know what you like and what you hate, what kind of movies you binge-watch, and the music you listen to. I want to find out how you got the scars on your knees, if it was from playing with your brothers and sisters? I want to hold you in my arms and listen to absolutely anything you want to tell me. But first," he said in that deep voice that had melted her insides from the very first time he'd spoken, "I want to give you more pleasure. So much that you'll never be able to forget our night together."

"There's no way I could ever forget it," she whispered against his lips right before he claimed them again.

She swore she could taste his desire—the desire to give her everything she wanted and needed, rather than the desire to take whatever he could get away with. Even though bringing her to another breathless climax would surely only leave him more frustrated.

His hands, his mouth found all her secret pleasure spots. Behind the curve of her knee. Along her spine. Even the tips of her toes were lavished with kisses. Until she was so aroused again that the barest brush of his fingertips between her legs sent her reeling back into climax.

He gathered her close as she fought for breath, but the brush of her breasts against his chest, and the way she could feel his heart hammering in his chest, only made her want him more.

"You amaze me, Lola." His words sent as much heat through her as his touch had.

Lifting her eyes to his, she said, "You amaze me too."

When their mouths found each other again, she was certain they wouldn't be able to stop this time. But she hadn't counted on just how strong his will was, because somehow he convinced her to leave the couch, put her clothes back on, and head out into the garden. The light had faded while they were inside and the stars were starting to twinkle from the sky above them as they created a comfortable, cozy haven with pillows and soft blankets, including the quilt her mom had made from the scraps of her favorite childhood dresses. They had also brought out a feast of fruit, cheese, crackers, and wine.

Though Lola's body was still humming with desire—and she knew his was too—she loved how easy being with Duncan felt. She'd never had a moonlit picnic in her backyard with anyone before, and every second with him, listening to the owls call back and forth while the moon rose higher and higher in the sky, was wonderful.

Once they had eaten, she lay in his arms, her head against his chest, drawing his arms around her waist as she told him funny stories about her childhood. She told him about the first time she used the sewing machine and accidentally sewed her dress to the tablecloth. She laughed as she recounted the Easter when she and all six of her siblings had an egg-throwing fight, and how her aim was so true that everyone in the family still looked a little nervous when she took a dozen eggs out of the fridge. She told him all about how she'd skinned her knees when she and her siblings were pretending to be Evel Knievel on the street in front of their house. He laughed when she said the scars had been worth it, though, because she'd jumped farther and higher on her bike than any of her brothers. She told him about her first gallery showing when she was fourteen, and how exciting it had been to see a red Sold sticker next to her artwork.

Though she tried to get Duncan to tell her stories about his past too, he always managed to bring it back around to her. But she didn't blame him for being reluctant to delve into his childhood, not when she couldn't imagine how difficult it must have been for him to lose his parents at such a young age.

"Tell me more," he urged her. "You've told me about your past. Now tell me how you'd like your life to be in five, ten, even fifty years."

"I have so much already," she said, her muscles loose and relaxed in his arms, her eyes growing heavy as sleep tried to claim her. "It almost doesn't seem fair to hope for more. But when I look out five years from now, on a professional level, I hope I'm still really loving my work and that what I do is still bringing a smile to people's faces."

"I have no doubt your work will always make people happy," he said. "And on a personal level, what do you want from the rest of your life?"

She liked his questions, liked the way he made her take a good look at her life. "I've traveled a bit, but I haven't seen as many places as I thought I would by now. I've been glued to my desk these past eight years, and while I don't regret the time I've spent building my business, in the future I hope I spend more time outside enjoying the beauty of where I live and also discovering other beautiful places. I also hope everyone in my family will stay healthy and happy—and I'd love to have more nieces and nephews. And of course, I hope there's peace and love for everyone all over the world."

"That's a great list."

"I'm not done. I haven't yet gotten to what I want most of all." She shifted to look into his eyes. "I hope you'll be beside me." Her voice was softer now, though no less sure. "Some people might call it crazy after only knowing you for a day, but I can see us together fifty years from now."

"At least fifty," he said, his deep voice sending heat moving through her, though the evening had turned cool.

They kissed again, but his intent to savor her meant he stopped the kiss before they lost control. Leaning back against his chest, she closed her eyes, just for a few seconds.

★ ★ ★

The next thing she knew, she was waking up to the

sound of birds chirping and the first rays of the sun rising over her back garden.

Still holding her, Duncan pressed a kiss to the side of her neck, making her shiver with need despite being covered in thick blankets. "Good morning."

"The best morning ever," she said, shifting slightly to run her fingertips over the rugged bristles across his jaw. She smiled into his eyes. "So have I convinced you yet?"

"Yes."

"You don't even know what you've agreed to, do you?" she asked on a laugh.

"Whatever it is, if you're recommending it, I trust it will be damned good."

She turned to kiss him, before saying, "Only good?"

He nipped at her bottom lip, turning her insides to liquid all over again. "Amazing." Another nip, this time at her earlobe. "Fantastic." His teeth gently raked her collarbone. "Stupendous."

It was all she could do to keep breathing, let alone think straight. Still, she somehow managed to say, "Okay, then have you agreed to let your new employee step into your role in your company so that you can focus on your talent and passion for cartography?"

He smiled down at her. "Twenty-four hours ago, I couldn't have imagined I'd be saying yes to that. But now?" He brushed the pad of his thumb across her cheek. "Now I can't imagine saying no."

She'd been so sure that her heart was safe from a fairytale, whirlwind romance. She was ecstatic about being proven wrong.

Lola threw her arms around Duncan, holding him tight, her heart feeling like it was going to explode with joy. She pressed her lips to his, wanting to kiss him forever. She felt warm and pleasured all over, her skin heated everywhere he touched her. And her heart? It felt so full. So happy.

Impulsively, the words fell from her lips. "I love you." After all these years of not being able to trust her heart, it felt so right to tell Duncan she loved him. But at the same time, she felt compelled to add, "I know maybe it's too soon—"

He stopped her from saying more with a kiss. A kiss that made her feel like she was the answer to every one of his prayers. "It's not too soon. I love you too." His mouth found hers again. "I think I fell in love with you the first moment I saw you smile. I fell even harder when you laughed." He traced her lower lip with one fingertip. "And then when I realized just how big your heart is…I knew I was a total goner."

Lola's heart had never felt so full. "I started falling when you didn't so much as blink when my matchmaking mother asked if it was difficult to leave your wife and children at home." They both laughed, and then she told him, "Every moment we've spent together since has only made me fall faster, and deeper."

He kissed her again, a kiss so passionate and full of emotion that she was surprised to see him frown when they drew apart. A muscle jumped in his jaw.

"Lola, there's something—"

The alarm on his cell phone went off, loud and jarring. They'd left the kitchen window open so that they would hear it.

Her heart sank. "I can't believe it's already time for you to leave."

He looked just as upset as she did. "I don't want to go."

They shared one more kiss. And then another. And one more still.

Lola savored every moment of pressing close to Duncan as they lingered over each other for as long as they possibly could. But too soon, he had no choice but to head to the airport, or else he would miss another flight.

Lola was sorely tempted to persuade him to stay, but the sooner he went back to Boston and convinced his new hire to take over for him in the office, the sooner he'd be back in Bar Harbor with her.

For good.

They kissed once more, and then they pushed off

the blankets and stood up so that he could go inside and shut off the darned alarm.

Before she knew it, he was giving her one final, sinfully sweet kiss…and then he was gone.

CHAPTER NINE

Lola wrapped her arms around herself as she stood in her front garden and watched Duncan drive away, wishing it was already Friday when he'd be back in Bar Harbor for dinner with her family. When he was near, her whole body responded to his presence. And now that he was gone, her normally full world felt a little bit emptier.

Her phone buzzed, and the text message brought a smile back to her face. *I miss you already. And I love you. So damned much.*

She didn't want to distract him from driving, so she would wait until he was safely at the airport to send him a message saying she missed him and loved him too.

No one had ever put her needs, her desires, her emotions first, the way Duncan had last night. Just thinking about the way he'd loved every inch of her, without taking anything for himself, made sensual shivers run through her, head to toe. Come Friday night after dinner with her family, she couldn't wait to make him feel just as good.

As she went to take a shower, she thought about how at the end of the previous week, she had been struggling to come up with new ideas for next season's designs. It wasn't that she'd lost her mojo, more that it seemed to have slowed down a bit. Now, however, she was bursting with energy, new ideas, and excitement. And most of all, with the urge to shout from the rooftops that she'd fallen head over heels in love.

Instead of shouting, however, she sang Ed Sheeran's *Perfect* at the top of her lungs in the shower.

Once she was out of the shower, she sent a group text to Cassie and Ashley. *Meet at my studio in 30 minutes? I'll bring coffee and donuts.*

Her sisters sent messages affirming they would be there, and then a text appeared from Turner.

Is that guy you were with last night still there?

Lola texted back a video of herself rolling her eyes. Turner had no business even asking that question, let alone getting an answer.

A half hour later, she had done her hair and makeup, put on a yellow dress, a cropped chartreuse cardigan, and bright red lipstick—plus heels that incorporated the same colors—and was heading into the local coffee shop.

Jonah, the owner, greeted her by name when she walked in. "You've got a special glow today, if you don't mind me saying." Lola had known Jonah, who was in his sixties and one of the friendliest people in town, her entire life. He was always sweet and had never made a pass at her, which earned him even more points in her book. "Good weekend?"

"The best."

She wanted to tell him everything, wanted to turn and say to everyone in the café, *I'm in love! I've met the most wonderful man, and I know we're going to have an incredible life together!* But she wanted to tell her sisters first, so she simply ordered three coffees and a bag of the best doughnuts on the East Coast, then headed for her studio, feeling like she was walking on air rather than four-inch heels.

Cassie and Ashley had let themselves in and were sprawled on the couch in Lola's studio when she arrived. But instead of falling on the coffee and doughnuts the way they normally would, both gave her long, knowing looks, obviously spotting her bright glow, just as Jonah had.

"You've met someone," Ashley proclaimed, a statement rather than a question.

Lola's youngest sister had been badly burned in high school by a boyfriend. After she got pregnant he did a runner, only to return a few years ago to insist on being a part-time parent on *his* terms. As a result, Ashley was hugely suspicious of romantic relationships.

Thankfully, both Zara and Flynn had managed to win Ashley over when they fell in love with Rory and Cassie, respectively.

Lola wasn't particularly worried about making her case for Duncan to Ashley, though. Not when Lola knew he would pass with flying colors.

When it came to Cassie, on the other hand, Lola wouldn't have to sell her older sister on Duncan at all, given that Cassie was head over heels in love herself. Flynn Stewart had come to Bar Harbor from Los Angeles with his niece when he'd become a parent in the wake of his estranged sister passing away from a drug overdose. Cassie had quickly taken both of them into her heart, and now the three of them were the happiest family imaginable.

"Is Ashley right?" Cassie was on the edge of her seat. "Have you met someone?"

Lola nodded happily. "His name is Duncan Lyman. He took my drawing class yesterday. He's so talented. And gorgeous. And we just stayed up all night together. Well, almost all night, since I ended up falling asleep in his arms." She stopped and gave a happy little sigh just thinking about how good it had felt to be held by him. "Anyway, he left an hour ago, but he'll be back on Friday to have dinner with all of us at Mom and Dad's."

Cassie jumped up off the couch and threw her arms

around Lola. "I'm so happy for you!"

But Ashley, who remained on the couch, tearing a glazed chocolate doughnut into lots of little pieces rather than eating it, didn't look quite as overjoyed. "Tell us more about him."

Lola refused to allow herself to be irritated by Ashley's reluctance to immediately embrace her joyous news. She understood how past pain could make a person unwilling to trust in love.

"Well," she began, "the most important thing is that we're in love with each other."

She'd known as she said it that it was akin to dropping a bomb in front of Ashley, but even Cassie's eyes grew huge.

Cassie was the first to recover from the shock of hearing that Lola had not only fallen in love, but so quickly to boot. "That's amazing, Lola! And I get it, because that's exactly what happened for me with Flynn and Ruby. Other people might think it isn't possible to fall in love so fast, but it definitely is. As soon as I met Flynn and Ruby, I knew they were going to mean everything to me."

But Ashley's eyes had only narrowed further. "I'm sure he's gorgeous and wonderful, but are you sure it's actually *love* after less than twenty-four hours together?"

"Yes, I'm sure. We both are." Lola wanted her sister to understand. "For the first time in my life, I'm not worried that a relationship is going to blow up in my face. When Duncan looks at me, he isn't seeing a sex object—he actually sees *me*."

Though Ashley nodded, she pulled out her phone and typed something into it.

"Are you looking him up online?" Lola asked, finally getting a little irritated.

"Of course I am. I love you." Ashley looked up from her screen briefly to meet Lola's gaze. "And I just want to make sure he's who he says he is." She pointed to her screen. "It says here that he runs a—"

"Venture capital firm," Lola finished for her. "He invests in companies that create renewable resources and prosthetic limbs and other innovative products that help people." Before Ashley could continue reading from whatever Web page she had pulled up, Lola continued, "He started the company five years ago after having worked with his brother before that. From everything he's told me, his brother isn't a great person. They are estranged now."

Ashley frowned. "But if his brother was a bad guy, why did Duncan work with him until five years ago?"

Lola hated how Ashley was forcing her to defend Duncan this way. "His brother is ten years older and raised him after their parents passed away when Duncan was six. They had a strong bond when he was a child, until his brother drove them apart. I don't know exactly what happened, but we all know how messy families can be. We're lucky to have such a close-knit family. And even then, it isn't always easy."

"I'm not judging him for his brother's misdeeds," Ashley clarified, "I'm just making sure there's no wife and kids hiding in—" She looked down at her screen again. "Boston." There was a new question in her eyes now. "Are you guys planning to have a long-distance relationship?" She looked slightly horrified. "Or are you going to move away?"

"I'm not going anywhere." Lola chose a pink frosted doughnut with rainbow sprinkles and took a big bite. "He's found someone to take over the day-to-day of his business in Boston so that he can move to Bar Harbor and pursue the passion he's pushed aside for so long. He's a magnificent cartographer," she explained.

Ashley opened her mouth to speak, but before she could, Cassie put a hand on their sister's arm to quell her next question. "He sounds wonderful, Lola. I can't wait to meet him at dinner on Friday."

Lola grinned as she told them, "Mom already met him at lunch at the café yesterday, when I brought my class in to eat during our midday break. She liked him so much that she went into full-on matchmaker mode. It was *so* embarrassing. Although, given that she ended up being one hundred percent right that he's the perfect man for me, I suppose I can't give her too much grief about it."

It was exactly the right thing to say to settle Ashley down. "If Mom liked him, that's good to hear. Although, remember that guy she set me up with last year?" Ashley made a face. "He kept asking me to send him pictures of my feet."

"He also had a habit of wiggling his nose like a bunny rabbit," Cassie said.

When they had stopped giggling, Ash asked, "Has Dad met Duncan?"

"Nope. And I'm a little worried Dad will come across as really overbearing on Friday." She looked at Cassie. "Remember how weird he was with Flynn the first time they met?"

Cassie nodded. "He was way too protective for my liking that night."

"Speaking of overprotective, you should have seen how Turner behaved last night when he let us into the Maritime Museum to look at the antique maps!" Lola took another bite of her doughnut before saying more, needing the sugar to sweeten her lingering irritation. "He all but tried to yank us apart when we kissed, then proceeded to send me a text this morning demanding to know if Duncan was still around. I was half expecting him to barge into my cottage last night to make sure Duncan wasn't having his wicked way with me."

She felt her cheeks go hot at the memory of all the delicious ways Duncan had *adored* her.

"The two of you have always shared an extra-close bond," Cassie reminded Lola. It was true that Turner and Lola were so close in age they were practically twins.

"I'm trying to cut him some slack," Lola said, "but is it too much to ask for everyone just to be happy for me? Especially when I never thought I'd find anyone who makes me feel the way Duncan does?"

At last, Ashley gave Lola a hug. "I *am* happy for you. I swear I am. Which is why I'm going to stop acting suspicious and weird like Turner."

Lola hugged her sister back. "You guys are the best. That's why I wanted to see you this morning. To share my happiness with you before I talked to anyone else about it."

"We're so glad you did," Cassie said.

"Now, enough about me. How are you guys?" Lola asked.

Cassie looked radiantly happy as she replied, "I'm awesome. Flynn's awesome. Ruby's awesome. And I was actually going to text you both about meeting this morning because there's something really important that *I* wanted to share with you before anyone else."

Lola instantly knew. In fact, given the way Cassie was glowing, Lola would have guessed her sister's big news immediately had she not been so caught up in her own joy.

Ashley beat her to the punch. "You're pregnant!"

Cassie nodded, and the three of them fell into a group hug, tears of joy in their eyes and on their cheeks.

"How long have you known?" Lola asked.

"I've done approximately eighteen tests since last night. All of them said the same thing, that Flynn and I are going to have a little brother or sister for Ruby!" Cassie looked radiantly happy. "I don't want to tell too many people for the first few weeks, until I see my doctor and know that everything is okay, but I had to tell you guys."

"It's amazing news, Cass. And am I right to assume that Dad will be walking you down the aisle soon too?"

"Flynn and I almost knocked each other over diving to the ground to propose. I had actually been working out for a while now how I wanted to propose to him, and it turned out he'd been doing the same thing. But doing it this way, when we'd just gotten the best news ever, was absolutely perfect."

Ashley passed their coffee cups around. "Here's a toast to my two favorite sisters." Cassie and Lola both laughed, as they were Ashley's *only* sisters. "To two women I love so deeply and dearly—may you both be this happy forever."

They tapped coffee cups, then sat in companionable silence, sisters who knew each other better than anyone else in the world. Sisters who had been with each other through thick and thin, bad times and good. Sisters who would *always* be there for each other, no matter what.

Lola couldn't wait for Duncan to meet Cassie and Ashley on Friday. Just thinking of him brought a new smile to her face.

Safe in the knowledge that he would be at the airport by now and out of his car, she finally sent a reply to his earlier text. *I can't wait to see you on Friday. I'll be counting the minutes. And I love you too.* Before hitting Send, she drew a heart on the screen, with her name written through the center of it, as a graphic signature.

She was delighted when, a few minutes later, he sent back a text with a drawing of his own. It was a map of two illustrated hearts, with the suit-wearing heart from Boston heading straight toward the dress-and-heels-wearing heart in Bar Harbor.

CHAPTER TEN

Duncan's focus was laser sharp during the workweek. The first thing he did was thank Gail for giving him Lola's drawing class as a birthday gift. She was clearly pleased that he'd enjoyed it so much and said she couldn't wait to see his next map. He spent the rest of the week giving his new employee, Anita, all the tools and information she'd need to fill his shoes at the helm of his company in Boston—and quickly—so that he could begin his new life in Bar Harbor with Lola.

For the past five years, he'd deliberately kept his company small so that he knew every detail of every deal, with Gail as his only full-time employee to help manage the office and assist with clients. He would never again let himself become so overloaded, or hire so many people to work for him, that he missed seeing crimes committed directly under his nose.

Not that he could imagine Anita ever doing anything illegal. She had graduated from Harvard Business School five years earlier and was enthusiastic, open to listening to new approaches and new ideas. She also had experience running her own startup, which she'd sold in her late twenties. Married with a young child, she was more than capable of having a full-on career and a well-rounded personal life. At last, he was ready to let go of the reins he'd held so tightly for the past five years.

Ready to start anew.

Fortunately, Anita was thrilled at the chance to take on the extra responsibilities Duncan wanted to give her. Throughout the week, they worked long hours while Duncan brought her fully up to speed on the finer details of each client. But even while he was working, Lola was there with him in his head and heart—both in the sweet digital doodles she sent him several times a day and when he simply closed his eyes and thought about her.

For the first few days back in Boston, the rush of falling in love with Lola was enough to keep the darkness from his past from creeping back in. And late in the evenings when he finally found time to sit at his drafting table, he was hit with a rush of inspiration. He knew exactly what he wanted to draw. Not a map this time, but a family tree. Lola had joked over dinner their first night together, while she was telling him about her family, that he wasn't there to draw the Maine branch of the Sullivans. He knew how much she'd love having exactly that, though. So he began his research of family trees and started sketching out ideas in pencil.

Unfortunately, as the days passed the familiar regrets and remorse, along with his fury at himself for having blindly trusted his brother, eventually came slipping back in through the cracks. Several times while on a video call with Lola, he came close to confessing everything. But each time, the thought of losing her stopped him cold.

When and how could he tell her the full truth without risking the love he'd only just found?

All week, the question plagued him. Worse still, with each day that passed, he felt more and more like he was lying to her by omission.

On Friday night, after dinner with her parents, he'd tell her everything. And hope like hell that she wouldn't run, that she'd somehow find a way to forgive him for his past mistakes.

If anyone could find the good in someone, surely it was Lola.

Meeting her was the luckiest thing that could ever have happened to him. And more than anything, he wanted to be a permanent part of her world. A bright and beautiful world where, in the face of love, nothing seemed insurmountable. Not even the darkness from one's past.

Come Friday morning, knowing he wouldn't have

the patience or focus to sit in his office while he counted the minutes until he was back in Bar Harbor with Lola in his arms, he decided to drop by the offices of several clients for face-to-face meetings.

His last visit of the day was with Dave Fischer, who had recently hit a rough spot in his research. Eight years ago, Dave's daughter had been born with a birth defect that left her without a right arm. A mechanical engineer before her birth, Dave decided to shift his focus into robotic limbs. His company had been Duncan's first investment five years ago.

Dave looked up from his bank of computer monitors when Duncan knocked on the door. He smiled in greeting, but Duncan could see that his smile was forced. He could also guess from the bags under Dave's eyes that the other man had been staring at his computer screen for hours on end, rather than getting the rest he needed for his brain to work at top speed. "It's been a while since I dropped by your lab. I hope this isn't a bad time."

Dave shook his head. "Nice of you to go out of your way like this. I wish I had better news for you, but I'm afraid I still haven't figured out why this last round of prototypes is a total bust."

Before Duncan could respond, Dave's daughter came running out, obviously having spotted him in the doorway to her father's backyard lab. While Katie usually wore her prosthetic in public, when she was just hanging around the house, she often went without.

"Duncan, look at what I can do!" She ran across the lawn, then tossed herself into a one-armed cartwheel, finishing with a front flip.

He clapped enthusiastically. "You amaze me every time I see you!"

She beamed from ear to ear, then upon hearing her mother call for her from the house, waved good-bye and ran off.

"You've got a great kid," Duncan told the man he'd come to see as more of a friend than a client.

"I know. She's the best." If anything, though, Dave only looked more discouraged. "I just wish I could do more for her."

"You *are* doing it, Dave. I know you're feeling down right now, but you and I both know the only way to get to a winning design is to try and fail a dozen times or more. You learn something crucial from each iteration, and this time will be no different. Why don't you take the rest of the day off to spend with your daughter and wife? Come Monday morning, I'll bet you return to the lab with a new outlook."

"Here's hoping." Dave pushed away from his desk, obviously on board with starting his weekend early. "What about you? Got any big plans for the weekend?"

Duncan knew he was beaming as big as Katie had after her cartwheel. "I'm heading to Bar Harbor to have dinner with my girlfriend's family."

"Girlfriend, huh?" Dave's eyes twinkled. "I thought you looked like a new man."

Dave was right. Duncan felt like a man who was finally ready to dream again, ready to hope. Just as long as his newfound luck held out. "Give me a call if you need anything."

"No way. You've got to make sure your focus this weekend is on impressing your lady's family." Dave winked, clearly feeling better now that he'd decided to take the rest of the afternoon off to spend with his treasured wife and daughter. "Have a good time."

"I will." As Duncan got into his car, he mused on how lucky he was to be able to support people who were building and creating such great things. The flip side was that it wasn't always a smooth process. So many times over the years, he'd wished the women and men he worked with didn't have the kind of struggles Dave was facing, even though it was an integral part of the entrepreneurial process. Often, the biggest gains and discoveries came out of the biggest disasters.

He made a quick stop at his office to drop off his laptop and pick up his weekend bag before heading to the airport. But he was surprised to find an unexpected visitor waiting for him. Though Duncan had never set eyes on the man before, he was certain that the stranger was associated with Alastair. The dead eyes gave him away.

For the past five years, Duncan and his brother had had no contact whatsoever with one another. Not since Duncan had confronted his brother with evidence of his crimes. Not since Alastair's goons had broken into Duncan's home to destroy all of his corporate paperwork and hard drives. Not since Duncan had accepted just how despicable his brother truly was. Alastair would do absolutely anything to evade arrest.

Duncan wouldn't have let this man over the threshold, but Gail hadn't known to keep him out. Not wanting to involve her in whatever Alastair had up his sleeve, just as he'd deliberately kept her out of harm's way for the past five years they'd worked together, Duncan gestured for his unwelcome visitor to follow him into his office.

He closed the door behind them with a firm click. Usually, Duncan didn't want his size to intimidate people. A head taller, and far broader than most men, he had to go out of his way to make sure others felt comfortable around him. Today, however, he deliberately pushed his shoulders back and widened his stance.

"We can skip the pleasantries," Duncan said. "Why

are you here? What does Alastair want?" They might be blood, but that was it. Alastair had given up all rights as a true brother a long time ago.

"Mr. Lyman has learned that you have brought a woman in to run your company with you," the man replied. He barely veiled his sneer at the word *woman*. "He would like to speak with you about acquiring your company."

Though on the face of it, the offer seemed shocking, it wasn't the least bit surprising. Only someone as self-absorbed and narcissistic as Alastair would think the brother he had betrayed would want to work with him again.

"I'm not interested." Duncan moved to the door and opened it. "I'll see you out."

"I've been directed not to return without the assurance that you'll at least think about it."

Duncan didn't bother to hold back his incredulous laugh, though there was no joy in it. "There's nothing to think about. The answer is no." He walked out, making it clear that the man had no choice but to follow him and leave.

Alastair had turned Duncan's life upside down when his crimes had cast a dark shadow over absolutely everything. But Duncan refused to allow that to happen again. He wouldn't let this unexpected visitor—or Alastair's preposterous buyout offer—steal his pleasure and anticipation in seeing Lola again, and meeting her family.

Not when he was finally on the precipice of a much brighter, much sweeter future with the woman he loved.

CHAPTER ELEVEN

Duncan drove away from the Bangor, Maine, airport like a man possessed. His plane had been late taking off from Boston, and he'd silently cursed every second of the delay. Though they had texted and video-chatted all week, Duncan was desperate to see Lola in person, to hold her in his arms, to feel her warmth, to hear the sweet sound of her laughter, to kiss her until they were both breathless. And though his brother's buyout offer kept trying to push to the forefront of his mind, he refused to let himself dwell on it. This weekend was all about his future with Lola, not a past he was leaving behind.

The drive from the airport was a beautiful one, the sky almost impossibly blue, the trees a lush, dark green, with hints of sea air coming in through his open window. It only served to reinforce his desire to move to Bar Harbor.

As he finally rounded the corner of Lola's street, he saw that she was standing on the front porch, waiting for him. She flew down her front path, her arms open wide, and as soon as he parked and got out of the rental car, he caught her and spun her around.

"Finally, you're in my arms again. I've missed you so damned much."

He kissed her before she could reply, and just kept kissing and kissing and kissing her without caring whether any of the neighbors were out watching. Let them watch. He wanted the entire world to see what true love looked like. Love that he could still hardly believe was his. Love that he was hoping with every fiber of his being he would be able to hold on to.

Because now that he'd found Lola, he'd found *everything*.

"*Wow.*" Her breath was coming in pants when he finally let her lips go. "That kiss was almost as good as sex."

He brushed his thumb across her lower lip. "Trust me, when I finally make love to you, you'll see that was *nowhere* near as good as sex."

A soft moan of desire escaped her lips. "I can't believe we have to leave for my parents' house right now." In her eyes, he could see that she was as desperate to be with him as he was to be with her. "Do you have any idea how many fantasies I've had about getting you into my bed...and keeping you there?"

"I've had all the same fantasies," he said in a low voice. "I've barely been able to think straight this week,

Lola. Not when I can't stop thinking about making love to you over and over and over again." He loved the way she shivered with anticipation in his arms. "What we've found together, it's so much more than a one-night stand, isn't it?"

She put her hand on his cheek, gently stroking his jaw as she stared into his eyes, her heart in hers. "It's forever, Duncan."

"*Forever,*" he echoed against her lips as they kissed again, a kiss so full of emotion it felt as though they had just spoken vows to each other on the sidewalk in front of her cottage.

Duncan nearly dropped to one knee right then and there. He didn't have a ring. And he wasn't prepared with a fancy speech. But he suddenly wanted to make their vows of *forever* official.

It didn't matter that it had been only five days since they'd met. All that mattered was how he felt about her and how she felt about him. Everything else just seemed like details.

But before he could ask her to be his forever, her phone buzzed loudly from the bag on her shoulder, the ring tone from Madonna's song, "Papa Don't Preach."

"It's my father. He's probably wondering where we are. We'd better go before he comes looking for us." With a roll of her eyes, she explained, "He's always been a little weird about me and my sisters dating new people. I don't think he ever truly trusts a guy until he can meet him face to face."

Together, they walked down the street, as her parents lived just a few blocks away. "Everyone is looking forward to meeting you," she told him, "although Brandon is in Asia, so he won't be here tonight. And if my dad does act a little weird, try not to read anything into it. It's just his usual father-daughter protective stuff. He was pretty awful with Cassie's fiancé, Flynn, when they first met, but they're super close now. His bark is far worse than his bite."

"Your father only has your best interests at heart," Duncan said. "You don't need to make excuses for anyone in your family. I know that anybody you're related to is going to be great."

He supposed he should have been nervous about meeting the family of the woman he intended to spend the rest of his life with. But when he was with Lola, Duncan actually believed he could start anew. That, at last, he could be absolved of his sins. That life could be a good, beautiful place. When he looked at the world through her eyes, it was a bright, beautiful place where any- and everything truly was possible, regardless of how dark or twisted the past was. And though he knew that belief would be put to the test later tonight when he told her the full story of why he'd left the family company and severed ties with his brother, when

Lola's hand was in his and she was smiling at him as though he was everything she'd ever dreamed of, his worries fell almost entirely away.

The three neighborhood blocks to her parents' house were lined with charming homes and cottages and mature trees. From what he'd seen so far, Bar Harbor village was a bustling community filled with locals who were happy to live year-round in such a beautiful area—and tourists who counted their blessings that they were lucky enough to get a chance to visit.

Duncan could easily picture himself living here. Even if he'd never met Lola, there was plenty about Bar Harbor that would have spoken to him. The water, the boats, the lush foliage, and so much open space. After a lifetime of being surrounded by buildings and concrete, small-town living was a very welcome change.

Ten minutes later, they arrived at the Sullivan's house. It wasn't the biggest or fanciest in the neighborhood, but it was the most charming. Duncan could envision seven children romping and playing outside, all of them growing up to be exceptional adults.

She took a big breath. "Okay, this is it."

"It's going to go great, Lola." Her kisses, and the love in her eyes, had fueled him with renewed confidence that they were meant to be together. The belief that nothing could tear them apart. "I promise."

"I know it will," she said. "It's just now that you're about to meet everybody, I want so badly for them to be on their best behavior."

Before he could tell her, again, that she didn't need to apologize for anything, regardless of how it went, Lola's mother opened the front door.

"Duncan, Lola!" Beth Sullivan hugged Lola, then drew him into a hug as well. "I'm thrilled you're back in town and so very glad you're able to join us for dinner. It will be wonderful to get to know you better. And everyone else is so excited to meet you."

"Thank you for the invitation. I'm looking forward to meeting everyone too."

Duncan wasn't surprised to see Lola's father waiting just beyond the foyer.

"Mr. Sullivan," Duncan held out his hand. "It's good to meet you, sir."

Ethan gripped his hand tightly. Hard enough that Duncan read it as a warning. "Welcome to our home, Duncan."

Duncan had met many powerful, intelligent men, but few had looked straight into the heart of him the way Lola's father seemed to as they clasped hands. It was as though Ethan Sullivan was trying to uncover all of Duncan's secrets.

Miraculously, Duncan still wasn't rattled. On the

contrary, he deeply appreciated the fact that Lola had a father this good and strong.

"What can I get you to drink?" Ethan asked. "Wine, beer, or we've got a fine Irish whiskey."

As the Sullivans clearly celebrated their Irish heritage, not only with their business but also at home, he said, "Whiskey would be great." While Duncan wasn't a huge drinker, he had no problem holding his own.

"Come meet everyone," Lola urged, shooting her father a look that Duncan easily interpreted as, *Stand down*. Her father shot back a look of his own that seemed to say, *Not a chance*.

Just then, Duncan was hit with a vision of Lola meeting his brother. It was all too easy to imagine Alastair eating Lola up with lecherous eyes, while making it clear that she was good for only one thing. Duncan's jaw clenched at the mere thought of it.

"Everyone," Lola said as she took him into the kitchen, "this is Duncan. Be nice or else." Her tone was dead serious, making him smile. Her father wasn't the only protective one in the family. Lola was equally fierce.

One of her sisters was the first to move forward, a welcoming smile on her face. "Hi, I'm Cassie. It's really great to meet you. This is my other half, Flynn." After the men shook hands, Cassie pointed beneath the kitchen table. "And this is our little girl, Ruby, playing on the floor with Bear."

Upon hearing her name, a cute child he guessed to be around eighteen months looked up and waved. "Hi!"

He knelt down to her level. "Hello. What a nice doggy you have."

"Bear Beary." Ruby put her arms around the dog's neck and snuggled in.

Duncan laughed at her adorable gesture, but was surprised when she held out her arms. "Up."

He looked behind him to see if she was speaking to her father, but when she poked his hand and said, "Up," again, he realized she was talking to him.

After getting a nod from Flynn, Duncan lifted her from the floor. She blinked at him for a few seconds, almost seeming to take his measure the way Lola's father had. Then she reached out a finger and lightly poked the end of his nose.

"Boop!"

Duncan reacted instinctively, mirroring her movements by gently touching her nose and saying, *"Boop!"* right back.

While everyone laughed, Ruby threw her arms around his neck and snuggled in.

Over her small shoulder, he saw Cassie smiling. "It's her new fun game," she explained.

"It's adorable."

Just then, Bear stood up and leaned against Duncan's leg, clearly angling to be petted. As Duncan scratched his head with his free hand, Lola laughed.

"Even dogs and babies can't resist you," she said, looking proud to be with him.

A few seconds later, Flynn reached for his daughter. "Come here, cutie."

"She's absolutely beautiful," Duncan told him as he transferred the little girl into her father's arms.

"Thank you," Flynn said. "She's a handful, and we wouldn't have it any other way."

Duncan could see how in love Flynn and Cassie were with each other and their little girl. Longing gripped him. Longing for a family like theirs. Like the Sullivans, all gathered together in the kitchen of their warm and welcoming family home. Duncan had never experienced a simple family dinner at the kitchen table with a mom and dad who asked him about his day at school. Even before his parents had passed away, he'd been raised by nannies.

Yet again, Lola's voice pulled him out of his dark thoughts. "This is my brother Rory and my friend Zara, who he somehow managed to convince to date him."

Where Rory was all movie-star good looks and swagger, Zara looked like an artist through and through. She wore thickly rimmed yellow glasses, bright orange combat boots—and every time she looked at Rory, there was pure love in her eyes, just as there was in his for her.

"This is my brother Hudson and his wife, Larissa," Lola said, introducing him to the next couple.

While they were both friendly, where Rory and Zara were clearly in the full flush of love, the opposite seemed true about Hudson and Larissa. Then again, maybe he was reading too much into the fact that they didn't have their arms around each other like Rory and Zara, and they weren't constantly giving each other loving glances like Cassie and Flynn.

Lola gestured for her other sister to come over to meet him. "This is Ashley. I don't know where her son, Kevin, is right now, but I'll introduce you to him once he makes an appearance."

"He's in the back room playing on his phone," Ashley said. "I keep trying to cut his screen time down, but it's hard when his father lets it be a free-for-all." Ashley smiled at Duncan, though her smile didn't quite reach her eyes. "Hello. I've heard so much about you. It's nice to finally meet you."

Duncan shook her hand. "It's great to meet you too."

Apart from Lola's father, Ashley seemed the most guarded. Borderline suspicious, even. Lola had explained about her sister's difficult relationship with

Kevin's father, so Duncan understood why she would want proof that he was good enough for Lola.

"And you already know Turner." Lola shot her brother a warning glance. "So that's all of us. I'd say it's definitely time for you to get that drink."

Her father handed Duncan his whiskey, then lifted his own glass. *"Sláinte."*

Following suit, Duncan spoke the classic Irish toast to good health and happiness, then drank the well-aged whiskey in one long swallow. Though it burned going down, since he clearly had some work ahead of him to win over Lola's family, a bit of Irish courage wouldn't go amiss.

Ethan went to refill his glass, but Lola put a hand over it. "Let Duncan have something to eat before you try to drink him under the table." Then she turned back to him. "You're in for a real treat tonight. You already know my mom is the best cook in the world, but what she makes at home is even better than what she serves at the café. You have to promise not to tell anybody in town, though. If they knew, all of them would demand her home-cooked food be added to the menu."

Beth laughed from where she was standing at the stove. "Lola exaggerates. I serve all the same things at the café. There's just something about being at home surrounded by family that makes food taste better."

He returned Beth's smile. "I've been looking forward to this meal all week." And though this wasn't likely to be a night of relaxed pleasure in the midst of so many assessing gazes, he was also looking forward to spending an evening in a warm family home with people who genuinely cared for one another.

Lola picked up a cabbage dumpling and held it to his lips. "Taste this."

He was overwhelmed by flavor. "That's fantastic."

"I told you," Lola said. "Best food in the world."

She wasn't kidding. He had eaten at some of the best restaurants on the planet, but he'd never had anything quite so delicious. "Where did you learn to cook like this, Beth?"

"County Cork, Ireland. There's a fancy hotel in town—you might have heard of Ashford Castle?—and I talked my way into the kitchen as a teenager."

"That's where I met her," Ethan said as he moved to give his wife a kiss. "They still haven't forgiven me for stealing her away and bringing her to America."

While Lola's parents had been married nearly forty years, when they kissed they almost seemed like teenagers just falling in love. Duncan knew that was exactly how it would be for him and Lola. They would never lose the spark that had drawn them together.

Lola and her siblings had been so lucky to grow up with their parents as an example of real love. He didn't doubt that there had likely been some bumps along the way. But love had clearly given them the strength to work through whatever issues cropped up.

Duncan reached for Lola's hand, lifting it to his lips and pressing a kiss to it. It was his way of silently saying, *Thank you for loving me. And thank you for inviting me here tonight to be with the people who mean the most to you.*

When she turned to kiss him, he knew she'd understood exactly what was in his heart.

And that it was all for her.

CHAPTER TWELVE

For the next several minutes, everyone worked in concert to get the food dished out and on the large dining table. The room looked out on a beautiful backyard where flowers were profusely in bloom. There was a green lawn where kids and dogs could play, and patio lights hung from the trees. Through the branches, Duncan caught glimpses of the ocean. It was a perfect place to live and raise a family.

Ashley's son came into the kitchen to wash his hands. "Kevin," his mother said, "this is Lola's friend Duncan."

Kevin nodded hello from the sink. "So you're the guy she can't stop talking about, huh?"

Half of Lola's family laughed, while the other half shot Duncan sidelong glances, curious to see how he'd react.

"I haven't been able to stop thinking about her either," Duncan replied easily.

No one in Lola's family had grilled him yet, but he had a feeling that as soon as they sat down, the questions would start coming.

Right on cue, while everyone was filling their plates, Hudson said, "I hear you're in investments?"

Duncan nodded. "I invest in small to midsize businesses with a focus on sustainable resources and innovative technologies."

"How long have you been in the industry?"

"Five years with my own company and another ten working with my brother at the firm our father founded." Duncan knew better than to leave off the period of time he'd worked with Alastair when they could easily find the information on the Internet. "When our interests diverged, it made sense to start my own company."

"You're based in Boston, aren't you?" Hudson's wife, Larissa, asked.

"I am. Although..." Judging by Lola's smile and nod that it was okay for him to tell everyone, he said, "I'm planning on moving to Bar Harbor in the near future."

Turner piped in, "What will you do about your business in Boston?"

"There are these things called phones and computers," Lola said to her brother, obviously still irritated with him.

"When someone's running a business, it usually helps if they oversee it in person," Turner countered, before shifting his penetrating gaze back to Duncan. "Or are you planning to walk away from this business too?"

Duncan had no doubt that Turner had read at least one of the interviews Alastair had given after Duncan left the family firm. Interviews that made it sound as if Duncan had followed "flights of fancy" rather than buckling down to do the difficult job of keeping a big venture business running. Though nothing could have been farther from the truth, Duncan had opted not to go public with the real version of the story.

Despite the fact that his brother's goons had destroyed all of Duncan's corporate records, and thus the evidence against Alastair, Duncan had gone to the FBI to tell them everything he knew. It wasn't until he was standing on the threshold of the building that he'd had to accept just how futile this plan was. Given that Duncan no longer had tangible data or proof to back up his claims—and certain that none of Alastair's partners in crime, whether willing or unwilling, would dare say a word against him lest he destroy their lives and families—the only person likely to go to jail for corporate fraud was Duncan. Because Alastair would surely do whatever he could to frame Duncan for the crimes, even though he'd had nothing whatsoever to do with them. And if Duncan went to prison, then he wouldn't be able to do a damned thing to help the people his brother had defrauded.

But while Duncan had done everything he could over the past five years to make his brother's wrongs right, he had never been able to sleep well knowing he hadn't actually taken away Alastair's ability to commit similar crimes.

Realizing Turner was still waiting for his response, he said, "I've recently taken on a brilliant new employee." Duncan turned to Lola to give her the good news. "Anita has quickly come up to speed, and I should be able to pass over the reins to her even sooner than I anticipated."

"That's fantastic!" Lola threw her arms around him, clearly overjoyed. "I'm so happy you'll be able to spend more time working on your maps." She told her family, "Duncan is an amazing cartographer. He works by hand in the old tradition, and when he came to my class, I was blown away by his talent and skill."

"Had you already planned to ask Lola out when you signed up to take her class?" her father asked.

Beth whacked her husband on the arm. "Ethan, don't be ridiculous." Lola's mother shot Duncan an apologetic look. "Please forgive my husband for saying that. We're all very happy that you're here. And if everybody could please stop grilling our guest, I'm sure Duncan would like to eat his dinner before it gets cold." Though Beth's voice had a soft Irish lilt, there was steel behind her words. Enough that further questions were swallowed, at least for the time being.

For the next half hour, Duncan got a chance to ask a few questions of his own. He found out where Hudson and Larissa lived in Boston—not too far from his own house. Rory told Duncan a bit about his bespoke furniture company, although he mostly extolled the virtues of Zara's eyeglasses-frames company. Ashley spoke about her role managing the Sullivan Cafés and boutiques up and down the coast of Maine. Cassie promised to put together a box of her special candies for him, while Flynn was incredibly modest about his award-winning screenplays and TV shows. And while Turner was reticent about his animation career, Duncan already knew he was at the top of his field.

Lola's family was an impressive bunch. Yet again, he was impressed by how Beth and Ethan had encouraged their kids to follow their creative urges.

Once they'd finished eating, Duncan helped clear the table and load the dishwasher. But though he'd already eaten several servings of Beth's delicious food, he should have guessed there would also be great desserts, given that Cassie's job was spinning sugar into magic.

"I've been venturing out a bit from candy lately and baking up a storm," Cassie said as she gestured to the pie, cake, and photo-worthy petits fours now in the center of the dining table. "Whatever we don't finish tonight, everyone should take home, because we have so many other cakes and pies at home already." Ruby, who was sitting on Cassie's lap, looked intent on eating her piece of chocolate cake as soon as possible.

Everyone served themselves, and then after a round of exclamations about how good Cassie's desserts were, she said, "I think it's time for the three of us to make our big announcement." She looked down at Ruby, who was still happily eating cake. "Right, sweetie?" Ruby smiled through a mouthful of chocolate frosting. Lola's and Ashley's eyes were shining as Cassie said, "We're going to have a baby!" She stroked Ruby's curls. "Another beautiful baby, that is."

Beth jumped up from the table on a happy sob to give her daughter and Flynn huge hugs, soon followed by everyone else's congratulations and cheers.

It wasn't until they sat back down that Duncan realized the distance between Hudson and Larissa seemed to have grown. He didn't think it was his imagination that they'd pushed their chairs farther apart, or that their smiles seemed forced.

"How far along are you?" Ethan asked Cassie.

"About ten weeks. I'll be seeing my doctor on Monday to confirm all the dates and everything else. I haven't had any morning sickness, fortunately."

"You are so lucky!" Ashley said. "Kevin, you were totally worth it, but OMG, was I sick as a dog when I was pregnant with you."

"It's true," Lola said to Kevin. "Your mom spent nine months face down in the toilet bowl."

Kevin made a face. "*Ewwww*, Mom, that's *so* disgusting." Then he grinned at Cassie. "But it's totally cool that you're going to have a baby, Aunt Cassie. I'll help babysit, like with Ruby, but I'm still not gonna change diapers."

Lola, who was laughing along with everyone else, let Cassie and Flynn know, "I have no problem with diapers or middle-of-the-night duty." She beamed at the happy couple. "I'm so excited by the way our family is growing!"

Duncan wanted to have what Flynn and Cassie had. A family of his own. A child he would love and raise with affection, a little girl or boy with Lola's beautiful eyes and bright spirit.

"We have one more announcement," Flynn said. He and Cassie both looked ecstatic as they said, as one, "We're engaged!"

More hugs and tears ensued. And then Ethan said to Beth, "You know what we need to do to celebrate, don't you?"

"Of course I do," Lola's mother said, grinning. "We've got to get out the instruments. And we need to dance. We can clean this up later."

"You're going to think we're like the von Trapp family singers in *The Sound of Music*," Lola told Duncan. "Or the Brady Bunch when they sang and danced in that Christmas special." But he could see that she was as excited as the rest of her family about celebrating Cassie and Flynn's great news in a classic Irish way.

Within minutes, the living-room furniture was pushed aside, and Turner was holding Irish pipes on his lap, which looked quite different than Scottish bagpipes. Ashley was holding a flute and Hudson a fiddle.

"If Brandon were here," Ethan told Duncan, "he'd be on the bodhran, an Irish frame drum. Tonight, we'll have to make do by stomping our feet and clapping our hands." Lola's father picked up a guitar. "Why don't we start with a jig?"

Within seconds, Duncan felt like he'd been transported to a pub in Ireland, the catchy, joyful music filling his soul.

Beth took Lola's hand, saying, "It's time to kick up our heels."

Lola shot Duncan a look that seemed to say, *What can you do but join the madness?* Then she followed her mother to the impromptu dance floor.

And what glorious madness it was.

Duncan had seen Irish dancing on TV, but watching it from mere feet away blew his mind. Lola threw herself wholeheartedly into the dance, her movements perfectly coordinated alongside her mother, both of them exceptionally talented dancers.

The last thing he expected was for Lola to reach for him. "Dance with me. We can do one where the man and the woman play off each other." After Ethan passed his guitar to Cassie so that he could join Beth in the dance, Lola said, "Just follow my lead."

Duncan's heart was soon pounding as he jumped and spun and pulled Lola into his arms, her laughter the most beautiful sound he'd ever heard. Though they were surrounded by her family, it felt like it was just the two of them, dancing and laughing and loving each other.

As he swung her close, he whispered in her ear, "I love you." When she whispered it back, he was happier than he'd ever been.

The doorbell rang just as the song ended. "Moira!" Lola's mother sounded thrilled to find an unexpected guest at the door. "What a wonderful surprise. If you had told us you were coming up from Boston, we would have held dinner for you. You're here just in time to dance."

"My weekend cleared up at the last second, and I thought it would be fun to surprise you." Moira smiled fondly at everyone. "Hearing the music, seeing the dancing through the window, felt like walking into the local. I almost wondered if I had been magically transported to a pub back in Ireland."

Moira and Beth had similar accents, and Duncan deduced that they had grown up together. And from the way Lola rushed to give her a hug, he guessed this was the second mother Lola had told him about, the one whose failing business had contributed to her ill health. Fortunately, she looked like she'd recovered from her bout with cancer.

"Moira, I'm so glad you're here tonight." Lola took her hand and brought her over to Duncan. "There's someone I'd like you to meet. This is—"

"Duncan Lyman." Moira's smile fell away, her face suddenly ashen. "What are you doing here?"

Duncan didn't believe he'd ever met Moira, nor did her name ring a bell. But from the look on her face, he had a bad feeling that he was inextricably connected to her all the same.

"He's here with me, Moira," Lola said, looking confused as to why her close friend was acting so strangely. "He took one of my drawing classes last weekend, and we—" She looked at Duncan, her eyes full of emotion. "We fell for each other."

But Moira was shaking her head and backing away as though she couldn't stand to be this close to him. "He…" When she looked as though she was going to faint, Ethan helped her to one of the couches, while

Beth brought her a glass of whiskey. She downed it in one gulp.

"What's wrong, Moira?" Ethan asked.

But Moira just stared at Duncan, her face even more pale now, if that were possible. "Brilliant Funds was yours, wasn't it?" Her question came out barely above a whisper. "And you were instrumental in all of our failures."

The earth actually seemed to stop spinning as Lola turned to Duncan with shock—and disbelief—written all over her face. "Duncan?" She looked like she was going to be ill. "Is this true? Did you have something to do with Moira's business failing?"

Everyone in the room was silent as they waited for Duncan's response. Standing in the middle of the Sullivan family, with Moira gazing at him in horror, Duncan felt as though an invisible fist were slamming into his gut, over and over and over again.

Brilliant Funds had been a startup incubator that had promised half a million dollars of funding to each company it worked with as long as company owners first put in one hundred thousand dollars of their own money and then proved their product's marketability over the first six months. Though Duncan's signature had been on the contracts, the company had been his brother's baby, so he'd had nothing to do with the fund. Unfortunately, Duncan had found out too late that Alastair was defrauding and embezzling from the clients of Brilliant Funds.

Lola had told him he was a good man. She'd had faith in him. She'd trusted him implicitly. She'd given her heart to him. And now, he was going to completely betray her trust, her faith, and her love with an honest answer. "Yes, Brilliant Funds was a subsidiary of Lyman Ventures, the company I ran with my brother."

That was all it took for the woman Duncan loved to jump away from him...and for doubt and stunned disappointment to replace the love in her eyes.

The anguish on Lola's face made it feel as though a knife had plunged straight through his heart. If only he'd told her everything before tonight, then maybe he could have found a way to make her understand that he'd never meant to hurt anyone—and that he had spent years trying to fix what his brother's crimes had broken.

But before he could explain anything to Lola, he first had to make his apologies to Moira.

After Duncan's corporate records had been destroyed, he hadn't been able to piece together enough information on one of the six companies that had signed on. Now he knew that Moira's company was the one that had slipped through the cracks.

Though the current situation couldn't be more fraught, he was glad that he'd finally found Moira. At last, he could make amends for what Alastair had done to her and her company.

"For five years," he began, "I've tried to find you—"

"You could have done that easily with a simple Internet search," Moira cut in, red blotches of color staining her cheeks.

"I promise you, if I could have accessed any information about you and your company, I would have. Unfortunately, all of your files were—"

"*No!*" Moira pushed up from the chair. "I'm not going to listen to your excuses. I don't want to hear them. It's taken me a long time to rebuild, but I have. And I won't let you drag me back into the past."

"Please, if you would just let me explain. I'm so sorry for—"

"You heard Moira." Lola stepped in front of him. "She wants you gone." Lola's eyes were full of pain. Anger. And deep betrayal. "I do too."

Duncan felt like his insides were completely shredding as a knife twisted around and around. "I don't want to hurt Moira again. And I swear I never intended to hurt her five years ago either."

But Lola wasn't interested in listening to his pleas as she walked barefoot to the door and held it open. "Leave. *Now.*"

Was there anything he could say, or do, that might convince her to let him explain? But given that even the previously docile dog seemed to be snarling at him now, he knew he wasn't going to get that chance.

Only little Ruby was still smiling, her wide eyes innocent as she looked up at him. But he wasn't innocent. No matter how many apologies he made, no matter what he did to make amends, he hadn't saved Moira from Alastair's schemes.

And Lola was right to want nothing to do with him.

The truth that he'd known all week, but had tried to shove back into the darkness, was that he didn't deserve her love. *This* was exactly what he deserved— her disgust and fury.

"I'm sorry." He said the words to Moira and to Lola's family, but most of all to Lola. "More sorry than you'll ever know."

He stepped outside, and the door behind him closed with a bang, the lock slamming shut. The night had grown cold and dark, wet and windy. The perfect mirror to the way he felt inside.

Because nothing, and no one, would ever compare to the joy that he'd known—and had just lost—with Lola Sullivan.

CHAPTER THIRTEEN

Lola was shell-shocked. *Beyond* devastated.

But her broken heart didn't matter now. All that mattered was Moira.

Beth knelt at Moira's side, clasping her hands tightly. Ethan had his hands on her shoulders, a comforting presence behind her.

Lola's voice was thick with regret and concern as she said, "Moira, I promise you, I had no idea who Duncan was. Are you all right?"

Moira nodded, but it was halfhearted at best. "I've let the Lyman brothers steal away so much time and energy and health from me already. I won't let it happen again."

"We won't let it happen either," Lola vowed. "If I could turn back time, if I had known last weekend what he and his brother had done to you, I would never have let Duncan sign up for my class, let alone spent time with him outside of it."

Moira reached for Lola's hand. "You have nothing to blame yourself for. How could you have known who he was, when I only just learned it myself?" Her mouth tightened and her brow furrowed even deeper. "I hadn't realized the Lymans were behind Brilliant Funds until my assistant recently digitized my old contracts and pointed out Duncan and Alastair Lyman's signatures buried deep in one of the many documents I signed. I know this is no excuse, but five years ago when my own lawyer said everything looked fine, I was so excited at the prospect of attracting the attention of a startup incubator, especially one willing to put half a million dollars into my brand, that I signed the contracts without reading the fine print myself." Her expression was bleak. "Believe me, I've never made that mistake again. And I have a different lawyer now too."

It wasn't until Moira had nearly lost her business that they had found out about her deal with Brilliant Funds. Though Lola hadn't known what startup incubators were at the time, she'd learned that they promised mentorship, connections, and manufacturing help for growing companies. Brilliant Funds had promised to match Moira's nonrefundable hundred-thousand-dollar investment in the incubator with five times as much in six months, after she proved that there was a strong demand for her innovative hand-bags that incorporated a phone charger and wifi booster inside sumptuous leather fabric. Unfortunately, at the five-and-a-half-month mark, they had cut her loose, saying that though they'd done everything they could to help her, the market for her products wasn't there. Moira had gambled her life savings on their promise to help grow her business, but that gamble had failed.

In the aftermath, Moira had blamed herself for not having a good enough product. But Lola had always suspected foul play behind the scenes. According to her research, some startup incubators were run by greedy crooks looking to take advantage of people's desperation to succeed at their dreams. Clearly, given Moira's reaction to coming face-to-face with Duncan, she now seemed to believe that the Lyman brothers *had* played a nefarious role in taking her money without ever intending to actually invest in her business.

"This is the first time I've ever met Duncan, though I've seen his picture in the Boston papers plenty of times," Moira continued, "and I only met his brother once at a startup networking event. It was a shock to learn they weren't simply investors in Brilliant Funds, but owned it outright. Honestly, the more I go over everything that happened during the five and a half months I worked with Brilliant Funds, and how they pressured me to put in even more money before they booted me out of the incubator, I'm more and more convinced that there was something shady going on.

But," she added quickly, "the last thing I want to do is rewind history and go back to that dark place I was in for so long afterward." She looked exhausted. "I think it's best if we all forget what happened tonight and just move on with our lives."

"Why don't I get you settled in the guest cottage with a warm drink?" Beth suggested. "I'll bring you a plate of food."

"I couldn't possibly eat," Moira said. "But a drink would be wonderful." She looked five years older as she walked away with Beth.

Lola sank into the seat Moira had just vacated. Her father poured another glass of whiskey and handed it to her. "I've been such a fool," she said. "If only I had been less trusting, less charmed. If only I'd spent five minutes digging into Duncan's past, surely I would have put the pieces together."

"You can't beat yourself up, Lola," Hudson said. "Who knows if digging into the guy's past would have turned up anything? Even Moira said his name was buried deep in her contracts. It's just a crazy coincidence."

"A *horrible* coincidence." Pride was all that held back her tears. Like hell she'd let Duncan make her cry! "I can't stop thinking about the look on Moira's face when she saw him and realized I was *dancing* with the enemy."

Only in the last year or so had her friend started to be like her old self, full of energy, and enthusiasm, and positivity. If seeing Duncan tonight had taken that away from Moira, Lola would never forgive herself.

She'd never forgive Duncan either.

"At least you found out before things went too far," Ashley said. "I mean, you've only known him a week."

That was true on the surface. But while Lola had known Duncan for only a week, she'd loved him as deeply as if she'd known him a lifetime.

Somehow she would have to forget him.

Forget what it was like to be held in his arms.

Forget his passionate kisses.

Forget that she'd felt as though she'd finally found her other half, the missing piece of her heart.

Though her siblings offered to stay with her, she insisted that she would be fine on her own. Knowing better than to argue, they all put on their coats and gathered up their things, giving her hugs and saying that they knew everything would seem better in the morning.

But how could she give away her heart one day, then take it back fully intact the next? Even if it turned out that the man she had fallen for was a liar, and a traitor, and a cheat, how could she forget her happiness and give up on her dreams of true love that quickly?

While her father saw everyone out, Lola headed

toward the guest cottage to check on Moira. Her mother was sitting on the edge of the bed, the two women talking quietly.

Lola stood in the doorway, not sure of her welcome. "I wanted to see how you were doing before I head home."

Moira held out her hand. "Come here, my darling girl."

Lola threw herself into Moira's arms. She felt like sobbing, but she couldn't. She needed to be strong for her friend, given that she had been the one to bring Duncan back into Moira's life.

Moira stroked her back. "Everything's fine. I was shocked at first, but don't worry about what happened for even one more second."

Lola needed to nod and smile so that she wouldn't make things worse for Moira. "Okay, but if you need anything, anything at all, I'll be there for you."

"You've always been there for me, Lola. You've done more for me than I can ever repay." Before Lola could speak, Moira held up a hand. "I know there's nothing to repay because we're family, maybe not by blood, but blood doesn't matter. I love you as much as I would a daughter."

"I love you too."

Her heart heavy, her chest tight, Lola walked out into the kitchen to gather up her things. Her father was waiting for her.

"Honey, if you don't need to rush off, stay and talk with me for a few minutes."

Before he could try to absolve her of blame in the same way Moira just had, she said, "How could I have blown things so badly?"

He pulled her into his arms and squeezed her tight. "You didn't."

"We both know that's not true."

But her father didn't look like he agreed. In fact, he looked more pensive than anything. "I don't know much about Duncan, obviously, but from what I saw of him tonight, he didn't seem like a liar."

Surprised by her father's words, Lola reminded him, "You heard Moira. She thinks there was something fishy going on with the startup incubator." Lola didn't modulate her bitter tone. "She thinks all Duncan and his brother wanted was her money."

"Perhaps," her father said. "Or perhaps there's another explanation for Duncan's involvement. One that none of us could guess at."

"You're not actually saying I should give him a second chance, are you?" She was stunned that her dad wasn't jumping down Duncan's throat. He'd never liked any of her boyfriends. But now that they had proof that one of them had done something bad—Duncan had admitted it in front of everyone!—her father was practically taking Duncan's side? "You are the very last person on the planet who I would think would advocate for that. You've always been so protective of us, especially me, Ashley, and Cassie."

"Of course I'm protective of you. You'll always be my little girl, no matter how old you are. But you're also one of the smartest, most intuitive people I know," her father told her. "And I think you need to give yourself a whole heck of a lot more credit, because you're also a great judge of character."

"Really?" She snorted. "Then what about all the losers I've dated? The ones you've *hated.*" And, she silently thought, what about Frank, the older man she'd never told anyone in her family about? No question about it, at eighteen she'd been a terrible judge of character.

He waved his hand in the air as if those guys were of no consequence. "None of them were anything serious. You were just growing up, coming into your own, then biding your time until the right man came along." He let his words sink in before he added, "The only man I've ever seen you look at like he matters to you is Duncan. And I'm just not convinced that your heart could play you wrong like that."

"Even with the evidence proving otherwise?"

"I can't shake the feeling that there's more to this situation than meets the eye. The question is, what actually happened five years ago? What exactly was Duncan's involvement?"

Lola's insides felt brittle and bruised. She felt like she'd gone ten rounds with a boxing champ. Her father was trying to help, she knew that. But she also knew that she couldn't take anything else in tonight. "I need to go home and sleep. I can't think straight about anything right now."

Her father hugged her tight again. "If you want to go for a hike tomorrow, or punch some bags at the gym, or even get stinking drunk in the middle of the afternoon, you know where I am."

She finally let her tears fall. Her dad was so great. She'd get through this because her father and the rest of her family would all rally around her until her broken heart had healed.

CHAPTER FOURTEEN

Though she'd barely been able to keep her eyes open by the time she crawled into bed, Lola hardly slept on Friday night. Come Saturday morning, she was surprised to find Cassie, Flynn, and Ruby on her front porch.

"Any chance you could help us with our baby group this morning?" Cassie asked after giving Lola an extra-tight hug. "The organizer called in sick, and now Flynn and I are responsible for ten eighteen-month-olds on our own."

There had to be someone else they could have asked to help, but frankly, it was a huge relief to have a reason to get dressed and do something that didn't involve thinking about *him*.

For the next two hours, she herded moms and dads and their little ones from the park's sandbox, to the small jungle gym, to the hand-washing station, to snacks, and finally to blankets for naps. All the while, Cassie and Flynn did their best not to shoot her too many worried glances.

Little Ruby settled in on Lola's lap instead of her blanket. "La-la sad."

Lola had to work like crazy to keep her eyes from filling with tears. "I was sad before you came to see me. But now that I'm with you, you're making me so happy." She gave the little girl kisses all over her face and on her tummy, making Ruby laugh so hard that even Lola couldn't help but laugh.

Thank God her family understood how much she'd needed this break from being alone with her thoughts. Which was why she wasn't surprised to see Rory and Zara swing by the park as the Saturday-morning baby group was wrapping up.

"We just painted our living room, and it looks *terrible*," Zara said, linking her arm with Lola's. "Rory says you're brilliant at wall colors."

As she agreed to head off with them to pick new paint, she knew this was part two of the Sullivan family plan to ensure that she made it through to Monday without drowning in her sorrows. For the next several hours, she helped them repaint their living room walls. By the time they finished, it was time to eat takeout Thai food in front of the TV.

Lola fell asleep in front of *Die Hard*—one of her favorite movies—blissfully tuning out everything that had happened the day before.

On Sunday morning, while she was staring at a

plate of bacon and eggs she couldn't possibly stomach, Turner arrived at Rory and Zara's. He must have gone to her house beforehand, because he had her hiking gear with him.

"My hiking group is headed up Gorham Mountain today. I thought this would be the perfect day for you to join us. Visibility should be exceptional, so I also brought your camera."

It was another *fait accompli*, but she didn't mind. Panting her way up a steep mountain and taking pictures of stunning vistas would be a good way to spend a Sunday morning that would have yawned on depressingly otherwise.

Though she lagged far behind the rest of the group, it was a beautiful hike. The panoramic views of Mount Desert Island, Frenchman Bay, and the outer islands never ceased to stun her. And fortunately, she could blame any tears on the wind.

When she got home, Ashley asked if Lola could come help Kevin build Buckingham Palace out of Popsicle sticks for his history class. For the next couple of hours, Lola diligently arranged and glued each Popsicle stick into place, architecting a wobbly, and very sticky, rendition of Buckingham Palace alongside her nephew.

She fell into bed exhausted again, hoping to sleep in her own bed as dreamlessly as she had the night before at Zara and Rory's house. But as she tossed and turned, she couldn't stop thinking about Duncan...and how stupid she'd been to trust him. She'd thought he was different, when it turned out that everything he'd said to her had been a lie.

He'd known exactly how to play her so that she'd believe his lies. Even going so far as to stop them from having sex that first night so that she'd think she actually meant something to him.

How could he have lied to her face so blithely, telling her, *Every day, I do whatever I can to be a good guy.*

And how could she have believed him?

Worst of all, though, was the part of Lola that still didn't want to believe Duncan could have played a part in destroying Moira's business. A desperate and foolish part of her that wished there was a good explanation for what had happened.

Though she knew better, she couldn't help going over and over what Duncan had told her about his brother and the secrets he'd kept from him. And yet, if Duncan had been innocent of any wrongdoing, wouldn't he have told her the truth the night they'd stayed up all night talking and professed their love to each other? If he had really loved her, wouldn't he have known he could trust her with absolutely anything?

At last, sunlight filtered in through her bedroom drapes. She dragged herself into the shower, doing her makeup and hair on autopilot. Though she'd barely eaten all weekend, her stomach was so badly twisted that she wasn't the least bit hungry.

While Lola was in the shower, her mother called to let her know Moira was doing better this morning after a somewhat difficult weekend.

A renewed burst of fury hit Lola. Though she had a ton of work to take care of at her office—Monday mornings were always crazy-busy—it would have to wait.

Duncan owed Moira more than apologies and explanations, whatever those might be. He owed her money. He owed her powerful, influential contacts. He owed her everything he and his brother had promised when Moira had signed up to work with Brilliant Funds.

Lola was damn well going to make sure Duncan gave Moira absolutely *everything* she deserved!

She hadn't thought Duncan was someone who would do whatever it took just to get richer. She'd thought he truly cared about trying to make the world a better place. She'd thought he had a heart. A soul.

But no. All he cared about was money.

And he clearly *didn't* care who he harmed to get it.

She didn't plan to stay overnight in Boston. She didn't pack a bag. She was simply going to force him to agree to make it up to Moira financially, no matter what it took, and then she was going to get the hell away from him.

Lola was on the road when Cassie's call came through her car's phone system. She picked up, saying without preamble, "I'm going to Boston to confront the bastard and make him do what's right for Moira."

"I had a feeling you were going to do something like this," Cassie said. "But you don't need to do this alone, Lola. I can go with you."

Lola had fallen for Duncan all on her own. Now, she needed to rip her love for him out of her heart by herself too. "Thanks, Cassie. But I've got this."

"I know you do. You can do anything you set your mind to. But if you need backup for any reason, just call, and I'll be there as soon as I can."

"You don't have to worry about me. I'm not going to let him get me down. But I am going to make sure that he does the right thing for once in his life."

"I don't envy him," Cassie said. "You're one tough cookie."

"Damn straight I am!" Lola hoped her laugh sounded real. "Now go make some cookies of your own."

Lola hung up, more determined than ever that this impromptu visit would get Duncan out of her system. Because if there was one thing she couldn't stand, it was being a sad sack in everyone's eyes. Since her experience dating Frank at eighteen, Lola had made sure to be tough enough that no one could hurt her. Though she'd made the mistake of softening for Duncan, she'd *never* make that mistake again.

CHAPTER FIFTEEN

Duncan's red-eye flight back to Boston Friday night had been a blur of self-recrimination and guilt. By the time he walked into his house at three a.m., he'd realized it had never felt less like home. Though he could easily have purchased a much bigger house on more land, his home wasn't ultramodern, nor was it a mini manor house like the ones his father and brother liked to live in. Duncan had simply wanted to create a comfortable home for himself, somewhere he could return to at the end of a long day in the office and let the stresses of his workday fall away. But compared to the Sullivan family home and Lola's cottage, his own house felt empty and cold.

Devoid of family. Lacking energy.

And most of all, missing love.

He'd forced himself to go to bed even though he knew he wouldn't sleep. He'd never be able to shake the memory of Lola's horrified expression when he'd admitted to owning Brilliant Funds. He'd *promised* he wouldn't hurt her. It killed him that he had. And as he lay in the darkness until Saturday morning finally dawned gray and drizzling, his mind continued to race, turning over one idea after another. How could he convince Lola that he hadn't been lying when he'd said he was one of the good guys? That he loved her with all of his heart. And that he was a changed man from the one who had blindly trusted his brother.

Was there any plan that might work? Would Lola ever forgive him for the role he'd played in hurting Moira?

His gut clenched at the thought of Lola falling in love with someone else. A great guy who would make all her dreams come true. Duncan had wanted to be that guy. He had thought he *was* that guy.

There was something he could do, though. He could make amends to Moira by doing whatever it took to undo the destruction his brother had wrought.

After taking an ice-cold shower, he called Gail and asked her to rearrange today's meetings for later in the week. Next, he let Anita know that he needed to take care of several unavoidable business matters this morning, so she should operate as he intended them to go on—with her as an equal partner.

His calls made, he opened his laptop and spent the rest of the weekend researching Moira's business, making a comprehensive list of what he could do to help her, and preparing to call in every contact and favor he could on her behalf.

Throughout the weekend, the family tree he'd been making for Lola seemed to mock him from the drafting table. A week ago, he'd been so full of hope, so sure that his luck had finally turned.

How wrong he'd been.

After forty-eight hours of little to no sleep, though his limbs felt like they were made of lead, he put on a suit Monday morning and headed out to chase down every lead on his list. Duncan was determined to make a positive difference on Moira's behalf.

Even if it never changed the way Lola saw him.

And even if she still hated him forever.

* * *

Lola had always liked visiting Boston. Though she wouldn't have wanted to live in the big city, it was always a fun rush to absorb the energy all around her for the day. But this afternoon, she barely noticed the hustle and bustle all around her. She was wholly focused on her mission to kick ass.

Duncan's ass.

She was surprised to find his office building wasn't a glossy high-rise. Instead, he worked out of a converted Victorian house, painted dark gray with white trim, and with a surprisingly lush garden out front.

Her fury only grew bigger as she realized this was

exactly the kind of office building and garden a person would have if he intended to trick someone like Moira into thinking he wasn't a cutthroat, heartless businessman. She bet he even served cups of tea and biscuits on little flowered plates during meetings. Just like the vicious wolf disguising himself in Grandma's nightclothes.

Anger fueled her as she wrenched open the door. No surprise, the woman at the reception desk had a kind expression to go with the garden and the unassuming office. Duncan was ticking off every dastardly box, one after the other. All his office needed to make the unthreatening image complete was a puppy running around the corner looking adorable and cuddly.

"Hello, I'm Gail," the woman said with a smile. "How may I help you?"

"I'm looking for Duncan Lyman." Lola's words were hard-edged, and there was no smile on her face or in her voice. It wasn't normally in her nature to bite someone's head off. But nothing felt normal anymore.

Not since Duncan had crushed Lola's hopes, dreams, and heart to smithereens.

The woman remained smiling as she said, "I'm afraid Duncan isn't here right now."

Damn it! Lola had wanted to catch him off guard, which was why she hadn't called to let him know she was coming to Boston. And if she was being totally honest with herself, she'd also been afraid that she'd crumble if she heard his voice. That was why she had blocked his number since Friday night, in case he tried to call her. The truth was that it had taken her the entire trip from Bar Harbor to steel herself to see him again.

"When will he be back? I need to see him right away."

"Is he expecting you?"

"No." Lola followed up the word with a harsh laugh. "I'm sure I'm the very *last* person he's expecting to see."

Remarkably, Duncan's assistant still didn't look flustered. "Perhaps if you could tell me what you need to speak with him about, I might be able to be of better service."

"He cheated one of my friends, causing her to nearly lose her business."

At last, the woman's composure began to crack as she frowned. "Duncan? Cheating your friend?" She shook her head. "I'm sorry, but I find that terribly hard to believe."

"He's already admitted everything." Each word fell with a hard, staccato beat. "I'm here to make sure he does the right thing by my friend."

His receptionist pushed back from her desk. "If you

will excuse me for a moment, I need to have a quick word with my colleague. What did you say your name was?"

"Lola Sullivan."

The woman's eyes widened. "I knew you looked familiar! I saw your picture on your website when I booked your drawing class as a gift for Duncan."

Lola was taken aback to realize this woman knew who she was. "You sent Duncan to my class?"

The woman nodded. "He absolutely loved it. I haven't seen him look so happy in the five years I've worked with him."

Lola's gut twisted even tighter at the memory of how happy she'd been too. Only to find out that her joy with Duncan was based on lies. "Whether or not he enjoyed my class is irrelevant," she insisted. "He still has a lot to answer for when it comes to the way he treated my friend."

For a moment, Lola thought Gail might defend Duncan again. Instead, she said, "Could I get you a cup of tea while you're waiting?" She gestured to the floral teacups and cookies on the sideboard. Just as Lola had predicted.

"No, I don't want anything." Only Duncan's blood.

Though Lola didn't take a seat on one of the plush seats, she couldn't stop herself from studying the framed maps on the wall. Hand-drawn, they depicted bodies of water near Montauk, New York; Charleston, South Carolina; and Baltimore, Maryland. Duncan's signature was on the bottom right corner of all three maps. She hated having to admit that, although he was scum, his talent was still undeniable.

Lola had never been a waffler. And with Duncan, everything had seemed so clear at first. So positive. So perfect. So joyous. Until Moira had unmasked him as the villain, and she'd realized just how wrong she'd been about him. This morning, she'd been so sure that nothing would sway her from seeing him as a villain. Yet, as she stood in his office looking at the maps he'd drawn, her heart twinged.

No. Lola refused to let her heart soften toward Duncan. Turning her back on his art, she crossed her arms firmly across her chest.

Sixty seconds later, Gail returned to the reception area with another attractive woman. Lola admonished herself for feeling at all jealous of the people Duncan worked with. She wasn't interested in him anymore. Clearly, she needed to get a grip on her emotions, and fast.

"Ms. Sullivan, it's nice to meet you." The woman held out her hand. "I'm Anita Greene, and I work with Duncan. Gail has just filled me in on your situation, and if you could spare a few minutes, I'd appreciate it if you could join me in my office."

Lola had come to Boston to make sure Duncan set things straight with Moira. But now that she was here, she realized she also needed to warn his employees about his true nature. Okay, so neither woman looked anything but nice, and happy to boot, but that could be because he was biding his time before he took advantage of them.

Lola followed Anita into her office. The other woman gestured for her to take a seat. "Before we discuss the reason you're here," Anita said, "I want you to know this is my second week on the job, and I'm still working to get a handle on everything. If there's an investment or partnership that I'm not aware of, I apologize, and I promise I will do my best to get up to speed quickly."

"Look," Lola said, "you seem like a nice person, as does Gail. And I get it, because I was also taken in by Duncan. I think you both deserve to know that he has done some really bad things."

Anita looked concerned. "I'd appreciate it if you could give me more information."

"My friend's name is Moira Kennedy. She's the founder of MKS Digital, a digital handbag and accessories company. She was involved with a startup incubator named Brilliant Funds five years ago, which was owned by Duncan and his brother. They took a great deal of her money, promising to quintuple it once she'd proven her product's marketability. Not only did they not give her a dime, but in less than six months, after she had changed her entire business plan and product line to suit them, her business was on the rocks, and they told her there was nothing more they could do for her. It took her years to salvage her reputation within the industry."

"I'm very sorry to hear this," Anita said, sounding genuinely upset. "While I'm afraid I only know the broad strokes about the period of time when Duncan worked with his brother, I can unequivocally tell you that *this* company is wholly aboveboard."

Lola wasn't surprised Anita was defending Duncan. After all, who wanted to believe they had been taken in by a scumbag? She certainly hadn't, even though Duncan had admitted it in her parents' living room on Friday night. Still, she had to ask, "What makes you so sure?"

"I have a background in forensic research and accounting," Anita explained. "Before accepting this position, I combed through Duncan's account books, files, and client records. I feel confident that I would not have missed anything unlawful."

Lola was reminded of her father's questions about whether there could be some explanation for Duncan's involvement—and supposed wrongdoings—with Moira.

No. Lola couldn't give in to her doubt. She needed to remain firm, strong, on task. This was about helping Moira. Nothing else.

"Even if this company is aboveboard," Lola said to Anita, "that doesn't erase Duncan's past misdeeds. And given that he has flat-out admitted to wrongdoing with regard to my friend, I would appreciate it if you would tell me where he is. I just drove in from Bar Harbor, and I need to talk to him immediately."

"I'm afraid I don't know his exact whereabouts, but I'm happy to call him to find out. And I want you to know that I promise to look into everything you've just told me."

"Thank you. But you don't need to call him for me." Lola's heartbeat sped up, knowing she would be hearing his voice again soon. Steeling her heart to lock down completely, she said, "I'll call him myself."

CHAPTER SIXTEEN

Duncan picked up halfway through the first ring. "Lola, I'm so glad you called." His deep voice resonated through her the same way it always had, turning her insides to liquid. "I've spent all weekend hoping you'd let me apologize and explain everything."

This was precisely why she had blocked his number Friday night. For all her fury at the way he'd betrayed her and Moira, she *still* hadn't trusted herself not to give in and pick up his call, if only to hear his voice one more time. And she'd been right not to trust her physical reaction to him. Despite what he'd done, just hearing his voice made desire rise up inside of her again.

Squashing every ounce of emotion and attraction, she said, "I'm not interested in hearing more lies about what a great guy you are." Her tone was flat, with none of her usual warmth. "I'm here in Boston to talk about Moira."

"You're in Boston?" He was clearly shocked. "Where? I'll come straight to you."

They needed a more even playing field than his office—somewhere impersonal where she couldn't make the mistake of letting emotions get in the way. "I passed a Starbucks two blocks from your office. I'll be there in ten minutes."

She hung up on him before he could reply. She had never hung up on anyone before, not even her brothers or sisters when they were being annoying. Lola went out of her way to be a good, kind, friendly person. But Duncan had pushed her too far. Farther than anyone had ever pushed her.

Because she'd never let herself love anybody else.

Only him.

Lola had let her heart tumble head over heels. She'd let herself be consumed by emotion and passion. And now she was paying the price.

Which was why it didn't matter how strong their connection had felt, or that just so much as looking at Duncan, let alone touching or kissing him, had set a thousand flames alight inside of her. If she had known the truth about him, passion would never have mattered. And she wouldn't have dropped her guard to let him in.

Regardless of his apologies and explanations, she would *never* make that mistake again.

Despite her dark mood, as she walked the two blocks to the Starbucks, she couldn't keep from breathing in the sweet aroma of blooming flowers on this softer edge of the business district, while also noticing how rushed everyone seemed as they hurried to wherever they were going.

It had been too long since she'd come to the city. Lola had always been inspired by people-watching—how strangers dressed, or did their hair and makeup, even the way some of them put their dogs in fancy outfits to match their own. This trip was an accidental reminder that there was a whole big world she needed to make time to see and experience.

She wouldn't thank Duncan for this reminder, but she wouldn't let him mar it either.

After ordering a cup of tea, she sat at a table for two that faced the window, then pulled out the sketchbook she always kept in her bag. Though she was on edge as she waited for Duncan, she was pleased that the creative part of her still felt inspired. She couldn't stand the thought of letting Duncan—or any other man—steal her creativity.

As her pencil moved quickly over the page, it was comforting to know that regardless of how heavy her heart felt, the core of who she was remained and would come out of this stronger than ever. It was a much-needed epiphany in what had otherwise been a horrible three days.

While she sketched, several men tried to catch her

eye. One asked her outright if he could buy her a cup of coffee. Having spent most of her life dealing with these kinds of interruptions, she let each know she wasn't interested with a small smile and a shake of her head. Fortunately, none was especially pushy today. Sometimes, a man would sit down and try to start up a conversation even after she'd made it clear that she wasn't interested, which was never a fun situation.

And then, she felt it. The air in the room actually seemed to change.

Duncan must have arrived.

Everything stilled inside of her as she looked up from her notebook, instantly attuned to his large, strong presence as he walked in. Her heart raced as she couldn't help but drink him in, broad-shouldered and strikingly handsome in his dark suit and crisp white collared shirt.

And yet, where once everything had felt so right between them, now nothing did. She had a million things she needed to say. But as she looked at him, all she could wonder was how she could have been so terribly wrong as to trust him.

She took a deep breath to try to ground herself before she spoke. "I didn't want to ever see you again." Though she knew her blunt statement had hurt him, she wanted him to know exactly where she stood. She also needed to remind herself that she hadn't come back to forgive him. "But I had to come to Boston to make sure that you give Moira everything she should have gotten five years ago."

His normally tanned knuckles were white as he tightly grasped the back of the chair, then slowly sat across from her. "I promise I will do everything I can to help her. That's precisely what I've been working on since I returned to Boston—solidifying my relationships with manufacturers, retailers, suppliers, and other important contacts on her behalf." He paused a beat before adding, "I know I don't deserve a chance to explain, but now that you're here, Lola, I hope you'll reconsider giving me that chance."

She hadn't planned to give him *anything*. Especially not a second chance. But hearing that he was already working to fix things for Moira softened Lola's heart before she could stop it.

Then again...what if he was telling more lies to try to convince her that he wasn't a bad guy? And here she was, a fool to believe anything that came out of his mouth. How many times was she going to get her heart crushed by Duncan before she actually learned her lesson?

She shook her head. "I can't trust you anymore."

A muscle jumped in his jaw. "I can understand why you feel that way. But I swear I'm telling you the truth when I say that I plan to help Moira however I can. I've spent five years wanting to find her so I could make things right."

Despite knowing she needed to stay completely shut down, Lola couldn't stop herself from saying, "Then why didn't you? Surely you could have found her contact information before now."

"Brilliant Funds was my brother's pet project, one that he insisted he didn't need any help with. By the time I finally copped to the fact that he was embezzling the initial investments into the fund, my access to the records—along with anything with Moira's name and company information on it—was revoked."

"Are you really asking me to believe that you couldn't find any information about Moira or her company because your brother shut you out of the company? The one you *ran* with him?"

"Yes." Frustration played out across his face as he explained, "Until now, I've never been able to discuss this situation with anyone except my lawyer from that time, who turned out to be dirty, as well."

A part of her—a huge part—was desperate to hear more. Especially given the fact that Duncan had previously told her his brother had *erased* him from his life. Was this why?

But she was afraid that if she opened herself up to him, even the tiniest bit, he'd somehow spin everything around so that she'd end up forgiving him…and foolishly fall back into his arms.

Which was why she made herself remind them both, "Like I said, the only reason I'm here today is to make sure you provide Moira with the funds and contacts you should have given her five years ago. That's as far as anything goes between you and me. I don't care about your past anymore. And as for your future?" She forced herself to harden her heart, expression, and tone. "Your future is definitely *not* going to have me in it."

CHAPTER SEVENTEEN

Duncan was overjoyed to hear Lola's voice again—and to see her beautiful, expressive face. But even as he gave silent thanks for this chance to be close to her one more time, his chest squeezed tighter and tighter as the ache inside of him grew.

She wanted nothing to do with him. And she'd made it perfectly clear that there would *never* be a future for them.

It was no less than he deserved. The perfect karmic payback for not stopping his brother from hurting so many others.

But it still hurt like hell.

"Would you consider coming back to my office to go over the plan I've been putting together for Moira and her company?"

He could see Lola weighing the benefits of being surrounded by strangers versus being alone with him. Finally, she nodded. "The less distractions there are, the sooner I'll be able to go home."

Duncan hadn't been looking for love when he'd

walked into Lola's class. But meeting her, falling for her, had changed everything. Loving Lola—and being loved by her—had started to heal his wounds, even the deepest scars. Now, losing her love had torn those wounds wide open.

Whoever had said it was better to have loved and lost than never to have loved at all was wrong.

Dead wrong.

Walking toward his office with Lola beside him, her hand no longer in his, was a brutal contrast to days when they'd taken any excuse to touch. To laugh. To share dreams and plans. Now there was a block of ice between them. One that would never melt.

The silence was oppressive. Duncan had never felt the need to fill empty spaces with conversation. But now he found himself asking, "How was your drive to Boston? Or did you fly?"

"The drive was fine." Each word was sharp. "I was so furious, though, that I wasn't paying as much attention to the road as I should have."

While he didn't like knowing how angry he'd made her, he was glad that she was at least sharing her feelings with him. "I take it you met Gail and Anita?"

"They both seemed nice." She sounded surprised. "Is Anita the person you hired to take over for you?"

"Yes," he said, happy that Lola was even the slightest bit interested in his life.

"You should know that I told her you're not the man she thinks you are." Lola was beautiful even when she was furious. "I told her you have plenty of skeletons in your past and that she and Gail should be wary of trusting you."

Duncan's heart sank even further, but not because he was angry at Lola. She wasn't trying to get revenge on him. She was simply concerned about Anita's and Gail's welfare as his employees.

His voice was low, and as even as he could hold it, when he said, "While I've only ever spoken to my former lawyer about what happened with Brilliant Funds, I swear to you that I have been absolutely forthright about everything else with Gail and Anita and my clients. I've done everything possible to make certain that my past mistakes have not and will not affect them or their careers."

Lola's eyes blazed as she stopped in the middle of the sidewalk. "You have the audacity to ask me to believe that you're doing a good job of keeping your employees out of harm's way? When all the while you've kept them completely in the dark about the Brilliant Funds embezzlement scheme that destroyed Moira's business and anyone else who was unfortunate enough to sign on with the incubator!"

There hadn't been a day that went by when he hadn't wanted to come fully clean with his staff. But his brother was too powerful, too vindictive, too vicious.

"If I could tell them everything, I would. But I know how far my brother is willing to go to stay in power. If any of them said a single word against him—to a colleague, a family member, the press—he wouldn't blink at destroying their careers and turning their entire lives inside out." Duncan ran a hand through his hair, wishing for the millionth time that things were different. "And you're right. Moira wasn't the only company owner harmed by the incubator. A half-dozen companies shared the same fate. The only difference is that I was able to locate the owners of those other companies to make amends."

Neither Gail nor Anita were in sight when Lola and Duncan entered his building and headed into his office. Lola was clearly still brimming over with indignation, her body practically vibrating with it. As grateful as he was at being given the gift of this extra time with her—he would happily take Lola's scowls over nothing at all—knowing that this was likely the very last time he would see her made it brutally bittersweet.

"Can I get you anything to drink before we start?" he asked.

"No, I just want to get to work." Lola chose the farthest possible chair from his desk.

As he sat, he worked to corral his emotions so that he could focus. But nothing he did made it any easier to know how much Lola hated him. "Over the past forty-eight hours, I've learned that Moira had a solid domestic customer base when she first joined Brilliant Funds. Within six months, however, her customer base had dwindled to almost nothing."

"She said the fund manager insisted that she change her designs."

Duncan nodded. "I'm guessing my brother was behind those changes, because he wanted to make sure her company didn't meet the bar required for the half-million investment promised to her if she could prove the marketability of her product." Lola continued to look absolutely furious as he spoke, and he didn't blame her. He wanted to tear his brother apart for what Alastair had done to so many unsuspecting people. "The good news is that five years on, Moira seems not only to have built her business back up, she has also expanded to retailers across the United States. I believe international expansion is the obvious next step, either in Canada or the UK, depending on how potential customers respond to her products in those territories. As I suspect she won't want anything to do with me or my current firm, I would like to give her the funds she was promised in her original contract—adjusted for inflation, of course—along with introductions to potential business partners in each territory." He looked at his notes one last time to make sure he hadn't left out any details, before lifting his gaze back to Lola's face. "How does my proposal sound to you?"

Lola looked surprised by his offer. Surprised enough that she was uncharacteristically fidgety, smoothing a hand over her hair, straightening her skirt, licking her lips. "It sounds pretty good," she finally replied. "But I also think it will be important for Moira to weigh in on whether she needs a similar influx of funds in the United States. That is, if she's even willing to go for this deal."

"I would agree with that. Although I'm afraid that even with no strings attached, convincing Moira to accept the funds and contacts from me won't be easy."

Lola didn't disagree. "Before I leave, I want you to put everything you've offered in writing and then sign it."

After quickly typing up his offer, and getting Lola's approval on the verbiage, he called in Anita. "Could you please witness my signature on this agreement?"

If Anita seemed surprised by the terms he'd laid out on the document, particularly the fact that all funds were going to come from him personally, she didn't let on.

Lola had just put the signed agreement into her bag and was standing up to leave when Gail poked her head in the door. "I'm sorry to interrupt," she said, her gaze shooting to Lola before moving to Duncan. "My babysitter just called to let me know George isn't feeling well. I'm afraid I need to head straight home."

"Of course," Duncan said. While he didn't have any children himself, he imagined there was nothing worse than one's child being sick. "Is he going to be all right?"

"He threw up, and he's got a temperature, but evidently the stomach flu has been going around his school. I'm sure he'll be fine in a couple of days."

"I'm glad to hear that. But please let me know if I can do anything for you or your family, Gail."

"I will, thank you." But instead of turning to leave, she said, "There is one big problem, however. I was supposed to help out at Serafina's fashion show tonight, and now I won't be able to attend."

Serafina was one of their most promising clients. A pioneer in sustainable fashion, she traced the provenance of every spool of thread and swatch of fabric, while also hiring women in disadvantaged communities to do her cutting and sewing.

"Don't worry," Anita offered. "I can rearrange my plans for the night and attend in your place."

"Normally, that would work," Gail replied, "but in this case, things are a little more complicated. I'm supposed to close out her fashion show in a wedding gown that has been fitted to my measurements." Gail looked doubly worried now, not only about her sick son, but also about a client they didn't want to let down. "I know how hard Serafina has worked for this opportunity to showcase her work to a broader pool of buyers, and I can't stand the thought of doing anything to ruin that."

"I wish I could do it," Anita said, "but you're right. There is no way I could fit in a dress made for you. I'm such a string bean the dress wouldn't fall right."

Gail looked worried as she asked Duncan, "What other options do we have?"

"I'll do it."

All of them turned to Lola in surprise, stunned by her offer to help a stranger.

Duncan wanted nothing more than the chance to spend a few more hours with her. It was beyond tempting to snatch at her offer and hold her to it. But trying to chain her to him by any means possible definitely wasn't the smartest path to reclaiming her heart.

"Thank you for the offer," he made himself say. "But we can find another solution."

"Gail and I are close to the same size," she countered, "and I hate the thought of a designer not getting the chance that she's worked so hard for."

Duncan warred with himself. A better man wouldn't let her make this sacrifice for him. But in the end, he couldn't find the self-control to let her go. And not just because of Serafina's fashion show.

The truth was that, despite knowing Lola deserved a man with an unblemished past, he wanted to fight for her. Wanted to do whatever it took to win her heart again. Even if it took him the rest of his life. Even if it ended up being impossible.

Because even the slightest chance of winning Lola's trust, and love, would be worth a lifetime of trying.

"Thank you so much for offering to help tonight." Gail gave Lola an impulsive hug. "You're a lifesaver."

"It's my pleasure," Lola said with a small smile. "Now go home to your little one, and don't give another thought to tonight's fashion show."

Soon, Lola and Duncan were alone again. "I can't thank you enough for going above and bey—"

She held up a hand. "I'm not doing this for you. I'm doing this for Gail and for your client. All I need to know is where to find the designer so that she can do a fitting before show time."

"I was planning to head over to Serafina's show in a couple of hours anyway, but I can go with you now."

"No need," she replied in a curt voice. "I'm sure you have important meetings or phone calls you need to make."

"I canceled my meetings to work on Moira's plan."

Lola frowned. She'd been frowning nonstop since the coffee shop. He hated seeing her look so unhappy.

All he'd ever wanted was to bring the same joy into her life that she brought to his. Not sadness.

"I'm still happy to go on my own," she insisted.

Knowing better than to keep pushing her when she was already selflessly saving the day, he said, "I'll call Serafina to let her know."

The phone rang only once before Serafina picked up. "Gail just told me you're sending someone else to wear the wedding gown." She wasn't bothering with pleasantries, and he didn't blame her. This was surely the last news she wanted to hear mere hours before her biggest-ever show. "I hope you're already on your way."

"Lola is going to head to the venue now," he clarified.

"Wait, you're not coming with her?"

He was about to explain that he would arrive closer to show time, when Lola put her hand on his arm. Obviously able to hear their conversation through his phone's speaker, Lola had a resigned look on her face as she mouthed, *You can come too.*

"I'll come with Lola right now," he said, his heart suddenly feeling a million times lighter than it had since Friday night, despite the fact that Lola still despised him. Five minutes ago, he'd been braced to watch her leave his life for good. Now, he would get a few more hours with her. "You're going to really enjoy working with her."

"I sure hope so." Serafina sounded frazzled, the way any designer would hours before a big show. Even before Lola had stepped in, he had been making plans to calm her nerves. He had a feeling, though, that Lola would know exactly how to make Serafina feel better without any help from him. She had a knack for making people feel comfortable, welcome, happy.

Just the way she'd made him feel happier than he'd ever been before.

CHAPTER EIGHTEEN

Lola couldn't believe how badly her day had spiraled out of control. She'd been so clear about her purpose when she'd been driving hell for leather to Boston. Find Duncan, convince him to do right by Moira, then get the heck out of town without being wowed by his charm, his gorgeous face...or by how much she wanted to feel his arms around her.

She wasn't anywhere near keeping to her plan, damn it!

On the plus side, he was fully on board with helping Moira. Unfortunately, instead of now being back on the road to Bar Harbor, Lola was in Duncan's car on the way to participating in his client's fashion show. It didn't help that she couldn't stop looking at his hand on the gearshift and remembering how good it felt whenever he'd touched her. It was torture being this close to him.

If only she wasn't such a soft touch. Having been a part of several fashion shows over the years to showcase her fabrics, she knew how devastated the designer must feel upon losing her most important model only hours before the show. She shoved away a voice in the back of her head that said the biggest reason she'd offered to help was because she wanted to spend more time with Duncan. She refused to admit that held even the barest hint of truth.

Steeling herself against the foolish emotions that kept trying to sneak in past her defenses—especially with Duncan sitting so close to her in his sports car that if she simply moved her left arm a bit, she'd be able to put her hand on his muscular thigh—Lola worked to refocus her thoughts on Serafina's fashion show. She hoped she would fit into the wedding gown without too many time-consuming alterations. Then again, if she needed to play seamstress, she would happily step in and put her sewing skills to the test.

At last, they pulled up in front of the Boston Center for the Arts and Lola was able to escape the close quarters of Duncan's car. She desperately needed space. Breathing room. And, most of all, time to get her head back on straight and remember that he was *not* the man for her.

She wasn't going to bother consoling herself with the thought that there were other fish in the sea. Nope, she was done fishing. She had learned her lesson, for good this time.

No. More. Men.

Serafina was instantly recognizable—she had a half-dozen pins in her mouth, a needle in her hand, and was still managing to give directions out the side of her mouth. Apart from her colorful hair wrap, she was dressed in head-to-toe black.

Catching sight of Lola and Duncan, she stuck the pins from between her lips into the pin cushion on her wrist. "Thank God. You'll be a near-perfect fit for the wedding dress! And it doesn't hurt that you're drop-dead gorgeous. My dress is going to look amazing on you." She turned to Duncan. "Where did you find this incredible woman?"

"It was pure luck." He smiled as he added, "Stars were shining down on me the day I met Lola."

He didn't hide the emotion in his voice, and it reverberated all the way through to Lola's heart. A heart that was supposed to be completely closed off to him.

With great difficulty, Lola managed to tear her eyes from his, before giving Serafina an overly bright smile. "Whenever you're ready to show me the dress, you can see what needs to be done to perfect the fit."

"I'll take you backstage to try it on." Serafina spoke to Duncan over her shoulder as they walked away. "Don't you go too far, because I have a couple of things I need to discuss with you once Lola and I are done."

"Don't worry," he replied. "I'm not going anywhere."

Though it sounded as though he was simply reassuring Serafina, Lola couldn't help but feel that his words were also meant for her. That he was saying no matter what had gone wrong, he was going to try to fix it, because he still loved her.

Desperate to stop thinking about the man whose eyes she could feel following her out of the room, Lola asked Serafina question after question about her company. When she'd first begun to design, where she'd studied, how long she'd been in the business? Within a matter of minutes, Lola had learned she was in the presence of a major pro who had designed for some of the biggest names in the business before striking out on her own.

"How have you liked working with Duncan's venture capital firm?" Lola needed to know if there were any warning signs that he might harm Serafina the way he'd harmed Moira.

"Duncan is *wonderful*." Serafina was unequivocal in her praise. "His staff is fantastic too. I've heard so many fiasco stories about investors since I made the decision to go out on my own three years ago. Which is why Duncan is the *only* one I would trust to come near my business with a ten-foot pole. He's never steered me or my company wrong."

It was on the tip of Lola's tongue to tell Serafina

not to make the mistake of trusting him. But where she'd been extremely forthright with Anita back at Duncan's office, something held her back this time.

While driving to Boston this morning, she'd been one hundred percent sure that he was a lying cheat. But after everyone she'd met today seemed to think he could do no wrong—and both Gail and Serafina had worked with him for years—her resolve and her certainty had begun to wobble.

Her father's words came back to her: *You need to give yourself a whole heck of a lot more credit, because you're a good judge of character. I'm just not convinced that your heart could play you wrong like that.*

"There haven't been any warning signs?" Lola asked. "You haven't gotten the sense that he's reeling you in before the fall?"

"No way." Serafina looked at Lola as though she had lost her marbles. "Trust me, after this many years in the business, I have an unerring radar for people who are out to rip me off. Even now, the way he recruited you to step in to help in a moment of crisis shows that Duncan is truly one of a kind."

"What do you know about his past?"

The other woman cocked her head. "After working so well with him for the past few years, I'd say I'm beyond the point of needing to question it." With that, Serafina unzipped a black garment bag.

Lola's mouth fell open when she saw the dress. "What a stunning wedding gown!" The classic silhouette with a fitted bodice and a full skirt looked like it had come straight out of a fairy tale. Yet it managed to look modern and edgy due to the beading, ragged edges, and asymmetrical hemline.

"Thank you." Serafina beamed. "Not to toot my own horn or anything, but it's my best work yet. I never planned to focus on wedding gowns, but when the idea for this dress popped into my head, I couldn't deny it. It's a bit of a change of pace for my business, but after discussing it with Duncan, we decided it was worth putting out there to see if any retailers bite."

"They're *all* going to bite." Lola was absolutely certain of it. "In fact, I have a recently engaged sister who would look amazing in this. Would you mind if I took a picture and texted it to her?"

"Heck, I'm this close to giving you the dress out of gratitude. So yes, you can absolutely send your sister a picture."

Lola snapped a couple of shots with her phone, then sent them to Cassie with a text. *I might have found your wedding dress. Or at least your wedding dress designer. I'll tell you more when I get back from Boston.*

Within seconds, Cassie wrote back, *That's one of the most beautiful wedding dresses I've ever seen! And also, what are you doing looking at wedding dresses? I thought you were in Boston kicking some ex-boyfriend butt? You haven't decided to walk down the aisle with him instead, have you?*

Lola quickly replied, *No time to talk now, but don't worry, I'm not letting myself be sucked in. I'm just helping out a fellow designer in need.*

She put her phone away, then stripped off her clothes so that she could put on the dress. After sharing a bedroom with her sisters since childhood, Lola wasn't shy about undressing in front of a stranger.

"You really are stunning," Serafina said as she took in Lola's lush curves. "No wonder Duncan couldn't take his eyes off you."

Lola hated knowing a part of her still loved knowing Duncan found her attractive. "There's nothing between us."

Serafina gave her a look that clearly indicated she wasn't buying it. Thankfully, she was far too focused on helping Lola into the dress to push it.

The exquisite gown was surprisingly light despite the beadwork and the many layers of fabric. Serafina efficiently pinned the bodice seams close to Lola's frame, which was a bit smaller than Gail's. Fortunately, Lola's heels looked like they would work well with the dress.

Serafina's walkie-talkie crackled just as she was finishing pinning the fabric, alerting her to an issue with the stage setup.

"If you could help me out of this," Lola suggested, "I'll start on these alterations. My degree is in textile design, but I spent a summer working in a Parisian couture house, so I promise my work will be up to par."

For the second time that day, Lola got a hug from a woman she'd only just met. "Thank you!" Soon, Serafina had efficiently undone the row of buttons down the back of the dress, helped Lola out of it, and given her the fine needles and thread needed for the alterations.

As she began to sew with tiny, precise stitches, Lola was glad for the intent concentration this work required. It meant she couldn't stew over Duncan. Even better, she could stay holed up in the back of the venue while Duncan was out networking on Serafina's behalf.

Every time she heard footsteps or a man's voice through the closed door, though, she thought it might be him. Every time it wasn't, she was simultaneously relieved *and* disappointed.

Ugh. Anger had been better than this waffling. Anger was straightforward, with no shades of gray, no lingering emotions, no second-guessing.

Just as she was finishing the alterations, her mother's ringtone sounded from her bag. "Hi, Mom, how are you? And how's Moira doing?"

"Much better, thankfully. She's starting to look and

sound more like her old self."

Though Lola was glad to hear it, she still couldn't shake the guilt over the part she'd played in upsetting her friend. "I have some good news for her, but I'd like to give it to her in person. Is she planning on staying with you for a while longer?"

"Yes, I've convinced her to stay a few more days."

"Excellent. I'm out of town right now, but I should be back no later than midday tomorrow to share the news with her."

"Where are you? I heard you had a busy weekend with your siblings, but grew worried when I didn't see you at the café today."

"I'm in Boston."

"Boston?" Her mother was clearly concerned as she asked, "Why?"

Beth could likely guess that Duncan was the reason. But Lola wasn't ready to answer her questions. Not until she'd tamped down the rogue emotions that kept threatening to rise up and swamp her.

"I can't talk, Mom." It was true—Serafina had just walked in to look at the alterations. "But I promise I'll call you back as soon as I know what time I'll be over tomorrow to see Moira. Love you. Sorry to have to rush off the phone."

Her mother hadn't raised seven children successfully by being thrown by a child who hurried to get off the phone...even if she was hanging up to try to hide her broken heart. "It's no problem, honey. Just be sure to let me know if you need anything between now and then."

Fortunately, Serafina looked radiantly happy with Lola's work. "You wouldn't happen to be looking for a job as a seamstress, would you?"

Lola smiled. "I'm not, but thanks for your lovely compliment. And I'm happy to help with anything else in your collection that needs alterations."

"All I need right now is to get you back into the dress. The show's going to start soon, and you'll be the final model to walk, right around the ten-minute mark."

Serafina had just begun to button Lola back into the wedding gown when she got another urgent call on the walkie-talkie, letting her know the first model meant to go down the runway had snagged her dress.

"Go," Lola urged her. "I'll close the rest of these buttons." If she strained her right arm and twisted her shoulder, she would hopefully be able to reach the buttons that ran along her spine.

She was trying to contort into a position even her super-bendy yoga teacher would find impossible when someone walked into the room. She instinctively knew who it was even before she heard his voice.

"I've been sent in to help you with some buttons."

Before Lola could tell Duncan that she would rather find a stranger on the street to do up the buttons—anyone but him—he had stepped behind her, his fingers gently moving over the silk and lace along her spine.

As her heart raced faster and faster, she couldn't stop breathing him in. Couldn't keep from noting how good he smelled. Couldn't keep from melting inside simply from how warm and solid and sexy he felt, even from behind her.

Thrill bumps ran up her spine as he slowly closed one button after another. Was he deliberately taking his time? Or was it just her imagination that he was *lingering* over her?

And then, for one of the topmost buttons, he had to brush her hair aside so that it wouldn't tangle with the dress. When his fingertips grazed the skin on her neck, she thought her knees would buckle with wanting him.

She tried to tell herself that desire meant nothing.

She tried to convince herself that needing him on a physical level had nothing whatsoever to do with her heart.

But she couldn't make heads or tails of any of those arguments.

Not when he was touching her like this.

And not when it was taking every ounce of her self-control to keep from turning into his arms and kissing him.

He didn't speak as he finished fastening the dress, and neither did she. Her mouth was too dry, and even if she had been able to form words, she didn't trust herself not to blurt out how badly she still wanted him.

Finally, after what felt like an absolute eternity of longing and desperation, he cleared his throat. "All done."

Just listening to his deep, sexy voice made every last cell in her body that wasn't already crying out for him leap to life.

She couldn't do anything but nod. Couldn't possibly turn to face him. Not when she knew that if she did, she would throw her arms around him and press her lips to his. And, worst of all, forgive him for everything he shouldn't be forgiven for.

Again, she held her breath, waiting. Waiting for him to either move closer...or move away.

At last, when she was almost out of self-restraint, he said, "I'd better go take my seat." His voice was rougher now—with desire, with emotion, with anguish.

Everything she was feeling too.

She held perfectly still until he stepped away and closed the door behind him. At the click of the latch, her breath rushed out, ragged and raw in her chest.

Her legs were trembling, and there was a fine sheen of sweat over her skin.

Never before had she denied herself something—*someone*—she wanted so much. If anything, she wanted Duncan even more now than she had when they were together.

But Serafina was waiting for her to take her place at the end of the lineup. Lola took a deep breath, lifted her chin, and headed out to the stage. Though Duncan's eyes would be on her while she walked the runway, she couldn't let it rattle her. She needed to do Serafina proud.

Lola's foolish heart had already done enough damage to Moira. She wouldn't let it ruin Serafina's show too.

CHAPTER NINETEEN

Duncan had wanted to beg Lola to forgive him, to believe in him, to love him. But with Serafina counting on them to make sure Lola was ready to hit the runway, he'd steeled himself to simply do up the buttons, rather than stripping the dress from her skin instead.

It was utter torment to be so close to Lola, to touch her again, knowing he could never have her. Not that any man would ever *possess* Lola Sullivan. She was a force unto herself. But if his past hadn't come between them, they could have been partners in life, in love. They could have had a family of their own. And every day for the rest of his life would have been so sweet.

For the past two hours, Duncan had done his utmost to focus on networking with retailer reps on Serafina's behalf. There was no question that she was about to make a huge splash in the international marketplace, especially if she continued to make wedding gowns on par with the one Lola was modeling tonight.

Duncan had seen Lola in the dress only from the back, but that alone had been enough to see that it was exquisite.

Lola was exquisite.

He took a seat in the back corner of the room, leaving the best seats to the customers, a mix of retailers and women who could afford to buy the entire collection without blinking an eye.

As the first model walked down the runway, Duncan was impressed by Serafina's talent all over again. She had escaped a dangerous marriage in her early twenties and had worked like the dickens to build her business. Now, she went out of her way to help women who needed a hand up.

Duncan was pleased to note the approving murmurs from the crowd, rapt with attention as the models walked in Serafina's dresses. Ten minutes in, the music and lighting shifted, becoming slower and softer. And then Lola emerged on the runway, taking away the breath of every single person in the room.

Though they were at a fashion show, the romantic expression on Lola's face made him almost believe she was walking down the aisle to become one with the man who meant everything to her.

Everyone's mouths continued to hang open as she paused at the end of the runway for the photographers. She was that stunning, that vibrant in Serafina's magnificent wedding dress.

Duncan was positive that Serafina would be besieged by orders. But no matter how hard he worked to remember that he was here tonight for business only, he couldn't erase the vision of Lola walking down the aisle toward him in that wedding dress.

* * *

Serafina held Lola's hand high as the crowd cheered the brilliant clothing collection. Beside her, Lola was grinning from cheek to cheek. Duncan was profoundly glad to see her smile again, even if he couldn't help wishing he was the one responsible for putting that smile back on her face.

When Lola went to change into her clothes, instead of giving in to the temptation to see if she needed help undoing the buttons on the back of the gown, he forced himself to do his job by making another networking round of the retailers and wealthy socialites.

When Lola emerged from the back, wearing her own clothes again, she was immediately surrounded by admirers. "You were my star of the evening," Serafina gushed. "I couldn't have done it without you."

"Your clothes are absolutely beautiful." Lola smiled fondly at the woman who looked to have become a new friend. "It was an honor to wear your wedding dress."

Not wanting to intrude, Duncan stood on the periphery until Serafina waved him over. "Congratulations on your best collection yet," he said.

"Thank you," she said. And then, she added, "Like I was telling Lola earlier, partnering with you is the best decision I've ever made."

Lola's expression was inscrutable. Did she believe Serafina? Or did she think he'd put her up to praising him?

"I always knew you would go far," he said, "and your success tonight proves you're going to eclipse even my highest hopes. I also want you to know that if you're looking to source new fabric in the future, Lola is a brilliant textile designer."

"Wait a minute." Serafina turned to look more closely at the fabric of Lola's dress, a batik style hand-drawn vegetable garden in an array of bright colors. "Did you design that fabric?"

"I did."

"I have been admiring it since the moment you walked in," Serafina exclaimed. "The only reason I hadn't mentioned it before now is because I was so frazzled before the show. If the rest of your designs are anything like what you're wearing right now, I'd *love* to work with you."

"I'd love that too. And thank you, again, for letting me be a part of your show. Now go mingle with your adoring public." Lola gave Serafina a hug, then edged away from the group, not seeming to notice the lingering stares from the men in the room.

"You did a great job tonight," Duncan told her. "I can't thank you enough." It killed him to speak to Lola as though she were nothing more than another colleague. "I know Serafina will be forever grateful."

She shook off his praise. "It was my pleasure to help her."

When she yawned, he realized how tired she looked. Probably because she hadn't slept well over the weekend after she'd learned the truth about his past.

Wanting desperately to make things right, he began, "Lola—"

She cut him off before he could say more. "I need to head back to Bar Harbor before it gets any later."

A flash of lightning, followed by a loud crack of thunder, surprised them both. Outside the windows of the art center, the trees were practically blowing sideways, and rain was falling in sheets.

"I had no idea a storm blew in while we were inside," Lola said at the same time that her stomach made a serious growling noise.

Though Duncan knew it was the last thing she wanted, he couldn't stop himself. "I know a place nearby where we could get something to eat while you wait for the storm to pass."

She looked like she was going to refuse. Until her stomach growled again at the same moment that a huge yawn overtook her. "I suppose a cup, or twelve, of coffee might be a good idea before I hit the road. Some food wouldn't hurt either."

Instinctively, he placed his hand on her lower back as they headed through the crowd to the exit. It wasn't until he felt her spine stiffen beneath his fingertips that he realized what he'd done.

He was just removing his hand when he realized they were being watched.

How had he missed seeing the man earlier? The same one who had come into his office, sent by his brother.

A chill moved through Duncan. And though he tried to shake away his uneasy sense that Lola was about to be pulled even deeper into the tangled mess of his life, he knew better than to underestimate Alastair. Only this time, Duncan had no intention whatsoever of letting his brother get the upper hand.

For Lola, Duncan would risk absolutely everything. Even his own freedom.

CHAPTER TWENTY

Lola knew she shouldn't be going to a restaurant with Duncan. And she definitely shouldn't be aware of every move he made, the raindrops on his eyelashes, or the fact that he was heart-stoppingly gorgeous.

On the contrary, she should be hightailing it back to Bar Harbor to put as much distance as possible between the two of them. Especially given that she hadn't been able to forget the heady sensation of his fingertips against her skin when he'd fastened the buttons of the wedding dress.

But she was starved. After not having any appetite all weekend, it had suddenly come roaring back to life.

At thirteen, like many teenagers she had tried a few fad diets, but none of them had done a thing to diminish her bountiful curves. It had been yet another reason to embrace her figure. Thank God she'd learned that lesson early, rather than wasting countless years fighting against who she was.

Right now, however, she was fighting *big time* against her inner urges. Embracing her curves was great. But embracing her unquenchable desire to be with a man who wasn't worth her time *wasn't* great. Which meant that she needed to eat as quickly as possible, then get the heck away from temptation.

Rather than continue on to whatever restaurant he had in mind, she pointed to the lit-up windows of the one they were in front of, only half a block from the Boston Center for the Arts. "This looks good." She headed inside before he could argue.

Lola was so flustered that it wasn't until they sat down that she realized the restaurant had white tablecloths and candles on every table *and* that couples were slow dancing to a live band at the back of the restaurant. She nearly groaned aloud at her choice. There must be twenty restaurants within a half mile of the fashion show, and somehow she'd chosen the most romantic one.

She studied the menu as if her life depended on it, when in reality the words were blurring together. Lola was always focused, never scatterbrained. But being this close to Duncan made it impossible for her to think straight, let alone corral her careening emotions and attraction to him.

"Good evening," their waiter said. "Would you like me to tell you our specials?"

"No, thank you." She didn't have time for a leisurely meal, didn't trust herself to be with Duncan a minute longer than was strictly necessary. She just needed to wolf down some food and go. "The meatloaf looks good." *Meatloaf?* She hated meatloaf. Whatever, she'd eat a couple of bites, and then she'd leave.

"I'll have the salmon." Duncan's deep voice reverberated over her skin, even though he had been talking about fish...not what he was planning to do to her in bed. "And two coffees, please."

In her desperation to avoid conversation after the waiter left, she picked up her water and guzzled it. She needed to do something, anything, to stop herself from asking Duncan *why*. How could she do that when she'd told him she didn't care about his past and that he no longer meant anything to her? How could she betray her desire to know more about him when she was supposed to be cutting him completely out of her life?

"Serafina is clearly very interested in working with you," he said, breaking into her tormented musings. "I had been planning to speak with her about you soon, but it was even better that she was able to meet you and see one of your designs in person."

Had he really meant to introduce them? Lola wondered. He sounded totally genuine. Then again, he always sounded genuine, didn't he?

"Serafina is extremely talented." Though she shouldn't have said anything more, she couldn't help adding, "You've done well surrounding yourself with excellent people, haven't you?" She didn't bother to hold back the bitterness and cynicism in her tone.

"I've tried to," he said. "In the past five years, at least."

Pushing aside all the questions about his brother that were so close to bubbling over, she asked instead, "How did you discover Serafina's work?"

"I was lucky. A friend from college bought one of her dresses in a store in the South End. When she told me what a hit her outfit was with her friends and that Serafina seeks out women in developing nations to help create her garments, I reached out to see if she would be interested in working with me." He paused a beat before saying, "If you would like to work with her, I won't stand in your way. I'll make sure you don't have to deal with me."

Of course Lola was interested in partnering with Serafina. But even if Duncan kept his distance, couldn't he see that just knowing he worked with Serafina would mean he would always be inside her head?

Thankfully, the waiter brought their coffees, so Lola could turn her focus from Duncan to the process of dumping in sugar and cream, then blowing the steam off the top. All the while, however, she could feel Duncan's intense gaze on her.

Ugh. Avoidance mode wasn't her style. She wasn't someone who hid from things, no matter how difficult.

It was long past time to buck up and deal with the situation calmly and coolly.

"Duncan," she said in as impersonal a tone as she could manage while looking into his eyes, "I appreciate that you're willing to work things out with Moira. I'm planning to run everything by her by midday tomorrow, and after that, she'll hopefully be in touch so that you can work out the finer details of the agreement."

She could easily read his expression, because it was exactly what she was feeling herself. Longing for things to be different, to go back to being as perfect as they had seemed just days ago. Longing for the happy ever after that had seemed like it might actually be within reach. Longing for the love they'd thought they'd found with one another.

"I'll do right by her, I promise."

Just then, a gray-haired couple approached. The man, whom she guessed to be in his seventies, reached out a hand. "Come dance," he insisted, leaving Lola no room to argue. Not that she would have, given the twinkle in his blue eyes and the fact that he had just given her the perfect excuse to put some distance between Duncan and herself.

The woman Lola assumed was his wife pulled Duncan up from his seat, as well. "We can't let them show us up, can we?"

The band was playing one of Lola's favorite big-band songs, "Lady Be Good." Lola let herself be swept up by the music and her very talented dance partner. As the band segued smoothly into "I'm Getting Sentimental Over You," it was lovely to let her guard down for a few minutes, to dance and laugh and pretend this last weekend had never happened. As long as she didn't accidentally catch a glimpse of Duncan looking handsome and charming as he swept his partner across the floor.

By the time she realized her partner was twirling her straight into Duncan's arms, the older couple was dancing away together.

Lola knew exactly what she needed to do: wrench herself away from Duncan, grab her things from the table, and leave. But now that his arms were around her, and his mouth was so deliciously close, she simply couldn't find the strength to do it.

Time stood still as they danced, and Lola was taken back to their first night together when they'd been so close. Being in Duncan's arms had felt like the most natural, perfect thing in the world. And no matter how she tried to tell herself it didn't feel that way anymore, she couldn't manage that big a lie. Not when all she wanted was to take his hands in hers, pull him off the dance floor, and kiss him the way she'd been longing to kiss him all day.

Neither of them spoke as she clasped her hands

around his neck and he moved his hands to cradle her waist and hips. The utter sensuality of their dance took her breath away. But even bigger, even more powerful, was the heightened emotion of the moment as they couldn't look away from one another, and both knew another kiss was inevitable.

His kiss was everything she knew it would be. Desperate. Full of longing. Sinfully sexy.

But it was also bittersweet after everything that had come between them since Friday night at her parents' house, when Moira had walked in and interrupted their joyous dancing.

Oh God. Moira.

Somewhere in the dance, in the kiss, Lola had let herself forget how Duncan and his brother had nearly ruined her friend's life.

Guilt gave Lola the strength to finally tear herself away, quickly cross the dance floor, grab her things, and dash out of the restaurant to hail a cab.

She could sense Duncan behind her and knew that if she looked at him again, she'd be lost. Thankfully, luck was on her side as a taxi skidded to a halt mere seconds after she raised her hand. Throwing herself into the backseat, she told the driver where to take her to pick up her car, her heart racing as they drove through the rainswept streets of Boston.

It felt like being in a getaway car after a bank robbery. Only she wasn't the one who had stolen something—it was Duncan.

He had stolen her heart.

And despite everything she now knew to be true about him, she wasn't sure she'd ever get it back.

CHAPTER TWENTY-ONE

It wasn't until Lola was on the freeway heading home that she felt like she could breathe again. By the time she got to her Bar Harbor cottage, it took all her remaining energy just to crawl beneath her sheets fully clothed to fall into an exhausted sleep.

When she woke at sunrise, she was momentarily disoriented. Too soon, it all came flooding back. Unfortunately, she hadn't dreamed her broken heart, as her brain replayed her best—and worst—moments with Duncan on continuous repeat.

Enough!

Determined to stop feeling like a heartbroken zombie, she stripped off her clothes and headed into the shower, hoping the hot water would wash some sense into her brain. After she dried off, she did her makeup more carefully than usual to hide the ravages of her nearly sleepless weekend and exhausting trip to Boston. If anyone knew how to transform themselves on the outside, even when they were shattered on the inside, it was Lola.

When she was confident that she had her game face on, and that her parents would be awake, she walked to their house. Her mom and dad were having breakfast, and they lit up when she walked in.

Her mother gave her a big hug. "Can I get you anything to eat or drink?"

So very glad for the warmth and comfort of her mother's arms, she said, "Thanks, but I'm fine."

The truth was that she was anything but fine. But what was the point of working so hard on her appearance if she was going to admit that the moment she walked in?

When her father hugged her, he held on a little longer than usual. Clearly, he could see beneath her mask. From the look in her mother's eyes, she guessed that Beth did too. Thankfully, neither of them said anything that might break Lola's composure.

"I've come to talk with Moira. Is she in the guest cottage?"

"We returned from a sunrise walk along the waterfront a half hour ago," her mom informed her. "I know she'll be thrilled to see you."

Not entirely sure that was true—especially given that Lola came bearing news of Duncan's offer—her heart started pounding hard when she saw Moira in the garden deadheading roses. "Hello, Moira," she said softly. "I hope I'm not disturbing you."

Her friend turned around with a wide smile, her arms opening automatically. "Of course you're not," Moira said as Lola stepped into her embrace. "As always, you're a sight for sore eyes. Although," Moira added as she pulled back to study Lola's face, "it doesn't look like you've been sleeping any better than I have." She stroked Lola's back, just as she had when she'd comforted Lola as a child. "Please don't lose sleep over what happened. You had no way of knowing who he was. It's just one of those strange coincidences."

"It was an *awful* coincidence," Lola said, her words drenched in guilt. Especially in the wake of her kiss with Duncan last night. The best kiss of her entire life, even when she included all of their kisses that had come before. "Again, I'm so sorry. But today, I have what I hope will be good news."

"Come inside, then, and have a cup of tea with me."

Lola followed Moira into the cottage, and as she watched her friend boil water and get out the teapot and loose-leaf tea, she tried to convince herself that everything was going to be okay.

Setting two mugs of steaming peppermint tea in front of them, Moira said, "I can't wait to hear the good news."

"I went to see Duncan yesterday. In Boston."

Moira's mug slipped from her hands onto the table,

splashing tea over the rim. "Why would you do that?"

"Because he needs to make things right for you." Hating that she'd caused Moira's rosy flush from the sunny garden to go pale, Lola rushed to say the rest so that her friend would see it truly was good news. "He's agreed to give you the money you were promised by Brilliant Funds. All five hundred thousand dollars. Not as an investment, but as a payment with no strings attached."

"I don't want it." Moira's voice was firm, her mouth a hard line.

But Lola was desperate for her friend to understand that Duncan could help her this time around, rather than harm her. "He also wants to give you every contact he has that will help grow your business in both the US and abroad. Everything you dreamed of five years ago can finally come to fruition. And you won't owe him anything."

Moira pushed away from the table. "I appreciate what you're trying to do." She sounded like she was working hard to stay calm. "Truly, it means so much to me that you want to help, just as you always have. But I'm doing fine on my own. I don't want anything to do with Duncan or his money. And I definitely don't want to be pulled back into the past. Not when I've worked so hard to move on from it."

Lola understood why Moira was reluctant to take

anything from Duncan, yet she still couldn't let it go. Not when Duncan's funds could make such a difference in her friend's business, and life. "Are you sure there's nothing I can do to convince you to reconsider?"

Moira's expression was firm. "I'm afraid not. The best thing for all of us is if we simply move on and forget about one another entirely."

Lola knew she should accept Moira's answer. She should give her friend a big hug, then drop the whole thing. Instead, she found herself saying, "Yesterday, I met a woman he's worked with for the past three years. Serafina is really happy with what he's done to help build her fashion business. I asked her a ton of questions, and she swore everything has been completely aboveboard. She even went so far as to say that working with Duncan is the best decision she's ever made." Words continued to tumble out. "I also met the women who work in his office, and they seem great too. So maybe—"

"Are you actually trying to convince me to trust him?"

Lola opened her mouth to deny it, even though she'd just been fervently pressing his case. Acting as though the praise from his coworkers, and dancing in his arms at the restaurant, and getting lost in his passionate kisses had somehow erased his wrongdoing.

So much for washing sense into her brain in the shower.

Lola stood, regret in every cell of her body. "I'm sorry, I shouldn't have come to you with this plan. And I definitely shouldn't be trying to convince you to work with him again." Had a secret part of her been so distraught at the idea of never seeing Duncan again that she'd been searching for any reason, any excuse to keep him in her life? Even if it meant convincing Moira to give him a second chance? Lola's chest clenched tight as she stood before the woman who meant so much to her. "I know I keep asking for your forgiveness, but I hope you'll give me another chance to get things right. I won't see him or speak to him again, I promise."

Before she could say anything more, Moira pulled her back into her arms. "You've got to stop beating yourself up. I adore you, Lola. I always have. And I always will. No matter what."

A few minutes later, Lola left through the side gate, deliberately bypassing the main house because she wasn't up to answering questions from her parents. During the walk to her studio, she reminded herself over and over that it was time to get on with her life. No more wallowing in misery. No more moping over a guy.

Once she was at her desk, she opened an email

window and typed in Duncan's address.

Subject: *Not interested*

Duncan,

I spoke with Moira. She is not interested in taking your funds or hearing your apologies.

Lola

She hit Send and watched the message disappear from her screen. Now their relationship was really and truly over.

CHAPTER TWENTY-TWO

Duncan's heart sank as he stood in his kitchen, coffee mug in hand, and read Lola's email.

Though he was hugely disappointed by Moira's response, he didn't blame her for refusing to associate with him and his money. How could he when it was exactly how he felt about his brother? Even worse, now that Moira had refused to accept his funding, he would no longer have any connection to Lola, however peripheral.

Renewed fury rose up inside of him at the damage Alastair had wrought on so many lives. When Duncan had first uncovered his brother's crimes, Duncan had been both stunned and angry. Then, when Alastair had gone even further by breaking into Duncan's home and destroying his corporate paperwork and hard drives, his fury had not only grown bigger and hotter, but he'd also realized that this was something even their blood bond couldn't withstand. He'd cut ties with Alastair completely that day.

Now, however, he couldn't let another day go by

without knowing whether Alastair's henchman had told him about Lola. Because if Duncan's brother realized how much she meant to him, would Alastair lash out at her as well? Would he try to hurt her in order to hurt Duncan?

Ready to pay his brother a long overdue visit, Duncan poured his coffee down the drain, grabbed his wallet and car keys, and was just about to head into the garage when the doorbell rang.

From the silhouette through the stained glass, Duncan was able to guess who it was. His instincts were confirmed when he opened the door to find Alastair standing on his front step, his face wreathed in a wide smile. Had Alastair always looked so small? Had Duncan always towered over him the way he did now?

As a child, given their ten-year age gap, Alastair had seemed larger than life to Duncan. But his brother now seemed diminished in so many ways, from the lines on his face, to his slightly hunched back, to his shoulders and the narrowing of his chest. Yes, his suit was bespoke and he had access to the best aesthetician in Boston, but neither of those things could turn back the clock.

"It's been too long." Alastair said it as though they were old friends who hadn't seen each other simply because their lives had gotten busy. Not because one of them was cheating, lying scum.

As Duncan stepped out and closed the door behind him, he was glad for the large trees and thick shrubs in front of his house, which would shield their conversation from neighbors who might be nearby.

"You're not going to invite me in?" Alastair asked.

Like hell. This wasn't a social call. Duncan wouldn't pretend that it was.

Ignoring the question, he said, "I already told your employee to pass on my reply to your offer. But if you mistakenly thought you could change my mind by coming here in person, I'll say it again: I'm not interested in working with you, now or at any point in the future. Whatever relationship we had ended five years ago. And don't send anyone else to my office or home to try to convince me. From this moment forward, I will not tolerate your presence, or the presence of anyone who works for you, in any aspect of my life—professional or personal."

His brother's expression barely changed, but Duncan thought he could see the strain behind Alastair's outwardly confident demeanor. After all, his brother never left his penthouse office for a meeting, not when he always wanted to make sure he had the home court advantage. The fact that he had come to Duncan's home today proved how far the power dynamic had shifted between the two of them. Duncan was no longer the little brother, in any sense of the words.

"Why don't you invite me inside for a cup of coffee and we can catch up and dispel any misunderstandings?" Alastair suggested.

But Duncan knew how his brother operated. If you made the mistake of giving him an inch, he'd take a whole hell of a lot more than a mile. He'd take absolutely everything from you, without losing one second of sleep over his actions, no matter how nefarious.

"I'm not going to play games with you." Duncan would repeat himself one final time to ensure there could be no misunderstanding. "I'm done with you and the family company."

At last his brother's smile fell, leaving only a calculated rise of one eyebrow. "This is because of your new girlfriend, isn't it? My employee who went to the fashion show last night couldn't say enough about her abundant..." He paused before adding a very lecherous sounding, "...appeal. After looking her up online, it seems her name fits her well. *Lola*. I can see why you've fallen in lust with her. With a face and figure like that, she's every man's wet dream. I'm disappointed that you seem to have fallen for her hook, line, and sinker, though. No doubt she's after your money and connections, just like women always are. She probably thinks if she gives you a few great blow jobs that you'll hand her everything on a silver platter. I tried to teach you better than that, Duncan, but I know firsthand it isn't always easy to think with the right head when infatuation strikes." He gave Duncan what was probably supposed to be an understanding look. "If you could see the forest for the trees, you'd know that the only move that makes sense is for your company to merge with mine. Of course I'm happy for you to remain CEO of the subsidiary company."

Duncan's hands threatened to bunch into fists at the confirmation that his brother had in fact set Lola in his sights—exactly what he'd feared would happen when he'd spotted Alastair's henchman at the fashion show. He forced himself to relax his fingers. And he didn't let himself growl at his brother not to so much as speak Lola's name, either. That was exactly the game Alastair wanted to play, and Duncan wouldn't lower himself to his brother's level.

Once upon a time, they had played on the same team, two kids reeling from the sudden deaths of their parents, just trying to keep their heads above water. But those days were long past. Ever since Alastair had changed from a boy intent on protecting his brother to a man intent on always coming out on top. Duncan had walked away from the business five years ago, but their emotional bond had disintegrated long before that.

And whether or not Duncan ever got to see Lola again, hold her again, *love* her again, he would protect her from Alastair. At all costs.

"You have two choices," Duncan told his brother. "You can stay out of my life. Completely out. Or you can continue your current course of action and pay the price." A price that would start with Duncan talking to the FBI.

Surprise flickered on his brother's face. No one threatened Alastair. No one dared. Until now.

Quickly reassuming his customary arrogance, he said, "As we're brothers, I'll pretend you didn't just say that."

It was meant as a warning. But Duncan had a warning of his own to impart. "I promise you, I mean every word."

For the past five years, instead of instigating an ugly legal battle against Alastair—a battle that would have been made even more difficult given the number of professionals in Boston controlled by his brother—Duncan had used his time, energy, and wealth to atone for Alastair's crimes with the people who had signed up to work with Brilliant Funds.

But things were different now. For Lola, there was no battle too long. And no risk too high.

"What would you do if you lost your power?" Duncan asked in a low, steely voice. "If everyone who you thought respected and worshipped you turned on you instead? Who would you be then?" He let an unspoken *no one* linger in the air between them.

The small flare of worry in his brother's eyes would have been imperceptible to anyone but Duncan. Of course, Alastair was full of bravado as he said, "It's a moot point. No one would dare be so stupid as to try to destroy me. Especially not my brother. A brother I've always gone out of my way to look out for, both back when we were children and as a wealthy adult who is a ripe target for gold diggers. So, despite any harsh words that have come between us, my door will always be open for you, and your company. Whether next year, or five years from now, I have no doubt you'll eventually see that our bond as brothers—and as a brilliant business team—can never be broken."

Alastair's response couldn't have been clearer. He not only wasn't planning to stay out of Duncan's life and business, but as he assumed Duncan's 'infatuation' with Lola had scrambled his otherwise sharp business brain, she had a bullseye on her back now too.

"Next year," Duncan said, "you'll be behind prison bars."

And then he walked back into the house and left his brother standing on his front step, waiting for a reconciliation that would never come.

CHAPTER TWENTY-THREE

On Wednesday, when Lola met Ashley for lunch, though they talked about everything but Duncan, Lola remained terribly distracted by thoughts of him. After they ate, they headed to her studio so that Ashley could pick up some fabric for a display in the café window.

Lola was unlocking the door, silently going back over every single second she'd had with Duncan, when Ashley said, "I'm planning to cut off all my hair on the right side and then dye what's left green and pink."

At last, Lola's brain registered what her sister was saying. "You're going to do *what*?" Of all of them, Ashley had the best hair, hands down. It was thick and lustrous, and chopping it off would be a crime.

In lieu of saying anything more about her hair, Ashley simply said, "Do you think it might help to talk about it?"

Lola groaned. "Sorry. I know I haven't been good company today. You shouldn't have to put up with me right now. No one should."

"Are you kidding me? For ten years, you've listened

to me complain about Kevin's father. The least I can do is be there for you now, even if all you want to do is throw things, then eat a gallon of ice cream. I have some plates I really hate. We could find a brick wall and let them loose, then stuff ourselves full of cookies 'n' cream."

After years of protecting herself from men who wanted only to get her into bed, Lola still couldn't believe how badly she'd screwed up by choosing to risk her heart with Duncan. She had promised herself she wouldn't waste any more of her life moping over him. She'd done a rotten job of holding to that promise thus far, so she would have to hit the restart button and try again.

"Thanks, Ash, but really, I'm fine. I just need to focus on my work, like I should have been doing the whole time, and it will be like it never happened."

"But it did happen. You fell in lo—"

"*No.*" Lola wouldn't let Ashley finish the word. Tamping down on her foolish, misplaced emotions, she forced herself to say, "He didn't mean anything to me."

The words were barely out of her mouth when the man she'd just claimed didn't mean anything to her, the man she refused to talk about, the man she would never admit she'd cried over, appeared in the doorway to her studio.

And that was when she knew for sure that no matter how hard she'd tried to scrub him from her heart over the past few days, she hadn't succeeded even the slightest bit. Not when she had to reach for the nearest piece of furniture to hold herself up on suddenly shaky legs.

"Lola, I know you don't want to see me again, but—" He suddenly realized Ashley was in the room. "Ashley, hello."

"Hello, Duncan."

As he turned back to Lola, his eyes were more intense than she could ever remember seeing them. Even more intense than when they'd almost made love the night they'd stayed up holding each other. She shivered remembering how much she'd wanted him. Shivered again at how much she *still* wanted him.

"Could we speak in private?" he asked.

"Whatever you have to say to me—even though there isn't anything left to say at this point—you can say in front of my sister." Ashley's presence meant Lola couldn't possibly make the mistake of throwing herself into his arms and kissing him the way she had in Boston.

She shouldn't even be *thinking* about his kisses when he would surely be able to read her thoughts in her eyes and flushed skin.

"I've come to warn you about my brother." His

voice brimmed with concern and protectiveness—and something that sounded far too much like *love* for her peace of mind. "Alastair has made it clear that he wants to be involved in my life again. I've told him to stay the hell away, but he's not inclined to listen." Duncan took a step forward, moving close enough for Lola to smell his woodsy aftershave. "After one of his employees saw us together at the fashion show on Monday night, Alastair now knows who you are and what you mean to me. I believe he may try to hurt you to get to me."

Despite the way Duncan had deceived her, hearing how vicious his brother could be made her ache for him. That couldn't change her response, though. "I don't need anyone to protect me. I can take care of myself."

"I know you can. I've never doubted how strong you are for a second. But Alastair doesn't play by the rules. The thought of anything happening to you—" His expression twisted with pain. "It would kill me, Lola."

She was doing everything she could to keep her heart closed, impenetrable. To remind herself that it didn't matter what he felt for her, because she felt nothing for him. But it was getting more difficult by the second when there were a million things she wanted to say to him, a million questions she wanted to ask, and a million kisses she wanted to give him.

Still, she forced herself to be curt and to the point. "I'll be fine."

He stared at her for a long moment, one so heavy with emotion she could have sliced through it with one of her cutting shears. "You mean everything to me, Lola." His deep voice resonated with emotion. "I'm sorry I couldn't be the man you needed me to be."

It wasn't until the door closed behind him that she finally let her breath go on a ragged exhalation. Shell-shocked, she lowered herself into the chair she'd been holding on to for support.

"You should go after him," Ashley suggested in a gentle voice. "It's obvious you two need to talk."

Lola shook her head. "We already said everything we needed to say to each other in Boston on Monday."

"For all your many gifts," Ashley said, "you've never been a compelling liar. It doesn't matter how many times you swear you're fine, or tell me that Duncan doesn't mean anything to you. It still won't make either of those things true. Which is why you need to go talk with him now, if for no other reason than to try to get some resolution for yourself. Until you hear him out, we both know you're going to lie awake wondering what he could possibly have to say to justify what happened to Moira and her company."

Lola's heart wanted nothing more than to dash out the door after him, but her head held her back. "I promised Moira I was done with him. If she finds out I'm meeting with him again…" She shook her head. "I've already hurt her so badly. I can't hurt her again."

"You never meant to hurt Moira," Ashley countered. "People fall in love every day. Sometimes, the man who seems right isn't. But then sometimes, the man who seems wrong turns out to be the right one after all." She paused before adding, "It seems to me that you owe it to yourself to hear Duncan out and find out once and for all if he really is the wrong man for you. Or if maybe, just maybe, he could be the right one."

Lola didn't have another rebuttal in her. She'd tried so hard to be strong. Tried even harder to shut down her heart.

But it was so damned hard to fight against her feelings for Duncan.

Ashley took both of Lola's hands in hers. "You know how strong my bad-guy radar is. But even though I was suspicious of Duncan at first, the truth is that once I met him, my radar didn't go off. Even after Moira told us who he is, the shocking thing is that I still didn't get a bad feeling about him. Which is why I have to wonder what role Duncan actually played in destroying Moira's business? Because I have a very difficult time imagining him willfully harming anyone. Especially you."

"Dad said the same thing," Lola murmured, almost to herself.

"Then go find Duncan and ask what happened between him and Moira," Ashley encouraged her. "And most of all, trust your heart. It's not going to let you down, Lola. I'm positive it won't." Ashley gave her a warm and loving smile. A smile that said she would always be there for her sister, no matter what. "You're magnificent, especially on the inside. If men have only ever seen your outer beauty, it's their fault, not yours. One day, you're going to meet a man who will see how beautiful you are in *every* way. In fact," she added in a soft voice, "there's a part of me that can't help but wonder if you already have."

Overcome with emotion, Lola held tight to her sister's hands as she said, "You're right. I need to know exactly what happened. I need to stop trying to act like I don't care."

"Text me or call me if you need anything."

But Lola was afraid that the only person capable of giving her what she needed was Duncan.

Only, could she ever trust him enough to let him?

CHAPTER TWENTY-FOUR

Lola found Duncan standing behind the seawall, watching a cruise ship sail out to sea. Mothers chatted nearby while their children giggled and blew bubbles into the sky. Dogs snuffled along the ground. And tourists holding ice cream cones marveled aloud at the beauty of the Bar Harbor waterfront.

But Duncan didn't seem to hear or see any of it. He looked as though he had the weight of the world on his shoulders and a dark cloud hanging over him.

Despite the warnings she'd given herself to keep her heart safe from him, Lola wished she could take his burdens, his sorrows, away.

"Tell me," she said as she moved into place beside him. "Tell me what happened. Tell me all of it, from the beginning."

She kept her gaze firmly trained on the water, but it didn't matter that she hadn't let herself look into his eyes. Seeking him out and asking to hear his story instantly shifted their dynamic and made the walls she had constructed around her heart crack even deeper.

He was silent for a long moment. Finally, he said, "It was always understood that I would work with Alastair once I graduated with my MBA. But that didn't make me love maps or atlases any less, or stop me from dreaming about the adventures I wanted to have. What I've always loved most about maps was how looking at them made me feel I would one day find my way to a safe, steady, happy place. To the kind of place I had always dreamed of. With you, I thought I'd finally found that place."

She couldn't stop herself from turning to look at him then. His expression was as ravaged as her heart felt.

"But that's not what you asked, is it? You want to know how I could have hurt your friend so badly." He ran a hand through his dark hair, leaving it standing on end. "My thirteenth birthday present from my brother was the book *The Art of War*. I thought it was a joke at first, that Alastair was messing with me because he knew I really wanted an illustrated atlas. But it wasn't a joke. Nothing was after that. He had recently taken over our father's company, and overnight he lost his sense of humor. He was all about business and power suits and drinks with the board. Instead of throwing a ball around the way we used to, he drilled me on negotiating strategy and structures of worldwide financial markets."

"Your brother quizzed you on finances when you were thirteen?"

"Our house never had that many games in it, even before our parents passed away. Our father believed they were a waste of time, and though Alastair used to sneak in balls and cards before they died, a few years later he obviously agreed that our father was right. But games weren't the only thing not permitted—" He abruptly stopped speaking. "I'm getting off track again."

"Whatever you have to say to me about your past," she told him, "I want to hear."

"You don't owe me this, Lola. You don't owe me anything."

"I still want to hear what you have to say." Because Ashley was right that Lola owed it to herself to find out if her instincts about Duncan's being a good guy had been wrong. Or...if there was a chance that her instincts might have been right all along. "What else were you not allowed to have?"

He went still. So still that even his hair barely seemed to move in the breeze. "Affection." Her heart broke for him as he explained, "For the first six years of my life, though my parents were barely there, at least I had my brother. And for a handful of years after they died, he was also there for me as a confidant, a father even. But once I turned thirteen, he became a drill sergeant more than a brother, unless I did something to please him—ranked first in my class, or outwitted a fellow student at school, or won a trophy. Everything I did, everything I worked for, was motivated by those moments when he was momentarily my brother again and we were laughing together, the two of us against the world." He drew in a ragged breath. "I shouldn't complain. I had everything I needed. A warm bed, and enough to eat, and a great education."

"But you didn't have the unconditional love you deserved." Lola's voice was gentle. "We can have all the food and shelter and education in the world, but we still need love to carry us through the good *and* the bad times." She had never taken the love of her family for granted, but now she was more grateful for it than ever.

Duncan was holding himself so rigidly beside her that she wanted to put a hand over his to let him know that it was okay, that she wouldn't harm him regardless of what he told her about himself. But though her fingers itched to move toward his, she reminded herself that it would be crazy to let down her guard again so soon, especially when she was still trying to piece everything together to make sense of it.

"You're right," he agreed. "There was no unconditional love in our house. It took me far too long to realize that, though. I was smart enough to get into

Harvard and Wharton for business school, but I wasn't smart enough to realize what love truly was."

She wanted to tell him that emotions had nothing to do with smarts, especially when his brother had disguised blind loyalty and quests for praise as love. Instead, she said, "What happened when you went to work with him?"

"I started out in the mail room. It was a much lower position than anyone else with an MBA, but I wanted to show Alastair that his faith in me wasn't misplaced. I worked every hour possible and deliberately worked in so many different departments that I started to see not everything at the company was perfect. Projects weren't always done to code, and the numbers on the spreadsheets didn't always add up. My brother was never concerned, though. He always had a reason, a justification that I could tell myself made sense. Somewhere in the back of my brain, though, I must have known that if one card started to fall, all of them would. And that it wouldn't just be the business that would be destroyed—it would be my relationship with him. Until…" He blew out a ragged breath. "Until I couldn't ignore the signs anymore."

"Was this when you started looking into Brilliant Funds?"

He nodded. "Five years ago, the startup incubator was abruptly shuttered. Alastair had made it clear that this was his pet project, but something didn't seem right, even though everyone had written it off as nothing more than bad luck during a period of economic uncertainty. This time, instead of taking my questions and suspicions to Alastair, I decided to investigate on my own." The cloud over Duncan seemed to grow even darker. "I discovered our charitable foundation was a front to hide the money being embezzled from the Brilliant Funds partner companies." His voice sounded hollow as he told her, "Realizing how wrong I'd been about Alastair all those years was brutal. I hadn't just looked up to my brother. I'd idolized him for the way he'd stepped in to be a father to me. Only to find out that he had been defrauding our clients and lying to me for years."

"I can't imagine how difficult that must have been for you."

His eyes were bleak as he turned to face her. "I tried to take solace in knowing that he wouldn't get away with hurting anyone else once I exposed his crimes. I also planned to make things right with the people whose businesses he'd destroyed. I found a lawyer, one I carefully verified wasn't connected to Alastair. But my brother's reach was even longer than I had imagined. Long enough that by the time I returned home from the law office, every corporate document in my possession—both virtual and paper—had been destroyed. My papers were shredded, my computer hard drives were smashed, and my company-issued phone and online backups had been remotely wiped."

"My God." Lola couldn't imagine being related to someone who could do that.

"I immediately went to confront him," Duncan continued. "And do you want to know the truth?"

"Yes. The truth is all I've ever wanted."

Regret was etched in the lines of his face as he said, "I'm sorry, Lola. So damned sorry for everything. You're the very last person I ever wanted to hurt."

Though her heart was breaking for all he'd endured, she still wasn't sure she was ready to forgive him for saying he loved her and then keeping so much from her. So instead of responding to his apology, she said, "What happened when you confronted him?"

"I thought he'd be upset. Scared, even. But it was the exact opposite. He was pleased that I finally knew the truth about him."

Though plenty of Duncan's story had shocked—and saddened—her, this took the cake. "Why do you think he reacted that way?"

"Maybe he was pleased that he'd raised me to be clever enough to see through his schemes when no one else did. Or maybe he relished the chance to show me that he would always be the victor, no matter what." Duncan stared out at the water as though the answer could be found in the rolling sea. "Whatever was really going on beneath his surface, he told me he was doing exactly what our father would have wanted him to do."

"Your father told him to embezzle from his clients, then lash out at his brother when his crimes were discovered?"

"The names Alastair and Duncan both mean *warrior*," Duncan explained. "From the day we were born, Alastair claims our father intended for us to head into battle—and to win every time. It didn't matter whether it was on the sports field, or in the classroom, or in the boardroom. Destroying the competition by any means necessary was the family brief. I was too young when he passed away to know whether Alastair was embellishing for impact, or if those actually were our father's intentions." Either way, Duncan looked utterly disgusted. "As of that day, the relationship we'd once had was forever lost."

"That must have been devastating."

Though he shrugged, it was clear how deeply losing the brother he'd once idolized had affected him. "He made sure I didn't have enough evidence to prove what he had done, and though I still planned to go to the FBI at that point, I soon realized that without hard facts to present to them, not only would they not believe a word I said, my brother would surely find a way to pin the crimes on me. If I went to jail, I wouldn't be able to undo the damage to the companies that had signed up with the fund. So instead of turning Alastair in, I did whatever I could to help all of them. Only Moira's name and contact information eluded me. You don't know how many times I wished I had done more than just sign off on the initial paperwork for Brilliant Funds, so that I could have found her and helped turn her business around." The chatter and laughter and smells of ice cream and lobster rolls continued all around them as he told Lola, "My explanations don't make me any less responsible for what happened to Moira, but I hope you'll at least believe I never intended to hurt her, or anyone else."

Looking into his eyes, she knew without a doubt that he had finally given her the full truth. "Why didn't you tell me all of this that night we stayed up together? You knew I was—" Her chest hurt as she decided to be just as honest with him. "You knew I was falling in love with you. How could you keep this from me?"

"I thought you couldn't possibly love me if you knew."

"Do you really think that little of me?" A fresh flush of anger ran through her. "I thought you were different, that you weren't like all the other guys who assume I don't have a brain, who think I'm not capable of analyzing information and coming to my own conclusions. I thought you knew that I'm capable of separating right from wrong."

"I've always known how brilliant and talented and strong you are, Lola. *Always.* I'm the one who should have been able to analyze my brother's behavior more quickly and seen him for who he really is, rather than staying blind to his faults."

Though she was still deeply conflicted over her feelings for Duncan, that didn't mean she could let him continue to tear himself apart over what had happened with Brilliant Funds. "He's your brother. Of course you wanted to believe in him. If I suspected one of my brothers or sisters was responsible for defrauding people, I wouldn't want to believe it either. Heck, I would hands-down *refuse* to believe it. Anyone who loves their brother or sister would."

But he obviously wasn't ready to be let off the hook. "I can't fix my past actions, but I can make sure Alastair doesn't hurt anyone else. Especially you, Lola."

For a moment, he looked like he was about to brush aside a lock of her hair that had blown in front of her eyes. She held her breath, waiting for him to reach for her.

When he didn't, she was more disappointed than she wanted to admit.

"Why would your brother come after me?" she asked. "I've never even met him."

"A man who works for Alastair—one of his over-muscled goons that he likes to use as an unspoken threat to his opponents—came to my office on Friday, right when I was about to head to the airport to see you in Bar Harbor, with an offer from my brother to acquire my company."

"You would never sell your company to him!"

"No, I wouldn't, which I made perfectly clear. Unfortunately, the man also came to Serafina's fashion show and he saw us together. When I realized that you could become a target due to your association with me, I knew it was finally time to pay a visit to Alastair to inform him in person that I won't tolerate his presence in any part of my life. That was when he showed up out of the blue on my doorstep, saying he wanted to sit down and resolve our 'misunderstandings.' But the truth is that he doesn't have one single stitch of remorse or regret for what he's done. All he really wanted was to make sure I knew he won't be swayed from his plans to take over my company. And that he'll stop at nothing to get it."

"Losing your parents, and then being betrayed by your brother...I wish..." Her chest clenched tight, aching for him. "I wish you could have been spared all of it."

But Duncan didn't so much as nod, and he certainly wasn't wallowing in self-pity. If anything, his anger was directed at himself. "After everything that's happened, Alastair still believes I'm going to come back, that it's just a matter of time until I see that he's right. The last thing he expects is for me to risk everything—including a jail term for myself—to go after him. But now that you're involved, none of the risks to my reputation, to my business, to my personal life, matter anymore. All that matters is making sure he doesn't hurt you." He blew out a harsh breath. "If only I had dealt with him five years ago."

"What if you needed to wait until you had the right team in place, rather than trying to take him on all on your own?" It was difficult for Lola to speak past the ache in her chest. She was utterly overwhelmed by just how much she meant to Duncan. Enough to risk, and to lose, absolutely everything. "What if all of this—your coming to Bar Harbor, the two of us connecting, Moira seeing you at my parents' house—is what will finally lead you to that safe, steady, happy place you've always dreamed of?"

"If I were ever to be that lucky..." But then he shook his head. "I can't imagine finding anyone who would willingly join my team knowing that Alastair will use every weapon in his arsenal to destroy them. I'm not exaggerating when I say that my brother will stop at nothing to make sure he remains on top. He thinks the best way to destroy me is to hurt you. But that's where he's wrong." Duncan's voice was fierce. "I would never let anything happen to you. *Never.*"

"My family will help." She didn't need to stop to think it over. "We'll be your team."

Duncan looked stunned by her offer. A moment later, however, he said, "I can't let you or your family get involved. Not when I know what Alastair will try to do to all of you."

But she was just as focused and determined. "Trust me, as soon as my family hears your story—particularly given that they all know and love Moira—they'll insist on helping. My cousin Rafe in Seattle is a private investigator who is absolutely brilliant at ferreting out information about people's wrongdoings they've tried to bury. And his brother Ian is a billionaire businessman who likely knows people who work with or have worked with your brother."

"I've never worked directly with Ian Sullivan, but I certainly know of him," Duncan confirmed. "Anybody in venture capital would."

"I'm sure my cousin Suzanne, who founded and runs Sullivan Security in New York City, would also be more than happy to get involved."

"Your cousin is Suzanne Sullivan? I use her digital security products in my office."

"She's a genius," Lola agreed. "So is my cousin Sophie in San Francisco. She's a librarian and is an absolute wiz at finding the most obscure resources and references. You've probably heard of her husband's company, McCann's Irish Pubs." Lola knew she was dropping a lot of extended-family information on Duncan all at once, but she needed him to understand the breadth of skill and talent that the Sullivans brought to the table. "And then there's my cousin Malcolm in London. I'll admit I don't know exactly what he does, but from all accounts, he's pretty highflying."

"I appreciate everything you're offering, Lola." She could see the truth of it in his eyes, that her support meant the world to him. "More than you could ever know. But—"

"I'm tough," she told him again. "I'm not afraid of your brother." And even though she *was* more than a little afraid of how much she felt for Duncan, she had to say, "Don't go back to Boston." They were the last words she'd expected to say to him today. But they felt right. A million times more right than sending him away. "Stay in Bar Harbor, and we can put together our war council from my studio."

"Lola—" He searched her face. "Are you absolutely sure about this?"

She nodded, her fingers already flying over her phone's keyboard. "I'm texting my cousins to see if we can arrange a meeting for first thing tomorrow morning." She hit Send before Duncan could protest. Within seconds, each of her cousins confirmed that they were happy to help and committed to participating in a video chat the next morning.

She was moving to put her phone away, when Duncan laid his hand over hers. "Thank you."

His touch was as electric as ever.

And despite everything that had come between them, she wanted to hold onto him and never let go.

CHAPTER TWENTY-FIVE

Though Duncan and Lola sat at opposite ends of her long worktable in the center of her studio, he didn't need to be directly beside her to be aware of her every move. She was so vibrant, so beautiful, and so giving that he'd fallen even more in love with her this afternoon.

He'd told her everything, and she not only hadn't run, she'd done the exact opposite and offered to help.

For years, Duncan's head and heart had been twisted in knots over the breakdown of his family. Learning of his brother's crimes, and then cutting ties with Alastair, had set him emotionally adrift and convinced him to build his walls thicker and higher than ever before.

Until Lola had broken through Duncan's defenses and taught him how to love with his whole heart.

Whatever happened from here on out—even if she decided she didn't want to be with him, or if the FBI threw him in jail—he'd always be grateful to her for showing him how to love without holding anything back.

For the rest of the afternoon, he worked on putting together a detailed informational document for her cousins on Alastair, Lyman Ventures, and Brilliant Funds. It was nearly five p.m. when his client Dave Fischer called.

"Dave, it's good to hear from you. How are things?"

"I wanted to call to thank you for your support last week. You were right that I was on the edge of a breakthrough, only I couldn't see it because I was tired and discouraged. After taking a couple of days off, I finally hit the sweet spot. Would you like to see my big new reveal?"

Duncan grinned. "I'd love to."

"Are you near a computer? If so, I can share my screen with you."

For the next few minutes, Dave walked him through his advancements on the prosthetic arm. It was hugely impressive how far he'd come in a matter of days.

Despite everything going on in his own life, Duncan had a massive grin on his face. "I couldn't be more pleased with everything you've accomplished, Dave, both this week and since we first began working together."

After they hung up, Duncan was surprised to realize that Lola was standing behind him, staring at the image of the prosthetic arm on his computer.

"I was walking to the coffee machine and couldn't help but stop to watch," she explained. "Is Dave one of your clients?"

"He is. When his daughter was born with a congenital defect to her right arm, he walked away from his career as a mechanical engineer and went back to school to study robotics and prosthetics. His inventions are going to revolutionize the industry."

"He's doing so much to help his daughter, but it's even bigger than that, isn't it?" Lola said. "His work is going to help so many people live more comfortable and active lives. And your support for what he's creating is a huge part of that."

But Duncan wasn't comfortable with Lola looking at him as though he were some kind of hero. As far as he was concerned, helping Dave and others like him proceed with groundbreaking work didn't make up for how blind Duncan had been to his brother's crimes. "Dave's a great guy. I'm lucky to work with him." He turned away from his computer. "I didn't mean to disturb your work, though."

"I'm glad I was able to listen in on his demo," she said as she poured them both cups of coffee. "Besides, I was ready for a break."

When she put down her coffee, then stretched her

arms over her head, he tried not to stare. "What have you been working on this afternoon?"

"I have at least a dozen things I *should* be doing, but I was so inspired by Serafina's collection that I wanted to get down some ideas for her immediately."

He gave a silent cheer at the thought of Lola and Serafina working together. Even if he could have only a peripheral place in Lola's life, he'd take whatever he could get. Because he already knew there would be no one else for him, no other woman who could replace Lola in his heart.

"Could I take a look?" he asked.

"Sure, although the ideas are pretty rough."

In only a few hours, she'd managed to synthesize Serafina's aesthetic with her own unique flair for color and shape. "Serafina is going to love this." He studied Lola's designs again. "In fact, I wouldn't be surprised if she came up with an entirely new collection around your textiles."

Though Lola looked pleased by his enthusiasm, she said, "I'd be happy if she decided to make a dress or two out of my fabric."

They had both turned back to their computers, when he was surprised to hear Lola gasp. "I just got an email from a law firm about the textile company I have always wanted to work with. They're offering to buy my company in a multimillion-dollar deal, while leaving me fifty-one percent ownership." Her eyes were huge as she reread the offer. "I would assume this was spam, but I know this law firm. They're legit."

"I wouldn't be too sure of that." Duncan's voice vibrated with barely leashed fury.

She turned to him, obviously confused by his reaction. "Wait a minute." She scowled as realization dawned. "You think your brother is behind this offer? And that the law firm, and the textile company, are in his pocket?"

Duncan nodded. "This is what Alastair does. He figures out what his opponents want, and he delivers beyond their wildest dreams so that instead of fighting him, they're forever on his side. Exactly where he wants them."

"I would *never* be on his side!" She shoved away from the table. "You've been glued to your computer all day, so you must have more than enough background information on your brother and his company to send to my cousins, right?"

Duncan nodded. "I uploaded the information to the group portal thirty minutes ago."

"Good. Because forget coffee, I need a much stiffer drink." She walked over to a cupboard fully stocked with the makings for cocktails. "Good thing I have my own cocktail bar right here. I'll mix us up some Long Island Iced Teas, and we can sneak them out to the seawall."

Just as they walked outside with their extremely strong drinks, a flash storm blew in, clouding over the blue sky and sending a torrent of rain down over them.

But instead of running for cover, Lola stopped in the middle of the sidewalk and turned to him. "How did you live with someone like your brother for so long and still manage to be such a good man?"

Duncan stared into her eyes, so big and beautiful as rain drenched them from head to toe. "I didn't think you thought I was a good man anymore."

Emotion was written all over Lola's face as she said, "I've started to reconsider that."

CHAPTER TWENTY-SIX

Lola had never experienced such a wide range of feelings in so short a time. First, she'd fallen head over heels in love. Then, when Moira singled out Duncan as being a bad guy, she'd been consumed with fury. And now, all she wanted was to kiss him...and just keep kissing him forever.

She shivered at the thought, knowing how good it would be. Only, wouldn't she be setting herself up for another heart-crushing fall if she gave in to desire when she still wasn't one hundred percent sure about him? Hadn't she vowed that she'd never let down her guard again unless she knew, without even a shadow of doubt, that she'd found the kind of true, pure love that her parents had?

"You're cold," he said. "We should go back inside and dry off."

But she didn't want to go back to her office. She needed to go to somewhere she could decompress. "Let's go home to have our drinks." Belatedly, she realized she'd said *home* as though it was both of theirs, not just hers. Of course her stomach rumbled right on cue. "And also," she added with a small smile, "I'm starved."

He fell into step beside her. "I'm a fairly good cook if you wouldn't mind letting me loose in your kitchen."

Given how badly she still wanted to kiss Duncan, she was sorely tempted to let him loose *everywhere*. No matter how hard she tried to steel her heart against him, he continued to touch her on an elemental level that defied rational thought. "That would be great," she said in as easy a voice as she could manage, given her conflicting emotions.

They entered her cottage via the mudroom, where she kept clean towels in case of flash storms like this. Duncan rubbed his towel over his head like he would a wet dog. By the time he hung it on a wooden peg, his hair stood up in all directions.

She laughed, a joyful sound that filled the small room, and when she mimed the height of his hair, he laughed too, but made no move to smooth it down.

It felt good to laugh with him again. So good that she knew she'd better move away fast, otherwise the kiss she'd almost given him out on the waterfront was bound to happen here. And her bedroom was *way* too close to risk that happening if she wanted to keep things platonic. At least until she was completely sure where her head was.

"I'll go find you some dry clothes."

"I doubt I'll fit into anything of yours." His voice was tinged with humor...and barely repressed desire.

She suddenly realized that her own clothes were sticking to her, outlining every abundant curve. Though he had seen her naked before, their one night together seemed like a lifetime ago.

"My brothers and father sometimes leave clothes here if they've helped me in the garden." She made herself back away, when all she wanted was to devour every gorgeous inch of him. "I'm sure I've got a pair of jeans and a shirt that will fit you. Just give me a minute, and I'll be back with them."

Though she quickly found the clothes in the back of her closet, she counted to sixty to cool herself off and bring her hormones back under control. Heading back to the mudroom, she said, "Here you g—"

She nearly dropped the bundle of dry clothes as she took in Duncan's magnificent bare chest and his muscular legs outlined by his soaking-wet pants.

Catching her surprised expression, he explained, "I thought I'd get going with taking the wet things off."

"Of course," she replied in a too-bright voice, all but throwing the dry clothes at him, even as she couldn't help but greedily drink him. "I need to get changed myself. Make yourself comfortable." She dashed off toward her bedroom, feeling breathless and overheated, even though she was still in her cold, wet dress.

My God, Duncan was gorgeous. She'd never wanted anyone the way she wanted him.

It would be so easy to strip off her wet clothes, walk back into the living room, and hold out her hand in an invitation to lose themselves in pleasure. How she wished they'd made love their first night together! If they had, then she wouldn't have to keep fantasizing about him, because she would know *exactly* how good, how wild, how perfect being with Duncan truly was.

Desire pulsed through her veins so strongly that, even though he was on the other side of the cottage, all of her senses felt intertwined with his.

She stepped into the shower, hoping the water would wash away her longing. But all it did was make her think of how his hands, and mouth, had run over her skin during their one night together. She turned off the shower with a fierce yank.

Lola rarely emerged from her bedroom without her hair and makeup done and her clothes and shoes carefully chosen. Tonight, however, she made the rare decision not to do any of that. Instead, she would let Duncan see a side of her that almost no one had ever seen before.

She so rarely wore a T-shirt and jeans that when she looked in the mirror, she hardly recognized herself, especially without makeup and with her hair pulled back in a ponytail. The guys she had dated in the past had given lip service to appreciating a more natural look, but ultimately, they'd all wanted her to look like a bombshell every second of every day.

How, she wondered, would Duncan react? Would he be disappointed? Or would he see that she was still the same person beneath the lipstick and mascara, without the formfitting dresses and sexy shoes?

Walking barefoot out of the bedroom, she saw through the window that Duncan had gone into the backyard. Just as quickly as the rain had come, it was now gone, the sky clear again. Before tonight, he'd always worn either a suit or slacks and a button-down shirt. But even in borrowed faded jeans and a T-shirt with a torn shoulder from when her brother had caught it in a blackberry bush, Duncan exhibited sexy strength.

He was walking down a narrow brick path between her vegetable beds when he turned and caught her staring at him through the kitchen window. She blushed as she waved, then headed out to join him.

His eyes lit, and his lips curved into a smile when she stepped outside and he took in her dressed-down look. "Lola, you're beautiful."

Perhaps it shouldn't have mattered what he thought. After all, being comfortable in her own skin was what counted most of all. But she couldn't deny how nice it was to know that no matter how she was dressed, wearing makeup or not, he still looked at her as though she was the loveliest woman he'd ever seen.

"I've never seen a home garden with so much in bloom," he said.

"I love being in the garden. On days at the office when it feels like my brain is going to explode, I love getting my hands dirty. By the time I head back to my studio, things rarely seem so difficult to deal with."

"I haven't spent much time gardening myself," he replied, "but now I'm thinking I'd like to change that."

She was hit with a clear vision of the two of them working outside together, Duncan pruning back roses while she planted rows of strawberries.

Apart from her siblings, she'd never had a true companion. Not just someone to get drinks and dinner and see a movie with, but someone who helped her pull weeds and harvest carrots. Someone who vacuumed the living room while she scrubbed the kitchen counters. Someone to fold the laundry with. Someone to watch the fireflies with on a warm summer's evening. Someone to cuddle with on the couch in front of a bad movie, before falling asleep in each other's arms.

Someone to simply *be* with, and love, no matter where they were, or what they were doing.

Duncan's voice broke through her thoughts. "I could make ratatouille if that sounds good."

"I'd love ratatouille."

Together, they harvested carrots, onions, brussels sprouts, celery, spinach, and tomatoes. When their hands were full of produce, they headed into her kitchen, working together with an ease that should have surprised her, but didn't. Her kitchen wasn't huge, but they cleaned and washed and chopped and sautéed as though they'd done this dance a hundred times before. With big-band music playing in the background, it was already just about the nicest evening imaginable.

Forgetting to be cautious about not setting too romantic a scene, she lit the candles on her dining table as they sat down to bowls of steaming ratatouille and glasses of red wine.

"This is really nice, Lola. Thank you."

"You're the one who cooked, I'm the one who should be saying thank you."

But she understood he wasn't talking about the food. He was thanking her for giving them this chance to spend time together again.

She was grateful for it too.

As they ate, he gestured to her wall of family photos. "Last time I was here, I noticed your big family photo wall. I wanted to ask you to tell me about your extended family, but there wasn't time. Now that I'm going to meet a few of your cousins over video chat tomorrow, I'm even more curious."

She almost let out an audible sigh of relief. Talking about her family was the easiest way to keep from blurting out not only how she didn't think she could keep her hands off him for another moment, but how she wanted so badly to trust him again that she was tempted to throw caution to the wind tonight and just let herself *feel*.

She pointed to one of the photo groupings. "In San Francisco, I have eight cousins and my fabulous aunt, Mary. Unfortunately, their father, Uncle Jack, passed away when he was in his early forties. We'll be talking with Sophie tomorrow morning. She's a twin and her sister, Lori, is pretty much her exact opposite. Lori's nickname is Naughty, and Sophie's is Nice. I adore them both." She pointed to another group of pictures. "I have five cousins in Seattle, plus Uncle Max and Aunt Claudia. We'll be speaking to Ian and Rafe tomorrow—those two there, with the fishing rods." She paused to take another bite of the delicious meal. "I also have four cousins in New York. Uncle William raised them by himself after his wife passed away. Suzanne will be on the call with us tomorrow." She sipped from her wineglass as they both continued to study the photos of her beloved family. "I'm also related to a bunch of Sullivans outside of the US via my grandfather and his brothers, including my five second cousins in London and their mom and dad, Simon and Penny. Malcolm will be calling in from London tomorrow." She laughed at the concentration on his face as he tried to keep the different branches of the family straight. "I think that's more than enough info on my family photo wall for the time being."

"It sounds like you're all close, despite the fact that you live quite far away from many of them."

"We are really close," she confirmed. "Even though my dad and his brothers moved to different parts of the country after they got married, they still wanted to foster connections between their kids whenever possible. For as long as I can remember, we've traveled to California or Seattle or New York for birthdays and graduations, and they've come here many times, as well. We Sullivans love any excuse for a celebration!"

"I've never met a family like yours," Duncan noted. "A family willing to help even when they don't know whether the guy they're helping deserves it, all because you asked them to pitch in. It's amazing—and incredibly inspiring—to meet people who are so open."

But she hadn't truly been open with Duncan, had she? She had railed on him for not telling her the whole truth about his past, but hadn't she done exactly the same thing? Hadn't she shown him only the public Lola Sullivan, while holding everything else back?

"You're right that my family is full of wonderful, open people. I just wish I could be as open as all of them."

"You are, Lola."

She shook her head. "It was so easy for me to come down on you for not opening up about your past, when the truth is that I haven't come completely clean about mine."

Though he didn't prod or pry, he did reach for her hand. It felt so good when his fingers wrapped around hers. Their connection was exactly what she needed when there was so much she hadn't admitted to anyone, not even her sisters or mother.

Not even, if she was being completely honest, to herself.

"I've always had such a great family and life that I've felt like I have no right to be sad or complain. Instead, it's been easier to simply pretend that I don't care about having so many bad relationships, that I'm not looking for the kind of forever love that my parents found with each other, and that my siblings and so many of my cousins have found. My whole life, I've let everyone think I'm too tough, too independent, having too much fun on my own to want to stop playing the field."

Duncan's eyes were intensely focused on her as she spoke. "Ever since you told me about what Frank did, I've wished I could turn back time to keep him away from you."

"But it wasn't just one particular man that I can pin everything on. I developed really early. And while I've never had to fight for attention, at the same time, I can never fade into the background. Believe me, when I was a teenager, I tried. For a few months, I wore baggy clothes that swamped me. All in blacks and grays. And I stopped speaking up in class." She shook her head. "Fortunately, I soon figured out that nothing I did to disguise myself worked. Plus, my mom, Moira, Aunt Mary, and Aunt Claudia—they all rallied around me. From that point forward, I stopped trying to pretend I wasn't born with this body and decided to fully embrace who I am. I love bright colors, not black. I love busy patterns and tons of layers, not minimalism. I love dangerously high heels, not flats. And the good news is that once I made these changes to embrace the real me, I was so much happier."

She took a sip of wine before continuing. "Except when it came to men." She sighed, thinking back to the years when she'd gone on dates every Friday and Saturday. "When I was younger and more idealistic, I wasn't nearly careful enough with my emotions, my heart, or my body. It's why I ended up with a guy like

Frank. Even after I broke up with him, I still went out with guys I shouldn't have given the time of day. Until one day, I woke up and realized I was sick and tired of feeling like the only worthwhile thing about me was how many positions I could get into in the bedroom. I hated feeling like my only purpose was to bring my date's sexual fantasies to life." She'd never admitted this much to anyone, and she appreciated that Duncan didn't interrupt as she finally got it all out. "On top of everything else, I never imagined that I would have such a hard time being taken seriously at work. Even now that I have an established business, plenty of men still dismiss me at a glance." Feeling more exposed than she ever had before, she said, "I'm not saying all of my experiences with men have been terrible, just that the hair-raising ones have been difficult to forget."

Duncan's expression had grown fiercer and fiercer as she spoke, and she got the sense that he wanted to tear apart with his bare hands all the men who had harassed, belittled, or used her. "But none of them ever—"

"No," she said quickly. "No one ever physically hurt me. But over the years, there have been so many hands that 'accidentally' brushed over my hips and breasts, so many loosely veiled sexual innuendos, so many leering eyes." She swallowed hard as she admitted everything to him. "Even though I act like it doesn't bother me, even though I tell myself I'm going to dress exactly as I please because I'm not going to let anyone else get the best of me, the truth is that while I might not be hiding my face and figure, I *am* hiding something. My heart." She looked into his eyes, letting him see what was in hers. "It wasn't until we met that I finally started to let my walls fall away. But even then, I was so scared to let you in. Which was why I pushed you away the first chance I could. It was the only way I could make sure that you wouldn't have a chance to see the real me...and then be disappointed that the reality didn't match your fantasy."

"You're so much more than a fantasy, Lola. Anyone who isn't a total fool would see that. You don't always have to go above and beyond to prove yourself." His soft, sweet, loving smile sent warmth moving through the center of her chest and radiating out to the rest of her body. "Anyone who matters can see that you're smart and funny and kind. Absolutely beautiful, inside and out."

She reached for him, lightly stroking her fingertips over the dark bristles of his evening shadow, before leaning forward and pressing her lips to his.

Just like his smile, it was a soft kiss. A sweet kiss. A loving kiss.

A kiss destined to lead to so much *more*.

CHAPTER TWENTY-SEVEN

Passion exploded as their pent-up need for each other burst free.

Last week, when Lola had fallen head over heels for Duncan and had finally let down her guard, she'd still held her deepest, most secret emotions and feelings inside. In the same way that Duncan had been afraid she would reject him if he bared his soul to her, darkness and all, she'd been scared too. Scared to admit, even to herself, that despite all her bravado about being empowered and strong, she *had* hidden large parts of her heart from everyone. Even her family.

As Duncan pulled her onto his lap, still kissing her, she relished both his touch and the hope that was blooming inside of her. Hope that he truly could be a love worth risking everything for.

Lola wasn't lost in Duncan's kisses—she was *found*. The passion, the emotion, the breathless need to be in his arms, was everything she'd once dreamed of before her dreams had been dashed by the grabbing hands and leering eyes of men who assumed she was nothing more than a brainless beauty.

Slowly, she took off his shirt, delighting in running her fingertips over the hard muscles of his chest. She loved how strong he was, and that he was clearly a very physically active person despite working in an office.

But instead of helping her get his shirt off, he cupped her face in his hands and looked into her eyes. "Are you sure about this?" His intense gaze searched hers for the answer. "Are you one hundred percent sure about me? About everything I've told you? About my past? About the future I want to have with you, more than I've ever wanted anything in my life?" He kissed her, one more quick kiss that stole her breath away all over again, before adding, "I don't want you to have any regrets."

She opened her mouth to tell him she was sure. That she wasn't going to have any regrets.

But the words wouldn't come, because there *was* still a part of her that couldn't stop seeing the horrified look on Moira's face when she'd seen Duncan in her parents' living room.

Lola wanted so badly to believe in him, with no reservations. But she didn't know how to flip the switch inside of herself that quickly, from *out* to *all the way in*.

At last, she found her voice, although it was clear from his expression that he already knew what she was going to say. "I'm almost there...but I don't want you to go. Not now."

"I don't want to go either." He brushed his fingertips over the curve of her earlobe, before pulling his hand away with obvious regret. "But you mean too much to me, Lola. I can't risk screwing things up with you. Not again."

Though it nearly killed her not to make love with him—she'd never wanted anyone this badly, not even close—at the same time she was amazed that he cared so much about her. None of the other men she'd ever been with would have put her first the way Duncan always did.

"We don't have to go to bed together. We can—" She had to wrack her brain to think of anything other than tearing his clothes off. "—watch a movie cuddled up on the couch, and then..." She made herself say the rest, even though it was the last thing her body wanted. "We'll go to sleep in separate beds."

Together, they put his shirt back on. At least hers weren't the only hands shaking. Duncan looked as close to the edge as she felt. His eyes were burning with desire, his mouth constantly returning to hers. Between stolen kisses they cleaned up dinner, topped up their glasses of wine, then settled on the couch in front of the TV, pulling a blanket over their laps.

That was when it occurred to her that she'd never done this with any man, never simply cuddled, never knew the pleasure of having strong arms holding her tight without it being a prelude to sex. Because even though she and Duncan were both dying to rip each other's clothes off, it was a revelation to know that they could relax together as friends too.

"Thank you," she whispered.

He didn't ask what she was thanking him for, simply drew her more deeply into his arms. "I'd do anything for you, Lola. Anything and everything."

★ ★ ★

Lola was smiling as she slept in his arms, and Duncan hoped she was dreaming of him.

He would happily have remained on the couch with her while the movie played on low volume in the background, their bodies intertwined beneath the blanket as the stars twinkled through the windows. But when she shifted and made a little groaning sound, he lifted her into his arms to take her to her bedroom so that she could sleep more comfortably.

She didn't wake up until he laid her on her bed. Her eyes fluttered open. "Duncan?"

Hearing her say his name in that husky, sleepy whisper tempted him to sink into the bed beside her and finally give in to desire. But he'd meant it when he said he couldn't risk losing her again. Especially when it had been only a handful of hours since he'd admitted the full truth of his past to her—and she'd done the same with him. Of course she'd need time to process what she'd learned. Time to decide whether she could risk trusting him again. *Loving* him again.

"Yes, it's me," he replied, barely above a whisper. "Once I get you into bed, I'll find my own."

"Stay," she said. "I want you here, in my bed."

He would have given anything to be able to stay with her. But he couldn't trust himself to just hold her tight all night long. Not when he knew that the first time they shared a bed, there wouldn't be any sleeping.

So, though it was one of the hardest things he'd ever done, even harder than hitting the Pause button earlier that evening, he stroked her hair and said, "I'll stay until you fall asleep."

Though she tried to fight her exhaustion, the difficult past few days had taken enough of a toll that she soon gave in to the need to sleep.

* * *

Lola woke to a pitch-black sky outside her bedroom window. Instantly, she remembered that Duncan was in her cottage. She wanted to throw the covers off and dash into the guest bedroom to find out if he was lying awake thinking of her the way she was thinking of him—and if every inch of him burned with need for her the way every inch of her burned with need for him.

But he was right that even being 99.9 percent sure about trusting him wasn't enough. Truly loving someone meant unconditional trust, and when she could look past her intense desire for him, she knew that she had that last bit of a percentage point to go.

For the first time in her life, there was a chance for a relationship to be perfectly right in a way nothing else had ever been. She'd never regret anything more than moving too fast just to scratch an itch.

If and when she and Duncan finally came together, it wouldn't simply be to satiate their need for hot, sweaty sex. It would be to declare themselves to each other in every way—body, heart, and soul.

Which meant that when she threw off the covers, rather than heading for the guest bedroom, she went to stand under the icy-cold spray of the shower until her skin felt like it had turned to ice.

★ ★ ★

Duncan heard the shower go on and grabbed his cell phone to look at the time. Four a.m.

He'd gotten sleep in bits and pieces over the last few hours, but mostly he had been kept awake by thoughts of Lola, barely a wall away. He desperately wanted to taste her and touch her and make love to her. But he also craved more of those beautiful moments when they were simply talking or holding each other.

He didn't have to wonder why she was showering in the middle of the night. Nor did he have to guess that she was likely standing under freezing-cold water. He'd done the exact same thing a few hours earlier.

If only he could stop the visions of water flowing over her naked skin and incredible curves, soap bubbles moving slowly across the very surface that he wanted to kiss and caress.

Duncan dropped to the floor beside the bed and launched into rigorous sets of push-ups and sit-ups. But though he worked up a sweat, he made no progress in purging the sexy visions from his mind.

Truth was, he'd never be able to do that. Not when he wanted Lola Sullivan in every way—her laugher, her bright outlook, *and* her lush curves.

All he could do, as night slowly turned to day, was hope and pray that nothing else would happen to ruin their chance at a beautiful future together.

CHAPTER TWENTY-EIGHT

Morning dawned bright and beautiful, and though Lola had been up half the night longing for Duncan, she bounded out of the bedroom and into the kitchen.

He looked absolutely gorgeous there, making coffee, and she didn't hesitate to move into his open arms. She might not be completely sure yet, but she was so close that she refused to deny either of them this delicious closeness.

Mmmm, his strong arms around her felt *so* good. Loving the steady beat of his heart against hers, she nuzzled his neck and breathed him in. She could hold on to him like this forever, just never let go and be perfectly happy.

Soon, his mouth found hers, and just as it had last night, passion leaped between them. By the time they finally dragged themselves away from each other, she was amazed they'd not only managed to keep their clothes on, but also hadn't just christened her kitchen island with their lovemaking.

One day soon, would they be able to love each

other with wild abandon and nothing between them except love and trust and faith and joy? No darkness, no half-truths about their pasts, no more trying to portray themselves as anything other than who they were?

Standing with Duncan as sunlight streamed over them, Lola had never wanted anything so badly in all her life.

"Since you made dinner last night," she said, "I'll make breakfast. What would you like?" It was a little weird to feel so close to him, yet not know whether he was a cereal eater, preferred a toasted bagel, or couldn't face more than a cup of black coffee in the morning.

"I'm happy with anything you've got on hand."

While she appreciated his easygoing response, she wanted concrete details. "Tell me," she said, just as she had the previous morning out on the seawall. She planned to keep saying it again and again until she knew him as well as she knew herself. "If you were at home, what would you eat right now?"

"Oatmeal, with raisins and brown sugar."

"I'll have that too. I'm usually a yogurt-with-granola-type myself, but it's nice to mix things up."

It was funny how happy making that oatmeal with raisins and brown sugar made her, probably because it was made entirely with joy.

"How do you like your coffee?" he asked her.

"With milk and two heaping spoons of sugar." She grinned over her shoulder from where she was stirring oats in a pot on the stove. "Three if you're feeling particularly generous."

"I'm not surprised you like things sweet," he said, grinning back at her. Then his eyes filled with renewed heat as he added, "So do I."

Both coffee and oatmeal were momentarily forgotten as they kissed again. Were it not for the buzzing of the alarm she'd set on her phone as a reminder that they needed to be in her studio in thirty minutes, she wasn't at all sure either of them would have had the self-control to let go this time.

Though they had an intense meeting ahead of them, once they finished eating, Lola felt as though she were floating down the street to her office. It felt so right to walk hand in hand, and every smile, every kiss, every little detail they shared about themselves seemed to build the trust between them even more.

At nine a.m., they connected with her cousins for the video chat. "Thanks so much for agreeing to help out," Lola began after everyone had made quick introductions. "Duncan is…" To say he was her friend wasn't enough, but calling him her boyfriend didn't seem right either. Not when they were still walking a tightrope between friendship and ultimate trust. She reached for his hand, something everyone could see on the video feed. "He means a lot to me. And after what I've learned about his past and how it intersects with Moira's business, I've decided that I want to help him make things right on all fronts."

"Thank you for agreeing to be part of this call today," Duncan said to her family. "Even if we don't go further, I appreciate all of you agreeing to meet with me simply because Lola asked for your help."

"We'll do anything for Lola," Suzanne confirmed. "And I'm even more curious about what's going on than I was yesterday, given the breaking news that just popped up online about your involvement with Brilliant Funds."

"What is it?" Lola asked, but Duncan was already searching for the news on his phone.

Within seconds of finding the story and quickly reading it, his expression darkened. "I shouldn't be surprised." His voice vibrated with barely suppressed fury. "Of course this is how Alastair would play it. Yet again, I've underestimated him."

He gave everyone the URL so that they could read the news themselves, then held out his phone so that Lola could scan it. The article implicated Duncan in the embezzlement scheme that had nearly destroyed Moira's company, along with the five other startups whose owners had signed on to Brilliant Funds. The story further accused Duncan of using those illegally gained funds to start his own company after breaking away from the family firm.

An anonymous source, described as a "close associate" of both Duncan and his brother, claimed that Alastair could no longer keep this information quiet when justice needed to be served. The source also stated that Alastair felt Duncan's clients needed to know about these allegations against him, and that was why he'd gone to the federal authorities.

Lola hadn't thought she could be more shocked by just how evil Duncan's brother was. She'd been wrong. "He framed you for what *he* did."

But instead of agreeing with her, Duncan said, "I can't expect you to believe that, Lola." He addressed the virtually assembled group next. "I can't expect any of you to believe I'm innocent after reading this. Especially when I'm sure the evidence Alastair has given to the FBI will look legitimate, particularly in light of the fact he destroyed my own evidence to the contrary five years ago." A muscle jumped in Duncan's jaw. "What's more, by bringing Moira back into the spotlight, he's made it perfectly clear that no one is off-limits. I have no doubt that he aims to destroy anyone who gets in his way or dares to come between me and him." The heavy weight on his shoulders and the dark cloud hanging over him were both back in spades. "I'm going to continue fighting him, to the very end, but this confirms that it will be better for me to fight him on my own."

Duncan pushed away from the table, his expression so bleak that Lola's heart broke into a million pieces as she looked at him.

In that instant, Lola *knew*. Knew with one hundred percent—no, one *thousand* percent—of her heart, mind, body, and soul that she trusted Duncan. That she believed him. And that she loved him.

Loved him unconditionally.

Loved him as she would love no one else.

Now and forever.

He would do anything to keep her safe—and she would do the same for him.

She reached for his hands and wouldn't let him leave. "I'm not letting you fight this on your own. I love you. I believe you. And I'm going to stand beside you for as long as it takes, through any hardship, no matter what your brother tries to throw at you, or me, or both of us, until you prevail."

Duncan's stunned expression quickly gave way to pure joy. *"Lola."* He looked as though she had just given him the greatest gift in the entire world. A gift he had never expected to have. "I love you so damned much."

She threw her arms around him and kissed him.

But though she never wanted to let him go, further declarations of love would have to wait, because there was no time to waste.

She turned back to the screen of her family's faces. "Are you guys still in?"

Ian nodded from his office in downtown Seattle. "If Lola's one hundred percent behind you, Duncan, then I am too."

Suzanne nodded as well, from her New York City headquarters. "It sounds like your brother needs to be taught a lesson about what family is really all about."

Sophie gave a thumbs-up from her desk at the San Francisco Public Library. "I'm in too."

Rafe, who looked every inch the dangerous-to-deceive private investigator, said, "Count me in."

Malcolm was the last to chime in, from London. Though he shared similar looks with his American relatives, his voice was all Brit. "What a bloody mess. But between the seven of us, I'm confident we can get this thing sorted."

★ ★ ★

Duncan was blown away, yet again, by Lola and her family. They were so good, so kind, so willing to take a risk on behalf of a complete stranger, all due to their faith in Lola.

Once upon a time, Duncan had thought his own

bond with his brother was that strong. It had taken evidence of his brother's crimes for Duncan to finally let go of his belief that Alastair was a good man. And yet, even now, the truth was that there was a part of him, way down deep, that didn't want to believe it.

After Duncan outlined what he knew about his brother's illegal activities, Ian was the first to weigh in. "I'll put out feelers within the American investment community. Based on what you've told us about your brother's belief that he's invincible, I wouldn't be surprised if he has his hands in other fraudulent activities, both in and out of Boston." Ian Sullivan was a hugely respected billionaire businessman known to be a straight shooter. Which was likely why Alastair had never worked with him, as Duncan's brother clearly knew to steer clear of anyone with a moral code. "I'm going to cancel my meetings for this morning and get straight to work on this. Now that your brother has sold you out to the media with this false story, I suspect the FBI will be knocking on your door in the very near future."

"My phone's been buzzing like crazy for the last half hour," Duncan confirmed. He did a quick scan of recent voice mails. "You're right—it looks like the FBI has been in touch, along with the SEC, my staff, and nearly all of my clients."

Everyone except for Alastair.

Rafe's expression was grim as he said, "If there's any way you can lie low in Bar Harbor with Lola and hold off on interacting with anyone but our family for twenty-four hours while I dig into your brother, that would help a lot. And you should know that regardless of how many law enforcement contacts or legal teams your brother might have bought off, it's doubtful that his paper and online trails have remained completely clean. What I find in cases where someone has pissed off, or screwed over, people badly enough, is that their enemies make sure to leave a little evidence behind to hang them in case an opportunity ever arises to get retribution. If there's any dirt on your brother, I'm going to find it."

"I'll check in with my European contacts to see if they've dealt with Alastair in any capacity," Malcom said from London. "I have a feeling it won't take long to find something incriminating."

"My instincts are saying the same thing," Suzanne agreed. "I'm already working on getting into his digital records." Before Duncan could protest, she said, "Don't worry, my sleuthing is untraceable. Even Rafe couldn't find me online and he can find everyone else." She grinned at her cousin from Seattle, who had laughed at her comment, and then Duncan could hear her fingers flying over her keyboard. "I've set up a fully secure online portal and file system where each of us can upload the information we find for easy reference." A moment later, the link popped up on Duncan's and Lola's phones.

"Whatever any of you need," Sophie said, "I'll be at my computer ready to search for it. I've let my boss know an important family matter is taking priority for the day. I will also pull up as much additional information on your brother as I can find to further flesh out the case against him."

Duncan was overwhelmed with gratitude for the Sullivans. "Thank you, again, for going above and beyond to help me." It was hard to believe that he not only wasn't alone anymore, but he had a brilliant—and very determined—team behind him. "I'll continue to put together information on the six companies that were hardest hit by their agreement with Brilliant Funds." Duncan wished he could do more, but with the FBI nipping at his heels, that would make it all but impossible to get people to talk to him.

"I love you guys," Lola said, and everyone sent back their love to her.

After they logged off the video call, Duncan's phone continued its constant buzzing on the tabletop. Ignoring it, he took her hands in his. "Your family truly is incredible. You're so lucky to have them behind you."

"They're behind you too. Behind *us*." Her expression grew fierce. "Between the seven of us, we are going to turn things around so fast, Alastair's going to get whiplash. He is going to regret everything he's done to you and the other people he's harmed." She tugged him up from his chair. "And now that Alastair is specifically using Moira and her company to implicate you in his crimes, we've got to tell her the truth about what really happened back then. She's still at my parents' house, so if we go now, we can catch her before she heads back to Boston—or before she hears about this."

"The last thing I want to do is ambush Moira when she's made it abundantly clear that she doesn't want any contact with me."

"This time, it will be different," Lola insisted, already heading for the door. "When she sees that I have one thousand percent belief in you, she'll know that she can trust you too."

"You have no idea how much it means to know that you believe in me, Lola. But just like I said last night, the last thing I want is for you to regret trusting me or loving me. Especially if I end up behind bars."

"You are *not* going to jail for being an accomplice to your brother's crimes when you didn't even know he was committing them!" she proclaimed. "And just like I told you last night," she continued in a gentler tone, "we've both made mistakes and held back when we should have trusted each other from the start. But now that we've shared everything, the past can't control us anymore." She gazed at him with so much love it stole his breath. "Remember how you told me the imperfections on a hand-drawn map are what give them their character? It's true about people too. Your imperfections are what make you *you*, rather than just some robot who never screws up."

"You don't have to pretend to be perfect with me either, Lola." Emotion poured from every word he spoke. "I love everything about you. Your good decisions and your bad. Your past, present, and future. Your smiles and your tears. Your happy days and your sad ones too. No matter what, I will always love you. Now and forever." He laid her hands over his heart. "And I will never lie to you, or withhold anything from you again."

Their kiss sealed their vows to each other. Vows to love, to cherish, and to rise above the pain they'd inflicted on each other. Vows that Duncan now knew would remain strong and unbreakable, no matter what happened from this point forward.

CHAPTER TWENTY-NINE

Lola had been fifteen when she realized that no matter how hard she tried to hide her curves, she would never succeed at fading into the background. She had been born to stand out, which meant that the only way forward was to love herself exactly the way she was.

Her new epiphanies were just as big today, only this time they were about Duncan. She would never succeed at hiding her feelings for him. Because she had been born to love him exactly as he was.

From the first day they'd met, her heart had tried to tell her, *Everything is okay now. He's The One. You can trust him. He won't hurt you. Not now. Not ever.* But she hadn't been totally willing to listen, not when she was still held down by past hurts. So when Moira had called out Duncan as the devil, Lola's unresolved fears had risen up, convincing her that she needed to shove him out of her life. It wasn't until she had finally confessed all of her secret fears to him that she realized they no longer had the power to control her. And now, with her past firmly in the past, her present joy—and dreams for her future with Duncan by her side—were bigger than anything she'd ever dreamed.

So big, in fact, that despite the seemingly insurmountable issues with Alastair, the FBI, and the SEC, Lola had more faith than ever before that everything was going to be all right. But in order to make sure that they gathered the strongest evidence possible against Alastair, they needed to speak with Moira immediately. What's more, if the media got to her before she knew the truth about what had happened, it could spell disaster for Duncan.

Lola texted her mother to find out if Moira was still at the house, and learned they were at the café having lunch. But by the time Lola and Duncan arrived at the café a few minutes later, Moira, Ethan, and Beth were all frowning at their phones instead of eating.

"The news," Duncan said in a low voice. "They must be reading it."

When her parents and Moira looked up and saw them standing by the entrance, Lola forced a smile that she hoped gave off a reassuring vibe. "Hello! Are you reading the lies Duncan's brother has told the press?"

The three of them looked at her like she was insane, speaking so cheerfully about something so awful. But Lola refused to be daunted. Not even when her father got up from the table and approached them, looking like a bear with a sore head.

Ethan Sullivan gave Lola a kiss on the cheek, then turned to Duncan. "We need to talk."

"Yes," Duncan agreed, "we do."

Though Lola would have loved to be present for their conversation in case she needed to be a referee between her extremely protective father and the man she loved, it was imperative that she speak with Moira about the poisonous story Duncan's brother had planted in the media.

Lola gave Duncan's hand a squeeze before moving to join her mother and Moira at the table, sliding into the seat her father had just vacated as Duncan and Ethan left the café.

"Remember, Mom, how I promised you that one day, if I magically fell head over heels in love like you and Dad did, I wouldn't fight it?" She let everything she was feeling show on her face. She was done hiding her real emotions, done pretending to be so strong and tough all the time. "I love Duncan. I love him wholly and completely, in a way that I never thought I could love anyone." Her heart swelled just saying the words aloud, finally speaking her truth to two of the people who mattered most to her. "All my life, no matter how many men have professed to care about me, they've all only cared about one thing...and it wasn't my heart. So I put up walls. Walls so thick and strong that no one would ever be able to break through them again to hurt me. But with Duncan…" She turned her head to look at him as he talked with her father in the park. "My heart knew it could trust him, even before my head did. Now I finally understand that the reason I never fell in love before is because I couldn't have loved anyone who wasn't worthy of it. And I could never have fully opened myself up to someone if they were going to hurt me."

"Lola, honey." Her mother's eyes were shiny with tears. "I wish I had done a better job of being there for you."

"Mom, you've *always* been there for me. But this was something I needed to figure out on my own." Lola looked out at the gorgeous man in the park who had completely captured her heart. "Actually, not on my own. With Duncan. I needed him by my side to finally see everything clearly." Lola turned to Moira. "I know this might sound crazy in light of the article you've just read and your past experience with Brilliant Funds. But I'm asking you to forget everything you believe to be true about Duncan and to listen to what he has to say."

Moira remained silent for long enough that it took everything inside Lola to hold tight to her belief that they were all going to have a happy ending. Finally, Moira spoke.

"From the moment I met you, Lola, barely an hour

after you were born, I could see that you had such a bright, bold light around you. You're brilliant and talented and beautiful—and you love with everything you are. I've always trusted you and believed that your instincts are spot-on." Moira's eyes gleamed with tears. "Do you have any idea how much I've learned from you? How to be proud about who I am. How to embrace my true self and not hide it for anyone or anything. And when everything fell apart, how to get back on my feet. But then on Friday, when I saw Duncan at the house, all my unresolved fury came rushing back—along with my self-recriminations over how stupid I'd been to fall for so many lies. It's taken until today for me to process it completely. I was actually planning to come find you before I went back to Boston so that we could talk things through again."

"You were?"

Moira nodded, then reached for Lola's hands. "The article I just read seems to prove that Duncan *is* responsible for nearly destroying my company. And yet…there's something I haven't been able to get out of my head since I walked into your parents' house last Friday night." She smiled as she told Lola, "The look on your face when you were dancing with him—and the look on his face as he spun you in his arms—was *exactly* the way your mother and father looked at each other all those years ago when they fell in love in

Ireland. It's the way Beth still looks at Ethan now. And it's the way I looked at Stephan before he passed away. The look of forever love." She seemed momentarily lost in a dream, as though she were back with her beloved husband. "Some people say a love like that is impossible to find, but I've always known it's out there for all of us, if only we can open up our hearts to it." She paused to take a deep breath, seeming to make her final decision in that moment. "If you think Duncan deserves to have me listen to him and keep an open mind, then I trust you, just as I always have."

Lola threw her arms around her friend. "I love you so much."

"I love you too, honey."

Tears streamed down all three women's faces as they gathered each other close and held on tight.

CHAPTER THIRTY

"Mr. Sullivan, I need you to know how much I respect Lola. And how much I love her." Though Ethan's eyebrows rose, he didn't interrupt. "Hurting your daughter is the very last thing I ever want to do." The thought of Lola in pain, in tears, twisted up Duncan's insides. "While I know that must seem hard to believe given my past with Moira and the news you just read, I promise you that I want only the best for your daughter."

While Duncan spoke, Ethan Sullivan's gaze remained steady. Neither happy nor furious. Surprisingly, Duncan got the sense that Ethan was assessing the situation from all angles.

Finally, Lola's father spoke. "You don't have any children, do you?"

"No." It wasn't until Duncan met Lola that he'd longed for a family of his own.

"One day when you do, you'll understand that the hardest thing in the world is to let go and allow your children to grow up and make their own choices, good and bad. You have no idea how difficult it is to watch them make mistakes, to see problems coming from a mile away when they don't yet have the life experience to see it themselves." Ethan's expression clouded over as though he was thinking back to some of his children's worst mistakes. Mistakes he clearly wished he could have prevented.

"I've always wanted to protect Lola the same way I protected her when she was little," he went on. "But as she grew older, and especially once she was a teenager, she pushed back on me and her mom. And why wouldn't she, when she had become her own person, no longer simply Ethan Sullivan's daughter or Turner Sullivan's sister? I love all of my kids equally, but I can also see each of their unique gifts and challenges. Lola is very talented, very creative, and very beautiful. So beautiful that other women have often been terribly jealous. And when it comes to men…" Ethan's frown carved deep ridges in his forehead. "Though my daughter has never come to cry on my shoulder or complain, I know dating and relationships have been difficult for her. I sure as hell haven't been a fan of anyone she's gone out with. No one has ever treated Lola with the same respect for her brain and her talent as they do for her beauty. And as one worthless guy after another has come through her life, Beth and I have worried that there might never be a man worthy of her. A man able to see beneath her outward beauty to truly appreciate the beauty inside." Ethan pinned Duncan with his sharp gaze. "I have to say, on paper, every single thing about you looks bad. Worse than all the guys she's dated put together."

"If I had a daughter," Duncan said, his voice resonant with emotions he couldn't keep in check, "I would want me out of her life. As far out as possible."

But instead of agreeing with Duncan, Lola's father did the strangest thing. He smiled. "Strangely, I find it comforting to have your past laid out in front of me, warts and all. With every other guy in Lola's life, I always had the sense they were trying to hide something. Putting on a pleasant veneer that would disappear the moment I turned my back. But with you, there's no veneer. Not now that your name is splashed all over the news. And yet, my daughter just walked into our family's café holding your hand and looking at you with love in her eyes." Ethan paused, his eyebrows rising. "That's where things don't add up. If you're such a bad guy, why would she let her guard down to let you in again? And why have several of my nieces and nephews texted me to let me know that they're working to help clear your name?"

Duncan wasn't surprised that Lola's father was already in the loop. He guessed Ethan Sullivan was aware of far more about his children's lives than they realized. "Lola recruited your family to help," Duncan explained. "Despite my voicing concern about drawing them into my mess, your daughter and your nieces and nephews have impressively strong wills."

"Lola would never turn her back on someone she loves," Ethan agreed, "especially if they're in trouble. And I'm not at all surprised that my nieces and nephews also insist on doing whatever they can to clear your name, despite your reservations about involving them." Ethan's determined expression reminded Duncan of Lola's. "I'd like you to tell me exactly what's happened—and why I should trust you within a hundred feet of my daughter ever again."

After five years of holding back the truth from everyone but his traitorous lawyer, Duncan was now able to cull it down to the essentials. "My parents passed away when I was six, and I was raised by my brother, Alastair, who is ten years my senior. We were close when I was younger, but as we grew up and he changed into someone I barely recognized, I wanted to believe he was a better man than he is. I joined Lyman Ventures, the family firm, after business school and worked with him until five years ago. That was when I discovered that several client accounts attached to the subsidiary company Brilliant Funds had had massive reverses in fortune. After doing some digging, I uncovered a trail of fraudulent activity, all of which pointed to my brother. Unfortunately, as the startup incubator was his pet project, I wasn't directly involved. And after I confronted Alastair with proof of his embezzlement scheme, he had all of my company records and contacts destroyed, which is why I was unable to find Moira to make things right."

"I can't imagine how difficult it must have been for you to accept your brother's perfidy," Ethan said. "In addition to Beth and the children, my three brothers have been the most important people in my life. I've mourned my late brother Jack every day since he died unexpectedly at forty-two."

"I'm sorry about your brother," Duncan said first. But while he appreciated Ethan's empathy, he wouldn't leverage it to let himself off the hook. "I should have seen what was happening at Brilliant Funds, and I should have stopped Alastair from stealing from the people who signed up to work with the company. During the past five years, without the evidence to give to the feds, I worked instead to make personal amends to the owners of the other companies that I could trace from memory. But now that Alastair has made it clear that absolutely nothing is off limits in his quest to come out on top—" Renewed fury rose inside of Duncan as he thought about what Alastair had said about Lola's being every man's wet dream. "No matter the cost, I need to stop my brother from hurting anyone else."

"The more you tell me about the situation, the more sense it makes that Lola has offered to help you. My daughter has a keen sense of right and wrong, and she can't stand to see evil win."

"Lola is an incredible woman," Duncan agreed, "and I can't tell you how sorry I am to have brought her and the rest of your family into this, as well as Moira, who has been through so much."

"Moira is from strong Irish stock, just like my Beth," Ethan told him. "Though I don't wish another rough patch on Moira, I guarantee she'll make it through with her head held high."

Duncan was glad to hear it. But there was something else he needed to say to Ethan. "There's no doubt that Lola would be better off without me. Better off without being drawn into my knock-down, drag-out fight with Alastair. Better off without worrying that I might end up in jail. But I've never loved anyone the way I love her. With all my heart and soul. With everything I am. And no matter what happens, even if she decides to push me out of her life again, I will always love her and only her. *Forever.*"

There was nothing more Duncan could possibly say to convince Lola's father that he was good enough for her. In fact, it would be perfectly reasonable if Ethan tried to tear him apart with his bare hands for daring to hold on to Lola's heart rather than relinquish it for a better man to claim.

Duncan was braced for the knockout punch when Ethan said, "Thank you for sharing all of that with me. That took guts. And if anyone knows just how much guts, it's me." For the second time in their conversation, he smiled. "I once gave a very similar speech to Beth's father to convince him that I would do whatever it took to make his daughter happy. Luckily for me, he gave me the chance of a lifetime to be with Beth. So I'll give you the same chance now. And if there's a way you can utilize my time and skills, I'd like to be a part of the fight."

Duncan was floored. His only experience with fathers, and father figures, had been with men who always put themselves first, even if they had to lie, cheat, or steal to get there. But Lola's father was risking so much on his daughter's behalf, with a man who, as he had said just minutes before, couldn't look worse on paper.

"It would be an honor, sir, to have you on my side."

Lola's father grinned even wider. "I've always relished a fight. Back in the day, I spent quite a lot of time in the boxing ring. Not so much because I was a fan of the sport. More because I liked winning."

Duncan could easily see Ethan Sullivan beating the

pulp out of his opponent, then taking the other guy out for a beer—or, more likely, shots of Irish whiskey. No harm, no foul, all in the name of good sportsmanship.

"Moira should never have gone through such trials and tribulations with her company," Ethan added. "But since we can't go back and undo what was done, I think it would do her a great deal of good to see that bastard brother of yours taken down."

The night Duncan and Lola had stayed up together, and she'd shared Moira's wisdom—that instead of spending their time wishing they could go back into the past and change things, they should focus on moving forward—Duncan had longed for such a thing to be possible. Longed for the past to stay in the past. Until today, however, he hadn't believed that the future could truly be bright given all the darkness and shadows that had come before.

At last, he believed it with every fiber of his being.

"Thank you, Mr. Sullivan." He'd been thanking Lola's family all day, filled with boundless gratitude for the support the Sullivans were giving him.

Her father grinned again, the expression so similar to Lola's. "Call me Ethan."

In his peripheral vision, Duncan saw Lola, Beth, and Moira walk out of the café and head across the street to the park. He couldn't quite work out what Moira and Beth were thinking, but thankfully, Lola was wearing a bright smile. What's more, she and Moira had their arms around each other, which he hoped meant they'd mended fences.

"Relax," Moira said to him, breaking the ice from a half-dozen feet away. "This isn't a firing squad. Lola has told me everything."

"Moira." Duncan wanted to physically reach out to hug her, but he had no right to do so. Not yet. "I hope you don't feel that I'm pressuring you to forgive me, or help me in any way, when you have every right to want nothing more to do with me."

She studied his face intently. "Honestly, Duncan, now that the shock of seeing you so unexpectedly has passed, I don't feel that way anymore. Truly, I don't." With the pallor of shock lifted, he saw how vibrant she was, with the same spark in her eyes that Lola and her mother had. "Like I said, Lola has filled me in on the situation, and I want you to know that I understand what it's like to be raised by family who want nothing more than to turn their own kin inside out, just for the hell of it. For the thrill of power. And to have control. It's why Beth and Ethan and Lola and her siblings are all so important to me. Though we're not related by blood, they're my *true* family. And I'm theirs." Moira smiled at Lola, Beth, and Ethan before saying, "And given your brother's latest chess move today, since he's clearly decided to drag me and my company into the mix, I'd like to tell you what I remember from my time working with Brilliant Funds. I'd also like to give you any papers that you think might be helpful in bringing your brother to justice."

Duncan had never known so many generous, giving people. "I appreciate your offer to help, Moira. More than I can say. And I'll accept it gladly. But if at any point you want to step away, please don't hesitate to do so. It's not up to you to help fight my battles."

"They're not just your battles anymore," Lola reminded him.

"We're all going to fight beside you," her father agreed.

Looking ecstatically happy, Lola threw her arms around her father. "I love you, Dad."

"I love you too, honey."

Beth had also softened toward Duncan, giving him a warm smile. "Whatever you need, even if it's just a hot meal or a few words of encouragement, be sure to let me know."

"Thank you." His words were slightly gruff, filled to the brim with gratitude. "Your support means the world to me."

"Me too," Lola said. And then, "Now that we've cleared the air, why don't we head to my studio and get cracking?" She winked at her mother. "And if you're in a baking mood, Mom, I for one would certainly feel inspired by some warm soda bread liberally slathered with butter."

Though Beth teasingly swatted Lola's behind, her eyes shone with love. And Duncan knew that no matter what happened from here on out, he'd always remember what real love looked like.

Because Lola and the Sullivans had shown it to him.

CHAPTER THIRTY-ONE

Though Duncan understood why Rafe had requested that he lie as low as possible for the next twenty-four hours, he needed to tell Anita and Gail not only why he'd left the family firm five years ago, but also explain that today's news was Alastair's way of trying to turn the tables on him. While Anita and Gail ended up being far more understanding than he felt he deserved, they did make him promise never to keep them out of the loop again.

Duncan now realized that he couldn't expect other people to trust him if he didn't fully trust them too. For so long, he'd been operating solo to protect himself from another betrayal. But after meeting Lola and her wonderful family, and being so warmly welcomed into their fold, Duncan finally understood he didn't need to live that way anymore.

While he'd been speaking with his employees, Beth brought over a veritable smorgasbord of food and drinks for Lola, Moira, Ethan, and himself. She was just about to leave Lola's studio when he stopped her to say, "Thank you."

"You're very welcome, Duncan." She gathered him in for a hug, one that meant more to him that he could ever express. "Now go raise some hell."

He was still smiling as he sat with Moira to take notes on her history with Brilliant Funds. When he tried to apologize yet again, she was adamant that the two of them had made their peace—and that the best possible way he could make things up to her was to help put his brother behind bars.

After they concluded their meeting, the four of them broke for lunch, and Moira and Ethan reminisced about the six months he had lived in Ireland.

"I was so desperate to convince Beth to go out with me," Ethan recounted, "that I tried to learn Irish Gaelic."

"It was very sweet of you to try," Moira said on a laugh. "But I'm sorry to say that you had the *worst* accent I ever heard. It didn't help that every other word you spoke seemed to be mixed up with one that sounded similar, but meant something very different."

Ethan chuckled, remembering. "I'm not sure I'll ever live down the time I thought I was talking about grabbing a bull by its horns when it came to my business by using the verb *adharcáil,* but actually told everyone that I was a lustful young man."

"In the end," Moira explained to Duncan, "Beth

only agreed to date Ethan upon his solemn vow to never speak Gaelic again."

Despite the threat of FBI and SEC investigations still hanging over him, Duncan found himself smiling and laughing. He'd never known anyone like Lola's family—they were focused and determined, yet relaxed and easygoing at the same time.

After lunch, Moira connected Duncan with the people she hoped could corroborate her experiences with Brilliant Funds. Come five o'clock, during a second video call with Lola's cousins to share what each of them had learned during the day, Duncan couldn't help but be amazed by how quickly they had been able to connect the dots on Alastair's crimes.

His chest ached as he wondered, yet again, what had happened to the sixteen-year-old boy who had vowed to take care of his six-year-old brother. Where had the person gone who had taught him to throw a ball and sail a boat?

Duncan's laughter during lunch suddenly seemed as though it had happened in a parallel universe as he took in the staggering extent of his brother's crimes. No matter the personal cost, or how many years it took, he wouldn't rest until Alastair was behind bars.

Ian's voice broke into his dark musings. "Given that we can't be completely sure which law firms in Boston might be under your brother's thumb, it would probably be best if you utilize my legal counsel in Seattle to fight any federal charges that might be brought against you. If the State of Massachusetts gets involved, we'll work it out."

"I agree," Rafe said. "And speaking of the feds, I feel confident that we will have enough solid information on your brother by tomorrow morning for you to let them know you're willing to cooperate in their investigation."

"I need to talk with my brother first," Duncan said. "I know there's virtually no chance that he'll confess, but I have to give him one more chance to finally do the right thing."

No one seemed surprised. Least of all Lola. "Of course you want to give him that chance. Why wouldn't you, when the two of you were so close before he turned toward the dark side?" She put her hands over his. "And I'm going with you."

But Duncan couldn't stand the thought of what his brother might do or say to Lola. "I know how strong you are, but I still don't want you dealing with him." If anything happened to her... His gut twisted in knots. "If he said or did anything to try to hurt you—"

"I know Krav Maga, remember?" Lola's expression was fierce as she added, "I have a few choice words I'd like to say to him before he gets locked behind bars."

Though Duncan still didn't like the idea of his

brother being anywhere near Lola, he knew nothing he could say would change her mind. Just as he would do everything in his power to make her happy and keep her safe, she felt exactly the same way about him.

"Okay," he finally agreed. "We'll go together." Duncan turned back to her cousins, Moira, and Ethan. "Thank you, again, for all you've done to help. If any of you ever need anything from me, anything at all, it's yours."

"Actually," Malcolm said from London, "while I was digging into your brother, I also dug into you, and I have to say I quite like the look of your investments. They're smart, forward-thinking, and you're working in sectors that I'm interested in moving into. Once this mess is dealt with, let's talk about possible ways we can work together."

"Ditto from me," Ian said from his Seattle office.

Duncan was honored by the possibility of working with Ian and Malcolm. "They're the first meetings I'll put on my calendar after this investigation wraps up."

"Now," Ethan said, "before everyone signs off, when can I expect the five of you and your families back in Bar Harbor? It's been far too long since we've had all of the Sullivans together in Maine."

"You know exactly what you need to do," Sophie put in. "Just throw a wedding, baby shower, anniversary, or birthday party, and we'll be there!"

As they all laughed and nodded in agreement, Lola said, "Actually, you should all keep an eye out for an invitation with a Maine postmark coming your way very soon." Then, realizing she'd already said too much about Cassie and Flynn's upcoming announcement to their extended family when everyone started peppering her with questions, Lola mimed locking her lips and throwing away the key.

CHAPTER THIRTY-TWO

After saying good night to her father and Moira, Lola and Duncan all but sprinted from the studio to her cottage. Though they still had the FBI and SEC investigations hanging over them, they knew three things for certain.

Lola loved Duncan.

Duncan loved Lola.

And tonight, for a few precious hours in the dark, nothing mattered but loving each other.

Once they were inside, Lola led Duncan straight to her bedroom, barely pausing to shut the front door, throw her bag on the counter, and kick off her heels.

"At last," she said in a husky voice, "I have you exactly where I want you."

Her hands trembled with anticipation as she reached for his shirt, yanking open the buttons. He was so broad, so muscular, so beautiful, that she had to kiss every inch of skin she exposed, until she had his shirt all the way off.

Though she could tell he was as overwhelmed by

desire as she was, he took her face in his hands, staring into her eyes as though he was trying to read her every thought. "Promise me you won't regret this."

"*Never*. The only thing I could ever regret is letting you leave again without making love with you."

Relief shone from his eyes, before increasing need quickly replaced it. The same unquenched need that had driven Lola crazy since the day they'd met. "You have no idea how many times I've dreamed of making love to you," he said, his deep voice sending thrill bumps all across the surface of her skin.

"You've been in every single one of my dreams too," she whispered back. "Dreams we can finally make a beautiful reality tonight."

Together, they moved to the bed, and he lay her back on it, gazing at her with such heat, she thought she just might go up in flames. He leaned over her, levering himself up on his forearms as he pressed his mouth to hers, kissing her so gently that his lips were barely brushing against hers.

Within seconds, however, their kiss spun out of control as their intense desire for each other swept them away. He smelled so good, tasted like heaven, and when he said her name in his low, rumbly voice that was so full of love, the very last vestiges of her self-control—and any remaining fears she had about giving all of herself to him—disappeared.

His hands were no steadier than hers had been as he slid her silk top from her torso, quickly followed by her bra. And then his lips were on her again as he pressed kisses over her bare skin. Every other man she'd been with had told her she was beautiful, but as Duncan whispered how sweet she was, how giving, how wonderful, Lola truly *felt* beautiful for the first time. Inside and out.

Together, they removed the rest of her clothes, and then they rolled over so that she was straddling his hips. Lola had to stop to stare, and to appreciate, the utter male gorgeousness beneath her. The breadth of his chest, his rippling abdominal muscles, the strong muscles of his arms and shoulders.

"You're mine," she said, claiming him as she'd wanted to claim him from the first.

"Always, Lola. I've always been yours."

She leaned forward to kiss him again, the tips of her breasts aching from their delicious friction against his bare chest, while his hands felt big and deliciously rough where he was clasping her hips. A low moan emerged from her throat as she rolled her pelvis against his.

Beyond desperate, she quickly undid his pants and pulled them off, along with his boxers. Their first—and only—night together, he'd given her such pleasure, touching her, tasting her. She'd longed to give him the same pleasure, but he hadn't wanted her to think that they were nothing more than a hot one-night stand.

Now that they both knew they were *forever*, she finally had the intense pleasure of kissing her way down his chest, nipping at him with her teeth, before laving the love bites with her tongue. His breath came in harsh pants, his muscles jumping beneath her fingertips, as she made her way lower. And lower. Until, at last, she wrapped her hands around his hard heat, her name on his lips as she lowered her mouth to him, swirling her tongue over his erection.

He was so big, so hard, so incredibly beautiful that her arousal jumped even higher. So high that she thought she might go delirious if she didn't have him soon.

Seconds later, she found herself on her back again, with Duncan's weight pressing her into the mattress. He slid his hands into her hair as their tongues tangled in breathless desire. She wrapped her legs around him, wanting to pull him closer.

With his mouth, he roamed her skin, licking over her breasts, circling her flesh slowly until he was teasing the taut peaks with his tongue and teeth. One hand was still threaded in her hair as he slid the other over her stomach and hips, her legs instinctively parting for his touch.

They both moaned as she bucked her hips against

his hand, their mouths finding each other again, their kisses growing even wilder. Her inner muscles clenched reflexively around his fingers, and she couldn't catch her breath.

"Come apart for me, Lola." His eyes, voice, hands all urged her to ever-increasing pleasure. "Come for me now…and then again and again and again."

His promise of never ending pleasure tipped her all the way over the edge, her climax breaking through her body as heady waves of ecstasy rippled from the top of her head to her clenching toes.

She was still catching her breath when she heard the tearing of a condom wrapper and forced her brain to clear enough that she could sit up to help him slide the latex down over his gorgeously hard erection.

He lifted her up onto his lap at the same time that she moved over it, their minds, their bodies, their hearts perfectly in sync.

And then…*oh God*…it felt like she'd been waiting for this *forever*…she lowered herself over him, taking him so that he filled her completely. So completely that she cried out his name.

They remained that way, with his hard heat throbbing inside her, their hearts beating against each other's chests as they stared into each other's eyes. Until she couldn't wait another second to lift her hips, the incredible sensations building as he cupped her bottom, his thrusts growing more and more wild while she moved against him. Faster. Harder. Both of them beyond desperate as they greedily drank in each other's moans and kisses.

Before she knew it, Lola was coming again, taking Duncan with her over the edge of ecstasy into a world so shockingly beautiful that she gasped aloud at the wonder of it all.

Not only the wonder of finally learning just how much joy and pleasure had been waiting all along inside their carefully guarded hearts...but also the wonder of true love.

★ ★ ★

Duncan loved Lola's spirit. She had more energy, more determination, and more *joie de vivre* than anyone he'd ever met. No matter how hard she worked, or how much she gave of herself, her inner light never dimmed.

He also loved her just like this—languid and sated from their lovemaking, her muscles pliant and loose from the pleasure they'd given each other, her eyes closed and a smile on her lips as she remained on his lap, naked and happy.

"Let's take a bath together," she murmured, her voice husky and lush with pleasure.

Her suggestion was a damned good one. Responding first with a playful nip at her bare shoulder, Duncan lifted her off the bed with her arms and legs still wrapped around him.

"Don't forget to bring another one of those," she said, pointing toward the condoms on her bedside table.

After scooping up protection, Duncan carried her into the bathroom, stunned all over again by her beauty, and also the look in her eyes. A look of such devotion. Devotion he wasn't sure he'd ever feel worthy of…but that he'd go to his grave trying to earn.

After turning on the taps, he reached out to run the backs of his knuckles down her cheek. He could see the pulse point at the side of her neck move faster, especially when he swept his thumb over her bottom lip. She reached for him, too, tracing the lines of his jaw with her talented hands, a beat before their mouths met in another urgent kiss, their desire for each other unquenched despite the intense pleasure of their lovemaking.

Duncan might have forgotten about getting into the bath altogether had the water not filled high enough to splash them as it fell from the tap. He turned off the faucets, then climbed into the water, holding out a hand for Lola to follow, drawing her hips and back against his chest.

Lying in the tub with Lola was every one of Duncan's most sinful visions rolled into one. She was utterly, beautifully uninhibited as she took his hands and curved them over her body, arching into his touch.

Duncan's whole world came down to Lola. To the feel of her slippery skin against his. To the little sounds she made as he played his fingertips over her aroused breasts. To her sweet scent, a tantalizing hint of vanilla and spice.

Picking up the bar of soap from the side of the tub, he slowly ran it down her arm, from her shoulder to her hand. He soaped up her other arm before moving to her legs, instructing her to lift them one at a time from the water, loving the way the tiny bubbles ran down her smooth skin.

Her hips began to move, grinding against his. But though it took him to the edge of his self-control, he continued to tease them both, moving the bar of soap along her collarbone and then her upper chest, without ever touching her breasts.

At last, he ran the bar from soft flesh to the taut peaks, making Lola's breath come out in a rush. He dropped the soap into the water, using his bare hands to trace a sensual path down from her chest to the vee between her legs.

Her head fell back against his shoulder as she gave herself up to his touch, her hips moving in time with his fingers as he played over her hot, slick sex.

"Again, Lola." He spoke the words into her soft hair. "Come for me again. Show me how much you love it when I touch you."

In the wild abandon of her climax, his name was on her lips as she cried out in release. Duncan wanted to give Lola a million orgasms, take her to the brink of ecstasy, then bring her over the edge of bliss, again and again and again.

But she obviously had plans of her own, because the next thing he knew, she had spun around in the tub and was raining kisses over his face, neck, and chest. Between kisses, she said, "I have an idea. Let's lock ourselves in my cottage and never leave."

"One day soon," he promised her, "that's exactly what we'll do. We'll make sure no one knows we're here so that we can make love all day long."

"And all night too."

He captured her mouth in another kiss as they sank deeper into the fantasy of a world where nothing could touch them, where nothing could ever go wrong again. And where kisses, and pleasure, and these oh-so-sweet hours of simply holding each other, were the most important things of all.

This time, she was the one ripping open the condom wrapper, and when she slowly slid it over him, it was nearly more than he could handle. The very second it was on, he curved his hands around her hips, lifted her over him, and thrust into her. Taking, teasing, loving Lola over and over and over while they gave each other fierce kisses.

Duncan matched Lola's cries of pleasure with his own hoarse groans, their hearts pounding in unison as they leaped together into their shared hopes and dreams of a long future together full of laughter, family, and boundless, unconditional love.

CHAPTER THIRTY-THREE

Waking up with Lola in his arms was the greatest feeling in the world. And as she yawned and stretched against Duncan, it didn't matter that he would be facing the equivalent of a Colosseum full of man-eating lions today at the FBI. He was happy.

The happiest man in the entire world.

Lola was the kind of woman painters immortalized and men fought wars over. A woman so beautiful—and brilliant—that jaws dropped whenever she walked into a room. And she loved him.

It was a *miracle*.

"Good morning," he whispered against her hair.

She snuggled in closer. "Good morning." Her words were a little husky as she came slowly awake.

He pressed a kiss to the top of her head. "I love you."

She tilted her face to his so that he could see her sleepy smile. "I love you too."

Despite the evidence they'd compiled against his brother, Duncan knew there was still a chance the FBI would file charges against him instead. Nonetheless, just being with Lola right here, right now, made him feel so damned good.

The alarm buzzed, loud and insistent, and though they both knew there was no chance of lingering in each other's arms today, it wasn't a slow seduction that either of them needed this morning. They simply needed to be as close as possible to one another as they hit the snooze button and reached for one another.

When they kissed, the air between them felt as though it would go up in flames. Their mouths were hot and desperate as their passion spiraled even higher and sweeter than it ever had before. Every cell in Duncan's body fought to get closer to Lola as she wrapped her limbs around him, then cried out his name as she held nothing back. "I love you," he whispered against her mouth and as she whispered it right back, he gave himself over to the greatest pleasure he'd ever known.

It took everything inside Duncan to finally tear himself away.

"The sooner we get to Boston," Lola said in a deliberately cheerful voice, "the sooner your name will be cleared *and* your brother will finally be taken out of commission."

Appreciating her positive attitude, no matter the hurdles ahead of them, he kissed her again, one more heady brush of his lips against hers before they went to shower and dress.

A short while later, they dropped into the Sullivan Café to grab croissants and coffee on the way to the airport. Beth gave them both huge hugs. "If you need anything, call us, and we'll be on the next flight to Boston."

"I have half a mind to go with you," Ethan said. "But you're going to be fine. I feel it in my gut."

Two and a half hours later, Duncan and Lola boarded their flight to Boston. As soon as they took their seats, Lola pulled a pencil box out of her bag, along with a notebook, just the way her mother had all those years ago in the park. "When I'm stressed out, nothing makes me feel better than drawing." She handed him a pencil and a blank piece of paper. "I don't know if it will do the same for you, but—"

He kissed her before she could finish her sentence. "It will. Thank you."

She put her hand on his cheek. "I know how hard it's been hearing all over again that your brother isn't the man you hoped he was. But I hope it helps, at least a little bit, knowing you have all of us now."

"It does help." Thanks to Lola's cousins, father, and Moira, they now had reams of evidence to take Alastair down. "The question is whether he'll find a way to circumvent the system like he has before."

"This time, we've made damned sure he can't!" she proclaimed.

During the flight, Lola sketched textile design ideas, while Duncan worked on a map of Bar Harbor that highlighted the places where his life had changed. Lola's studio. The Sullivan Café. The Maritime Museum. Lola's cottage. Her parents' house. The stone wall where they'd kissed in the rain. The bench in the park where he'd had a heart-to-heart with her father.

It wasn't until the flight attendant asked them to put up their tray tables in preparation for landing that Lola looked over at his paper.

"I love the way you've drawn your own unique map of Bar Harbor where it's not just about the nuts and bolts of the town, but what each location means to you. It's such a perfect way to bring a personal touch to traditional cartography."

He was just as impressed by her designs. "You are so gifted at expressing beauty. You're a remarkable woman, Lola Sullivan. In every single way."

"I'm just glad I finally met someone who sees it too," she said, making them both laugh.

She deliberately kept him laughing with stories from her childhood during the taxi ride to Lyman Ventures' corporate headquarters. Where Duncan had made the decision five years ago to work in a small building with a pared-down staff so that he could give each client his individual attention, Alastair liked nothing more than sitting at the top of a skyscraper with his name on it while hundreds of employees below him scurried to do his bidding.

Once they were standing on the sidewalk, Lola looked up at the tall building and raised her eyebrows. "Looks like your brother is compensating for something."

Duncan was surprised to find himself laughing again as they headed inside. He wasn't tense. He wasn't even angry anymore.

He was simply ready to finally move Alastair into the rear view.

Lola didn't look the slightest bit ill at ease either. On the contrary, she was absolute perfection in a dress made from one of her own prints, which had gold and silver threaded in a subtle floral design through a black base. Her heels were high, her hair was glossy, her makeup was flawless. She was utterly magnificent, and Duncan was beyond proud to be with her, and to love her.

"This is it."

Her lips curved up into a small smile. "Oh yes," she said, clearly relishing the opportunity to give his brother hell. "This is most definitely the end of the road. He'd better hope he doesn't provoke me, because my brother Hudson can attest to the fact that I give one hell of a noogie twist. It's been twenty-five years since the last one, and he's *still* a little afraid of me."

Weeks ago, if someone had told him that he would break into laughter just seconds before confronting his brother with the long list of his crimes, Duncan would never have believed it. But Lola had changed everything. Her sass, her confidence, and her belief that people should always be kind and fair, had transformed his entire outlook on life.

The office at the top of the building looked out over the Boston skyline. It was a magnificent view by any measure, but one Alastair had never appreciated for anything more than as a symbol of power. Wealth. Prestige. Duncan's brother liked knowing that he sat a head above every other person in the city.

But instead of scowling, with Lola at his side, Duncan was smiling as they walked into the corner office. Which ended up being exactly the right move to throw his brother off. Alastair would have assumed Duncan would enter guns a-blazing. But relaxed and smiling?

He would have never seen that coming.

"Duncan." Alastair's voice was smooth. He shifted his calculating gaze, which transformed into a leer as he said, "And you must be Lola."

In lieu of replying, she squeezed Duncan's left hand while he reached into a leather bag with his right. He placed the condensed report—a document with less than a quarter of the evidence they'd found, but all of it damning—on his brother's desk.

"This is for you," Duncan said.

Alastair was clearly dying to see what was on the pages in front of him, but instead of giving in to the urge, he continued ogling Lola. "You're even more beautiful than you appeared in the pictures I've seen online. A girl like you could go far with your looks. Especially if you're smart enough to sell them to someone who is willing to pay you what they're worth."

Alastair was so predictably egotistical and power hungry that Duncan wasn't sure he'd ever stop beating himself up for not having seen it sooner. He needed to try, though. Not only did Lola deserve him at his best, rather than being forever chained down by the past—*he* deserved it too. No matter how difficult it might be to finally let go of, and forgive himself for, his past mistakes, he was determined to prevail.

His desire to be a better man for Lola—and the fact that she was more than capable of defending herself—was all that kept Duncan from leaping across the desk and wrapping his hands around his brother's neck.

"You are even more of a dirtbag than I heard you were." Lola spoke softly, but there was steel behind her words, something Duncan knew she got from her mother. "A guy like you thinks he can get away with manipulating everyone around him for his own gain, but you always end up having to pay for what you've done. Especially if you're dumb enough to overestimate your own worth." She bared her teeth in a snarl, rather than a smile. "Looks like it's your time to pay...although there aren't going to be any pretty girls where you're going."

Duncan couldn't remember the last time he'd seen Alastair betray surprise. But Lola had obviously stunned him speechless, and not just because of her looks. She was whip smart. And one of the bravest people he'd ever known.

Working to recover his composure, Alastair turned back to Duncan and drawled, "She speaks remarkably coherently for such an attractive woman. It's nearly impossible to find that combination in the fairer sex. She might be a gold digger, but I can see now that she could also be an asset on your arm at parties...and certainly in your bed after the parties are over."

Yet again, Duncan was sorely tempted to land a solid right hook on his brother's jaw, but Lola's firm squeeze on his hand helped to remind him that Alastair would be far more thrown off if his insults were ignored. "I've come to tell you it's over. This is your final chance to admit to your crimes. There's no guarantee that the FBI will cut you any slack for coming clean, but I'm assuming you'll have better odds for leniency if you don't try to run from them."

Though his brother leaned back in his large leather chair and laughed, to Duncan's ears it seemed forced. "Perhaps you should take your own advice," Alastair stated in an easy voice. "Word on the street is that both the FBI and the Securities and Exchange Commission are both chomping at the bit to speak with you." He adopted a somber expression. "You should know that I've asked them to give you a chance to make things right with everyone you defrauded at Brilliant Funds. In fact, I've suggested that they let me oversee your restitution to the clients you wronged so badly behind my back. If you're lucky, you might be able to avoid a lengthy prison sentence by agreeing to those terms. Of course, I would still be happy to take over your company so that none of your clients suffer for your misdeeds." There was steel in Alastair's eyes as he added, "I'm on your side, Duncan. I always have been."

This time, Lola was the one who looked on the verge of leaping across the desk to wrap her hands around Alastair's neck.

Duncan turned to face her. "He can't touch me anymore," he reminded her in a low voice. "He can't touch *us* anymore."

"If you're not going to accept my offer," Alastair interrupted, "then I'm afraid you're on your own with the feds. And now, if you two little lovebirds could take your nauseating gushing outside, I have work to get back to."

Duncan had needed to make this final visit. To look into his brother's eyes one more time to see if the sixteen-year-old boy who had vowed not to let the foster system tear them apart was still in there. At last, he accepted that though he'd always be thankful to the boy his brother had been, he wouldn't miss the corrupt man he had become.

"For so long," Duncan said, "you weren't just my brother, you were the most important person in my life. And even when we didn't see eye to eye, I gave you the benefit of the doubt and respected your decisions, because I thought that's what family was. I thought that's what love was. But I've learned otherwise. Whatever respect and trust and love there was between us is long gone. Your actions, your crimes, have betrayed my trust in the worst possible ways. I wish I could say you'll one day feel remorse for what you've done, but I very much doubt you will. Still…" Duncan took a final long look at his brother, who had once been the center of his world. "I hope you can find happiness one day. Real happiness that comes from what's inside of you, rather than the illusive trappings of wealth and power."

With that, Duncan and Lola turned to leave. They were almost out the door when Alastair spoke again.

"When you get tired of slumming it, sweet Lola, I'll be here waiting to give you absolutely *everything* you could ever desire."

She whirled around, a furious goddess. "Duncan *is* everything I could ever desire. He is the man of my dreams. And now that I've seen just how vile you truly are, I love him even more for rising above you, in every possible way."

With that, Lola and Duncan walked hand in hand to the elevator. Before the door closed, Duncan could see his brother at his desk, looking red-faced with rage as he read through the papers Duncan had given him. No doubt, Alastair would spend the next several hours calling in every last favor to try to keep himself out of jail.

Once they were out of the building, Duncan drew Lola into his arms. "I'm sorry for everything he said to you, for the way he looked at you, for the way he dared to treat you."

"You have nothing to be sorry for. And it was really satisfying to tell him exactly what I think of him, especially when it clearly hit the mark."

"He's usually unflappable," Duncan agreed. "But he never counted on coming face-to-face with a woman like you." He gently stroked his fingertips over her cheek. "Neither did I."

"Just like I said in my parting shot to him, the fact

that you remained so honest and good with a father figure like him is truly amazing. Compared with that, the feds are going to be a breeze to deal with."

Only Lola would call meetings with two of the most powerful government agencies in the world—agencies that at the moment wanted his head on a pike—a breeze. But though he was mere minutes from what would surely be one of the most difficult, intense afternoons of his life, as Duncan held Lola in his arms in the middle of a busy Boston sidewalk and kissed her with all the love in his heart, he couldn't help but believe that justice and love would prevail.

If he'd learned anything from Lola's parents, her cousins, and from Lola herself, it was that in a battle between love and evil, love would always emerge the victor. Because love was *always* worth fighting for, no matter how hard, or how long, the fight.

CHAPTER THIRTY-FOUR

Spending ten hours a day for a week straight inside a windowless room with a team of lawyers, FBI agents, and SEC agents had to be one of the most exhausting experiences in the world.

Lola hated that she couldn't be in the meetings with Duncan. Though she and Duncan were staying at his house in Boston, Lola went over to Hudson and Larissa's home each day and paced a hole in their back lawn while Duncan was dealing with the feds. Thank God her brother and sister-in-law lived in the same city. They not only went out of their way to make sure Lola didn't go completely crazy with the waiting, they also made sure to help out with providing food for Duncan so that he didn't have to worry about anything other than his meetings.

On top of everything else, Lola was worried about Hudson and Larissa. For the past few years, she'd noted hints of strain between her brother and sister-in-law. Now, after spending the better part of a week with them, there was no denying the chasm between them.

Lola wished she could do something to help...but the truth was that she was barely hanging on herself.

Every evening when Duncan returned to his house from the latest round of questioning, he was even more stoic and silent than the day before. It had been a wonderful surprise when she'd found the family tree he'd been making for her on his drafting board. Hoping that drawing would relax him, she'd encouraged him to spend time working on it during the week. But she knew how hard it must be for him to concentrate, even on something he really enjoyed, when on top of his high-stakes meetings, he also had to accept the loss of his brother, once and for all. She couldn't imagine how deeply she'd grieve if she ever had to face such hard truths about one of her siblings.

Fortunately, that would never happen. In fact, as news had traveled through the Sullivan grapevine that the love of Lola's life needed additional backup beyond what her five cousins, father, and Moira had already given, Sullivans from around the globe stepped up to help.

Alec, who had transitioned from owning a billion-dollar fleet of private planes in New York to cooking at the garden restaurant he shared with Cordelia, called in favors from heavy-hitting business contacts on the East Coast. Harry, Alec's brother, utilized his research skills as a Columbia professor to join Sophie in chasing down any leads and financial information that the FBI and SEC had trouble confirming. Both Nicola, Marcus's wife in Napa Valley, and Ford, Mia's husband in Seattle, used their extensive music industry connections to get more details on Alastair's investments in the entertainment industry. Smith Sullivan and his wife, Valentina, also reached out to their extensive film and TV contacts.

While the FBI hadn't yet exonerated Duncan for his brother's crimes, Lola remained hopeful that it would happen in the very near future. Otherwise, wouldn't they have filed charges against him already?

Thankfully, at the end of the week, the FBI and SEC gave Duncan a break from questioning—and Lola was determined that they would make the most of it.

She had been longing for a lazy morning in Duncan's bed, a few precious hours where they didn't have anywhere to go or anyone to see. Time to cuddle together in his house while drinking coffee and reading the paper. Time to walk in a garden, hand in hand, while smelling the roses in bloom.

But as soon as they woke in each other's arms, neither of them could quell their urgency to let pleasure take over and banish the threats hanging over Duncan's head and their future.

His lips on her skin, his hands caressing her curves, made all her fears, her worries, disappear. And as he kissed his way down her body, she wondered how she could have lived without him for so long. When he finally levered himself over her, filling her with his hard heat until she was breathless, Lola didn't have one single doubt that Duncan was her destiny.

Wherever they were, as long as they were together, was *home*.

Their lovemaking temporarily helped them forget the uncertainty swirling around them, but as Lola came back down to earth, she remained overwhelmed by the deep emotions their lovemaking had stirred up.

As though sensing her disquiet, Duncan lovingly stroked her hair. "Before I leave Boston for good, there's one place I'd like to take you."

Anything he wanted to show her, anything he wanted her to understand about his life, his mind, his heart, she wanted to see. "I've always loved Boston. And I know I'll love it even more when I'm with you."

Her enthusiasm made him smile. "Despite everything that's happened here, I can't hold it against this city. At the same time, I know Bar Harbor is exactly the right place to begin anew."

Lola hadn't ever had to contemplate starting over. She'd always been safe and secure not only in the knowledge that she was in the right place, but also that her family would be there for her, no matter what. Now, they would all be there for Duncan too.

They had just finished dressing when there was a knock on Duncan's front door.

Her heart immediately leaped into her throat, hammering faster than ever. Was this the FBI coming to take him away in handcuffs?

For the second time that morning, Duncan reminded her, "Whatever or whomever is out there, everything's going to be okay. I promise."

She knew he was right, that no matter how tall the mountains were in front of them, as long as they had each other, they'd climb them together.

Thankfully, when Duncan opened the door and brought a package inside, she immediately recognized Brooke's handwriting on the label. Rafe's wife was an artisan chocolate maker who sold her homemade truffles at grocery stores, restaurants, and boutique stores throughout the Pacific Northwest.

"Hurry, open it," she urged Duncan.

She was practically drooling as he undid the packaging, then took off the lid of a lake-blue chocolate box imprinted with a pattern of green trees. The best chocolate truffles in the world were inside.

A note accompanied the sweet treats. *Lola and Duncan: In case you guys need a pick-me-up, here's some chocolate! Love, Brooke.*

Duncan looked seriously impressed, not only with Brooke's intricate truffle designs, but also their rich aroma. "Did Brooke make these herself?"

"No one can transform chocolate like Brooke can," Lola confirmed. "I haven't ordered a box of truffles from her for far too long—mostly because I can't trust myself not to eat the whole thing in one sitting—so this is a major treat. I know it's only nine in the morning, but as far as I'm concerned, it's never too early for chocolate."

Their moans and groans as they popped one truffle after another into their mouths rivaled the sounds they'd made in bed earlier.

"This is the best chocolate I've ever had," Duncan said. "How come I've never heard of Brooke's company?"

When Lola had first met Duncan, she'd thought he was too preoccupied in trying to grow every business he was involved with into a multinational, billion-dollar corporation. But now she understood that it wasn't money that drove him, but the urge to help people with great products change the world for the better.

"Brooke loves creating the chocolates by hand. It's more like she's making art than working in a commercial kitchen," Lola explained. "Plus, if she and Rafe are thinking about starting a family soon, she might not be interested in going into startup mode and upending their relaxed lake life in Washington." Actually, it was the perfect opening for Lola to let Duncan know that she'd changed her mind about a few things. "You might be surprised to hear this, but I've decided that I can finally see the benefits of working with a great investor. The only barometer I used to have when it came to investors was Moira's terrible experience, so I assumed they were all bad. But Serafina loves working with you. Same goes for Dave building the prosthetic limb—he's clearly thrilled to have your support for his work."

"Corporate and financial success used to be the only barometers I had to gauge my own happiness," Duncan responded. "But once I met you, I finally understood just how many other things there are to be happy about. Parts of life that have nothing to do with work, or business, or money. Picking vegetables in the garden. Taking a walk by the shore. Sitting side by side sketching." He looked at her with so much love it stole her breath away. "And I would give up every penny I have just to hold you in my arms one more time. When you kiss me, Lola, I have everything I'll ever need."

Cradling his jaw, she brought his lips down to hers. Duncan was exactly the kind of man she'd been hoping for all her life. After being in so many bad relationships, she'd started to believe good ones didn't exist. But now, here she was, in love with the most amazing man in the world.

"No matter what happens," he continued in his

gorgeous deep voice that shot through her veins like fine Irish whiskey, "getting to be with you every morning, and every night, has made this the best week of my life. It doesn't matter where we are or what we're doing. All that matters is loving you."

* * *

"I've been on the Harborwalk before," Lola said a short while later, "but it's never seemed quite this beautiful before."

Duncan agreed that the Boston sky had never been so blue, the sun had never sparkled more on the water, and the historic ships on display in the harbor had never looked quite so majestic.

"That first night we were together, I told you my brother and I used to come to the Harborwalk. But what I didn't say was that the first time was only a few days after my parents died." He remembered it so clearly. "It felt so normal, like we were still just two kids with nothing more to worry about than whether we'd score a goal at our next soccer game. That was the day we went inside the Tea Party Ships and Museum, and I discovered the hand-drawn maps." Lola squeezed Duncan's hand tight as he continued speaking. "I was only six, but even then I understood that bringing me here was his way of telling me we'd be all right, even without my parents to guide us. He wanted me to know it was okay to have adventures, and dream about the future, and even to have fun and forget that we weren't normal kids with normal lives anymore."

Emotion hit Duncan square in the middle of his chest. "He loved me. He really did. I may never know what turned him to the dark side. Was it being forced to step into a responsible-parent role at such a young age that he never really got to sow any wild oats? Did he have to get his thrills from cheating the system instead? Did he buckle under the pressure of having to protect me and keep the business going? Or was he simply so good at getting his own way that he couldn't help but get cockier and cockier as the marks got bigger and bigger?" Duncan shook his head, knowing the answers would likely always be a mystery. "But even after everything that's happened, I'll never forget the love between us as kids."

Lola put her arms around Duncan and held him tight, oblivious to the throngs of walkers skirting around them on the path. "It's wonderful that you can remember the good things. How close you once were. How well he took care of you. And the hope he filled you with when you needed it most."

This walk along the Boston Harbor was Duncan's chance to see the good in his past…and lay the bad parts to rest for good. Because now that he had made his peace with the past, he could finally look toward the future. By letting go of the guilt and shame he'd carried for the past five years, his heart now overflowed with joy and hope and boundless love.

Slowly, he went to one knee, making Lola's eyes grow wide with surprise—and what he hoped was pure joy. "Whatever happens from this moment forward, I know that I want to be with you for the rest of my life. Will you marry me, Lola? Will you let me love you with everything I am, forevermore?"

"I swear, I was just about to ask you the exact same thing." Her words were thick with tears as she said, "Will you marry me, Duncan? Will you let me make you the happiest man alive, as happy as I know you'll always make me?"

At the same moment, they both said, "Yes."

He stood, swinging her around and around in his arms. Barely thirty seconds later, his phone rang with the ringtone he'd assigned to the FBI.

They both stilled, instinctively knowing this was the call that would decide his—and his brother's—fate.

Lola slid down to her feet as he pulled his phone out of his pocket, seeing the lead investigator's name on his screen. "Steve, I take it you have an update?"

Barely five minutes later, Duncan put the phone back in his pocket.

"Alastair was just indicted. The FBI is getting a warrant for his arrest." The enormity of the situation hit Duncan like a sledgehammer. Despite his brother's money and connections, Alastair's future was going to be very difficult from here on out.

"Does that also mean...?"

"The FBI and SEC have concluded that I am wholly and completely innocent of any crimes." The evidence Lola and her family and Moira had helped Duncan pull together, along with the past week of closed-door testimony, had convinced the prosecutors that Duncan's intent had only ever been to build great companies with smart people.

"This is the best news ever!" Lola's cheers of joy caused everyone on the Harborwalk to turn and look at them.

Duncan pulled her close again, never wanting to let her go. "Deep down, a part of me always believed that maps could lead me to the place I was meant to be." He felt like the luckiest man in the world as he said, "And that's exactly what taking your drawing class for my maps did—it led me straight to you. Forever, Lola. That's what you are. *My forever.*"

"You're my forever too," she whispered against his lips, before kissing him with all the love in her heart.

Hand in hand with Lola on the Harborwalk, Duncan couldn't wait to begin his new life with her in Bar Harbor. While a part of him would forever regret the way things had turned out with his brother, at last his heart was free.

Free to love Lola Sullivan. *Forever.*

EPILOGUE

Cassie and Flynn's combined engagement party and baby shower was a joyous celebration. Ruby was in her element as the little girl happily went from one set of arms to another.

It was wonderful to see Lola and Duncan so totally in love as they embarked on their new life together in Bar Harbor. Duncan had settled easily into the family dynamic—even Turner was warming up to him.

The Maine Sullivan family tree Duncan had drawn for Lola now had pride of place in the café, hanging on the wall where everyone who came to eat or shop in the attached store could see it. Ashley knew that he had already been commissioned by a local who wanted something similar made up for her family. And after her father had shown Duncan's drawing to his two brothers and their wives, along with her Aunt Mary in California, each of them had asked if he could also fit their family trees into his schedule. Though Duncan hadn't originally planned on becoming a family tree expert, he seemed more than happy to add them to his map-making commissions.

Ruby pulled on the hem of Ashley's dress. "Up!"

Always thrilled to get a chance to cuddle the little girl, Ashley picked her up and they *boop*ed each other on the nose.

When Ruby wriggled to get down, Ashley set her on the floor, smiling as the toddler rushed off to see what her cousin-to-be Kevin was doing on the patio.

Ashley couldn't be more thrilled for Cassie and Flynn. But at the same time, it was impossible not to compare this beautiful celebration to the day she'd realized she was pregnant.

She'd been seventeen, and it had been a terrible shock to realize why she'd missed her period for several months. She'd never thought something like that could happen to her, or that her senior year of high school would be full of anything but carefree parties and getting ready to move away for college.

Instead, she'd tearfully told her parents that she was pregnant, then spent the next six months hiding out in her bedroom.

Kevin was the best thing that had ever happened to her, of course. But as a single mother, Ashley had completely missed the carefree years of dating and parties that so many of her friends and family had taken for granted. She'd been a working mom her entire adult life.

Ashley would never admit it to anyone, but she sometimes secretly wondered what it would be like to be just a little bit wild. To do something crazy, like date a totally unsuitable man. To hop on a plane for an impromptu trip without needing to spend weeks planning for babysitters and homework helpers. To throw caution to the wind and drink too much and kiss a man without worrying whether he would be a good role model for her son.

"Penny for your thoughts, Ash."

She smiled at her brother Brandon, who was on one of his rare trips home from setting up hotels in Asia or Europe or South America. Grateful for the glass of wine he'd brought her, she said, "It's a great day, isn't it? Cassie and Flynn deserve all their happiness."

"They sure do." Brandon took a slug of his beer. "Although I have to admit I never thought I'd see so many of our siblings looking this lovey-dovey."

"Still bound and determined to stick with the single life, I take it?"

She thought she saw something flash in his eyes. But it was gone as he grinned and said, "The single life is the only life for me."

She couldn't hold back a sigh. "Me too."

"Come on, Ash. You're bound to find a great guy one day."

"I'm not holding my breath. Besides, I'm perfectly

happy with my life."

Brandon put an arm around her. "I've got an idea. Come with me to Vienna for my next hotel opening." Before she could protest, he said, "Mom and Dad can watch Kevin for a few days. Besides, he's got to be more than ready for a little freedom. I know I sure was when I was eleven."

It was as though her brother had read her mind and knew how badly she needed to shake up her life. "Thanks for the offer. I'll think about it."

"Just say yes, Ash. What would it hurt to have a little fun for a weekend?"

Maybe he was right. After all, she was no longer a naïve seventeen-year-old girl who would foolishly fall for the first guy who looked her way. She was a reliable mom whose son was her top priority. What could possibly go wrong during a weekend in Austria?

"Okay," she said, clinking her wineglass against Brandon's beer bottle. "I'm in."

★ ★ ★

ABOUT THE AUTHOR

Having sold more than 9 million books, Bella Andre's novels have been #1 bestsellers around the world and have appeared on the *New York Times* and *USA Today* bestseller lists 91 times. She has been the #1 Ranked Author on a top 10 list that included Nora Roberts, JK Rowling, James Patterson and Steven King.

Known for "sensual, empowered stories enveloped in heady romance" (Publishers Weekly), her books have been Cosmopolitan Magazine "Red Hot Reads" twice and have been translated into ten languages. She is a graduate of Stanford University and has won the Award of Excellence in romantic fiction. The Washington Post called her "One of the top writers in America" and she has been featured by Entertainment Weekly, NPR, USA Today, Forbes, The Wall Street Journal, and TIME Magazine.

Bella also writes the *New York Times* bestselling "Four Weddings and a Fiasco" series as Lucy Kevin. Her sweet contemporary romances also include the USA Today bestselling "Walker Island" and "Married in Malibu" series.

If not behind her computer, you can find her reading her favorite authors, hiking, swimming or laughing. Married with two children, Bella splits her time between the Northern California wine country, a log cabin in the Adirondack mountains of upstate New York, and a flat in London overlooking the Thames.

Sign up for Bella's New Release newsletter:
www.bellaandre.com/Newsletter
Join Bella Andre on Facebook:
facebook.com/bellaandrefans
Join Bella Andre's reader group:
bellaandre.com/readergroup
Follow Bella Andre on Instagram:
instagram.com/bellaandrebooks
Follow Bella Andre on Twitter:
twitter.com/bellaandre
Visit Bella's website for her complete booklist:
www.BellaAndre.com

Made in the USA
Monee, IL
30 October 2020